Black Chokeberry

Black Chokeberry

MARTHA NELSON

Brown Books Publishing Group
Dallas, Texas

This is a work of fiction. Any similarity to real persons, living or dead, is coincidental and not intended by the author.

Black Chokeberry

Brown Books Publishing Group
16250 Knoll Trail Drive, Suite 205
Dallas, Texas 75248
www.BrownBooks.com
(972) 381-0009

A New Era in Publishing™

ISBN 978-1-61254-043-6
Library of Congress Control Number 2012932934

Printing in the United States
10 9 8 7 6 5 4 3 2 1

To Mark

Your strength, encouragement, and the precious gift of time

have made all the difference.

Thank you for loving me, and more than that,

for believing in me. I love you, Mark Nelson.

and

To Billy and Terry

Wherever you are,

there I am,

loving you both

with a Mother's heart.

Acknowledgments

Thanks to Sally Kemp, my wise and talented editor, for her guidance, patience, and willingness to read the manuscript one more time. Thanks to Laura and David Leach for opening doors and being my trusted friends; and to the wonderful editors, designers, and encouragers at Brown Books—especially Rayven Williams. Thank you for your brilliance and support all along this amazing way. To my wellspring in the wilderness and fellow writer, Tina Benson, my heartfelt thanks for knowing just what to say and when to say it; and the same to Robert Sanders, who loved Ruby instantly.

In particular, this story is written with a warm embrace to my sister-cousins, Mimi Brennan Bruckenfeld and Gigi Brown Scriggins, for their generosity, love, and enthusiasm in all of my life and particularly in this project, and as a tribute to my kind, fun-loving, generous, spirited, lifelong friend Bobby Jensen, who loved Oswego with a passion until the day he died.

Last but certainly not least, thanks to the most wonderful group of writers I know, the Twaddlers of Lake Providence: Pat Morrell, Gerri and Leonard Goodwin, Ken Glinski, Clive Arlington, Don LeBlanc, Laura Parra, Mary Lou Cross, Barbara and Bob Dirr, Diedre Jackson, and Jim Moore. Thank you all.

Black Chokeberry, *Aronia melanocarpa* (*Photinia melanocarpa*): A deciduous shrub of the rose family, native to the Great Lakes region. Seemingly phased by nothing, this shrub will tolerate anything thrown at it: swampy ground, dry sandy soil, drought, salt, and pollution. Songbirds, many species of small mammals, and upland game birds enjoy the dark bitter fruit in harsh winter months. This plant is recommended to those who are interested in trying something a little old-fashioned, but still a little different.

—**Christopher Lindsey**
Founder, hort.net

One

She reached into the nightstand and counted. Six Snickers, one Twix, five Milky Ways, and two twin packs of Mallo Cups. Breakfast, lunch, and dinner in a drawer.

There's a cooking show in there somewhere, but damn, fourteen won't be enough for the weekend. I'll have to go out.

Ellen Varner lay back on the pillow, stretching her legs and arms, catlike. The afternoon sun was behind the tightly closed bedroom blinds. "Stay there," she said. "Leave me alone."

Rubbing her eyes, she heard Henry trotting along the front of the bed. She appreciated his patience with her, his willingness to wait for her to wake up before he could go for a walk. He was just the kind of dog Ellen loved, a mix of German shepherd, with that unmistakable head and pointed ears, and hound dog, the lean medium-sized body covered with a strawberry-blond short-haired coat. At three years old, he was all muscle with a lot of puppy energy still in him. She had rescued him last summer; more accurately, he had rescued her. At fifty-two, her twenty-four-year marriage over, Ellen had needed a warm body near hers as she went to sleep and someone to care for when she woke up. Henry fit the bill perfectly.

He sat by the side of the bed now, his dark eyes never leaving hers, his long tail banging the floor, wagging frantically. His intense stare willed her to rise up, put on his leash, and take him outside, *now*. "All right, Henry, I get it," she said, stretching again, feeling the warmth of the sheets under her and not wanting to leave the safety of her bed. "I'm up."

Pulling on the limp navy-blue corduroy slacks she'd worn for a week now, Ellen reached for her leather Keds with the white ankle socks stuffed inside. Her slacks hung simply on her, no bulges anywhere, no stomach to hide with a long sweater, no fanny to cover, no pull at the waist. She moved the belt a notch closer, feeling it settle on her hips. She hadn't been this thin since her twenties. In fact, she had celebrated the start of the year at 143 pounds, dancing up a 2010 storm with her pals at a rockabilly party on New Year's Eve in Nashville. That wild prosecco night turned out to be the last one with Nashville friends. Two months later she moved back to Oswego, New York, the small city where she had grown up. Since that move, her life had changed completely.

Bending down, Ellen picked up the dark-green Land's End cotton twill jacket from the floor and put it on. The jacket was her favorite, the cotton like soft butter after twenty-five years of wash and dry, the diagonal pockets just big enough to keep her hands warm. She loved the gentleness of it, the dependability, the faded sameness, year after year. The jacket was the first thing she had bought when the weather turned cold that first year of marriage in New York. It had carried her right through Thanksgiving when she had to retrieve her heavy wool car coat from the cedar closet. She stopped to take a look at herself as she passed by the mirror on the back of the bathroom door. She was looking pretty good from the outside; but her legs and arms sported bruises all the time now, the result of large and small bumps against one thing or another—a doorway, the car fender, the bathtub faucet. She supposed she was anemic. Inside she felt incredibly light—fragile, really. Oh, well. It could be worse. She could have turned into a comfort-food crisis eater. In that case she'd be looking at a two-hundred-pound mess now. Instead, her lifelong pattern of losing her appetite in times of major change was fully engaged. Her throat closed at the sight of food. *So it goes.*

Moving downstairs to the vestibule Ellen lowered her voice, commanding Henry to *stay*. He sat instantly, his blond chin up and pointed out at her, giving her full access to his neck so she could attach the metal lobster-claw clasp easily to his blue collar. The leash in place, the front door open in front of her, Ellen hesitated.

"Wait a second, Henry," she said, "I'll be right back." She leaned down to give him a kiss between his eyes, then turned and hurried back up to the bedroom, opening the nightstand drawer. She reached in and put her fingers around a Milky Way bar. Nougat in her pocket, she walked quickly to the front door. She picked up his leash and locked the door, and they started down the front porch steps. "Let's see what's going on in our little burg today, Henry," she said. Walking briskly, they headed north down the hill, toward the lake.

Two

Ruby Bainbridge held the heavy drapes between her fingers, opening them just a crack to see the street. She stepped to the side so that she was in no danger of being seen, nervously jiggling her right foot behind her, a habit she'd had since childhood.

"Stop that movement," Aunt Eleanor used to say. "People will think you have to go to the bathroom all the time. Or, worse yet, that you have St. Vitus's Dance. Either way, it's not good. Please stop."

Ruby had tried hundreds of times to stop, but it was no use. She was fine with it now. It had taken her five decades, but at fifty-four she really didn't give a great big fat hairy hoot if anyone liked her nervous jiggle or not. "Live and let live" was her motto now. She craned her neck slightly, peering through the vertical peephole of the drapes to get a better look at Ellen leaving her house across the street.

How does she stand it? Always in and out with that silly dog. Thank you, Lord, that I don't own one of them.

She watched Ellen and Henry all the way to the corner, the dog anxiously sniffing the street lamp as if it were a wild rabbit, tugging at the leash hard enough to pull Ellen's arm right out of her shoulder, for heaven's sake. As they disappeared down the hill, obviously headed for the lake, Ruby sighed and closed the drapes. Not much going on this afternoon. She moved away from the parlor window, making her way to the kitchen at the end of the long hallway. Ruby knew the neighborhood would become increasingly quiet as the warm fall afternoons turned into frigid winter days, her neighbors shuttering their windows and sweeping their front porches of the last of the dried leaves, the summer furniture cleaned and wrapped in plastic for winter storage. In the winter months she'd hardly see anyone on her street, the horrid cold blasts of Canadian air pressing down on them, bullying them, using up their energy, forcing them to stay inside until the spring thaw.

"I know what's com-ing," she sing-songed. Reaching past the bright red apple-shaped cookie jar, she turned on the GE radio on the kitchen counter. The sound of big band music filled the kitchen. She loved those sounds, that swing. She never changed the station, keeping the dial right there. She started moving her hips with the rhythm, closing her eyes, feeling the clarinets in her soul.

"I'll get by-y-y-y-y, as long as I-I-I-I have you-u-u-u-u," she sang, her arms embracing a pretend partner, her legs enjoying the pull of deep dips as they moved in silky unison, circling, smaller in-between steps perfectly in time together, delicately light on their feet, mesmerizing to other dancers who stopped to watch, envious, charmed by the couple. "Po-ver-ty may come to me-e-e-e, that's true. But what care I-I-I-I, oh, I'll get by-y-y-y-y, as long as I-I-I-I have you-u-u-u-u-u."

A small applause as the band brought the number to a close. Ruby held on to the last waist dip then smiled shyly as her dream partner pulled her upright and released her. She reached for the counter to steady herself. The close footwork threw knifelike pains into her ankle.

"Oh, thank you, dah-ling," she said. She batted her eyelashes furiously, giving them her best Marilyn Monroe pose, waving to the dancers, blowing kisses. "You are simply delightful! I'm off now— see you next time!" Basking in their affection, she moved to the far end of the kitchen, to the long windows overlooking her small backyard. She stood still while her heart slowed down, the sun hot on her face, her upper lip moist from the dancing, her hair a little damp at the temples, the gray and white finger waves slightly frizzy from the exertion. She took a deep breath, exhaled through her mouth slowly, and felt her breathing relax. She watched a plump robin bob for worms, storing up energy for the imminent flight south, and listened, not unhappily, to a noisy blue jay screaming at everything that moved. She calmed down, glad that the gay excitement was now over—and a little embarrassed, although she couldn't say why exactly. She reached into her pocket for a tissue and felt the Swiss Army knife, cool and strong against her fingertips. She loved that knife. She had carried it with her everywhere since she was eleven years old, since her Girl Scout days. It was an old, trusted friend.

Tucking the tissue into her apron pocket she moved back into the kitchen. "Leg of lamb and *Dr. Phil,*" she said. "My favorite combination. Get after it, Ruby Bainbridge."

She went to the hall closet just outside the living room and pulled out the TV table, bringing it back to the eat-in part of the kitchen by the windows. She had a large TV and cable box lodged securely on the built-in shelf that once was the butler's pantry pass-through. Ruby had moved the TV out of the living room several years ago after Mother died, preferring the coziness of watching TV and eating in that small alcove. Everything she needed was right there for her. She could safely snuggle in, enjoy her meals in peace, and keep an eye on the birds and the TV all at once. She congratulated herself again on her good sense in using the space so wisely.

She slid the legs of the TV table sideways under her overstuffed chair, at an angle giving her room to get in later and pull the table around in front of her. She was proud to have figured out how to put *Dr. Phil* on a daily "record series" mode, which allowed her to access the show anytime. It had taken her two weeks to figure out that crazy machine, but she hadn't given up until it was done. She did the same for *Oprah*. *Boy, I love that Oprah*, she thought.

The remains of last Sunday's leg of lamb were tightly wrapped in aluminum foil in the fridge. Ruby loved lamb, hot or cold, and was sorry this would be the last of her leftovers. Still, she had managed six meals out of that small leg, a testimony to her frugality, her willingness to eat half of what she felt like eating. She ran her hands over her hips, smoothing her cotton dress, feeling the smallness of her body. Pride coming before the fall notwithstanding, she was proud as she looked down at her flat stomach, her still-good-looking legs.

Well, why shouldn't I be proud? I've worked hard to keep my figure. Pride isn't always a bad thing.

She reached for her favorite blue Fiesta dinner plate—an original Fiesta, not one of those new ones they sell at Macy's. She put a slice of Pepperidge Farm thin sandwich bread in the center of the plate, ready for the small handful of lamb to be spread out evenly, touching all parts of the little slice. It was true. She had never let herself go. It wasn't so much a matter of pride as it was a point of character. She believed in self-denial, the kind modeled by the nuns she had known as a child. They seemed to want nothing more than a calm demeanor, lovely, clean white fingernails, and pressed black habits. Always in control, always that tense secret-keeper smile on their lips. Ruby had wondered how they could bear the pressure of the headgear they wore, the stiff dimiti starched into the coif, the white band steadily pressing into the forehead, a deep crease etched into the skin by the end of the day, no doubt. She thought they must trap a lot of perspiration in those dimities. Wet, hot skin boxed in under there with no way to relieve the itchy, salty sweat. Yet they always looked serene, as if they'd just come from a sanguine Maundy Thursday midnight vigil. Those nuns were a discipline worth remembering, worth emulating.

It wasn't easy choosing food as her character builder. She loved food. She thought about it from the minute she woke up until the last forkful of dessert at night. She only allowed herself one forkful, never more. Sort of the way Dolly Parton says she eats, never denying herself anything, but only taking one bite, period. She was no Dolly Parton, which meant Ruby's bite was pretty big, maybe even obscene. The dessert fork she used was a large sterling silver service fork Mother had left her, the one on the Thanksgiving turkey platter year after year, the one that could carry almost a full helping of dessert, with a little practice. Ruby had lots of practice. She finely honed her ability to pile high the cake, ice cream, and whipped cream on the fork without them slipping off. The trick was to pile high, not wide. Tall and deep.

She looked at the sad cup of vanilla pudding she'd have to eat for dessert tonight. She loved pudding but it took her four days to eat a batch. Hot off the stove, she'd pour the pudding into half-cup ramekins to stretch them out for the week. But this was the fourth day and the pudding had pulled away all around the inside of the ramekin, the top part dried out despite the tightly pulled piece of Saran Wrap. She'd deal with that pudding later. Ruby had a dozen ways to perk up sad food. Disciplining herself to live on $1,800 a month, she knew all the tricks. Reaching into the second shelf, she put her hands on the glass jar of leftover gravy. She dumped the gravy into a white enamel saucepan, put it on the front burner of the electric stove, and turned it to high. In the cupboard she hesitated a minute, unsure if she wanted French-cut green beans or Jolly Green Giant yellow corn. Eenie, meenie, miney, moe, back and forth with her finger, landing . . . on . . . the . . . corn.

She cleaned the last bits of lamb from the leg and thought briefly that Ellen's dog would probably love that big bone. She was about to drop it into the garbage can by the sink, then hesitated. She didn't give a juicy spit for that silly dog, Lord knows, but it might be a good idea to keep the bone for, what was his name? Harold? Henry? Harley? She couldn't remember, having been close to the dog only once since Ellen had moved in across the street seven months ago. Ruby had to admit she was curious about the reclusive Ellen. She didn't want her as a friend. She simply felt it was her duty to keep tabs on what went on in the neighborhood. Too many things had changed on West Fifth Street in the past thirty years. Somebody had to keep track. The bone would be her calling card.

Three

Ellen stood on the Utica Street Bridge, looking down on the Oswego River as it rushed out, pouring itself into Lake Ontario. Two bridges joined the east and west sides in this small upstate New York city, one crossing the river on Bridge Street, the other—parallel to it and four blocks over—crossing along Utica Street. Ellen loved this part of downtown and had always parked the car to walk the bridges when she came home to Oswego. Now she could walk them every day if she wanted. After thirty-five years away, she had moved back home after ending her long marriage. It was still too soon to tell if the divorce and the move had been the right decisions, but she was stuck with both now, and that was fine. Nothing really mattered much anymore.

Holding tightly to the rail, she leaned over to look down on the men fishing along the river wall. The men wore light jackets and sneakers, their navy blue NY Yankee hats pulled low over their eyes, the wool brims tightly curved into an upside down *U*. It was a cool fall day, her favorite time of year in Oswego. Henry stood behind her, wagging his tail. He wanted to get to the lake where he could bury his nose in the smell of dead mooneyes that had washed up on shore.

Her mother's spot was still there, of course. Ellen focused on it, visualizing that frigid day forty-eight years ago when Mother, in her heavy wine-red winter coat, had stood quietly on the ledge a few feet above the rushing river, preparing to jump. Ellen imagined the scene, the men on the river's edge smoking cigarettes and fishing just like today, not suspecting a thing. She could only guess at their shock when they saw her mother dive easily into the frigid water, barely making a splash.

Exactly how and why it all happened remained a mystery to Ellen and her two younger sisters. At the time she overheard her grandparents say the girls were certainly too young at three, five, and seven for a frank discussion. "We'll just tell them their mother is sick and she'll be home in a little while, when she's better," they said. Wanting details, Ellen would sneak out of her bedroom and tiptoe down the front staircase to listen as family members whispered to each other in the living room about the suicide attempt, trying to figure it out.

She picked up tidbits in the stories about the two brave fishermen, one who jumped into the river, grabbing her mother before she sank, and the other man who pulled her out of the dark green water. A third man ran to the corner store and called the ambulance, which took her mother to the Oswego Hospital where she stayed until Mother's parents could arrange for her to go to a sanitarium on the lake near Rochester, an hour away. The expensive sanitarium was determined to be far enough out of Oswego to stop tongues from slicing up their daughter's life, yet close enough for weekly visits. It was the first of twenty-one years Ellen's mother would spend in and out of psychiatric wards, the grace of lithium finally stabilizing her schizophrenia.

Unable to cope with the situation, and unwilling to take on the responsibility of three young daughters, Ellen's father had abandoned his small family when Ellen was nine. He moved to Fort

Lauderdale where the weather was warm, and where he eventually found a nice enough woman who loved to drink as much as he did. Ellen and her sisters never saw or heard from him again. In 1970, Uncle Will called from Florida to tell them their father had died.

Ellen straightened up and gently patted Henry's head. How many times had she walked this bridge as a child? Hundreds? Thousands? She stretched her legs and moved across the bridge, remembering how she had gone from home to home as a child, staying with Mother's three sisters at various times and seasons. With each visit she had tried to dissolve into family routines as she settled into new beds, figured out how to negotiate the personalities of her cousins, and most of all, do what was expected of her. She stayed busy.

By the time she was eight, she had discovered the magic of books. With the turn of a page she could escape into family life on the prairie, drive around in a bright-red roadster solving crimes, fly high over the Atlantic, or engage the genius of a musical prodigy. It gave her an internal life she nurtured like a porcelain secret; by selecting books from different genres at the public library, she became Pocahontas in the summer reading group and attempted to emulate Bach and Chopin by working harder at the piano as she perfected her Burgmuller fingering exercises.

She loved the summer days in Fruit Valley when she'd tuck into the morning room at Aunt Maggie's where no one was likely to venture in and tell her to go outside and play. At night she would get in bed to read, snuggling in with her mischievous cousin Mitzi, who eventually sent them both to sleep giggling from her hair-raising ghost stories. She rode bikes and horses, packed picnic lunches, swam and played golf at the country club with her pal Teresa, and in the heat of July went on trips to Canada and the Adirondacks with Aunt Maggie and Uncle Sean's family. She was always deeply sad for days when the school buses roared into action and she had to return to town, to her city cousins—although the reunion with cousin Ginger made that worthwhile.

She had missed her sisters, who grew up together at their grandparents' home on the east side, but nothing could change that. In time, picking up bits and pieces of adult conversations, Ellen surmised that her grandparents had decided three children were simply too much for them to take on in their seventies when Mother had become ill. They decided that Ellen would be the traveling child. And although it had stung when she heard it, Ellen knew she fit the description her cousin Gloria ascribed to her one holiday season as Ellen unpacked her red Amelia Earhart weekender suitcase next to her cousin's bed.

"You certainly are the gypsy child," Gloria had said.

Ellen turned again to the river to watch one of the men reel in a fish, a nice, big lake trout. She could almost hear the sizzle of butter in the cast-iron pan where the fish would land for supper. Her mother had loved a haddock fish sandwich around the lake at The Stands, at either Mulcahey's or Rudy's, and then a maple-walnut ice cream cone at Stone's Candy Shop for dessert, with a small box of chocolate raspberry creams to go. Ellen would take her to those places when they both came home for visits. Mother's illness made conversations unpredictable. One minute she'd be fine; a second later her mind would leapfrog, taking her to places Ellen couldn't understand. As a result, they never talked about anything meaningful. Ellen didn't have to be told why her mother never returned to Oswego after being released from the hospital the year Ellen graduated from college. The town was too small and her mother's life had been too big to ignore. Instinctively Ellen knew Mother was protecting herself from familiar streets and houses, from people and family and friends with their unsure stares, the questions in their minds showing up in their eyes. Mother knew she had no answers to give them.

Instead she chose to live with strangers. She was settled into a sheltered environment in the home of a middle-aged couple who were paid to watch over her in their home downstate, in Utica. Mother's dad had created a trust fund for his daughter's lifelong care, and with medication, Mother was well enough to do occasional hospice service. She told Ellen she enjoyed that work, the privilege of sitting and waiting quietly, sponging pale faces with cool water, her spirit unaffected by the shallow breaths of her dying acquaintances, her mind in neutral, praying for their release from terrible diseases. Her skill as a linguist in Latin, German, and Greek had been destroyed years before, her *summa cum laude* brilliance erased by her illness.

Ellen breathed in the river air deeply. Her mother's life was an enigma, breathtakingly sad. The life everyone thought she would have had disappeared by the time she was thirty-four. And yet, it was a life with a sweet spot.

No matter what that damn disease did to her thoughts, my mother never lost the core of her soul. In a mental hospital, at someone's bedside, or facing the stigma at home, she always brought gentleness with her. Her inherent kindness survived the terrors.

Her mother had died peacefully in an Oswego nursing home three years ago. When the call had come that Mother's time was short, Ellen booked a flight from Nashville. She arrived late the next afternoon to find an empty bed in Mother's room, with a neatly packed box of her clothes sitting on the dresser. The harsh battering of dementia and Alzheimer's disease had taken their final toll in the early hours of the morning. She was eighty-six. Ellen always would regret that she had been too late to hold her mother's hand at the end.

Hearing a shout from below, she looked down to see another large trout being carefully reeled out of the river. Two of the fishermen shuffled over to take a closer look, peering down into the water as if they expected to see more fish circling around, ready for the hook.

Look up here, you guys. I'll volunteer for the hook. My life is in such a shambles that I'll happily dive into that water and swim with the salmon until you yank me up or the current pulls me away.

But she wouldn't be doing any swan dives today, and she knew it. In truth, nothing suicidal was an option even though she had toyed with the idea many times since her divorce. It would be too messy, too public, and her two sons would be horrified.

The most serious threat had come three weeks after she'd left Nashville for Oswego to begin again. News of Matt came in an e-mail from Ellen's cousin Julie.

I just couldn't stop laughing when I opened my e-mail this morning. Got the one from Matt about his wonderful new girlfriend! That didn't take long. So much for broken hearts. Just a typical man . . . on to the next one before sunset. Didn't skip a beat. You are well rid of him. Love, Julie.

That Matt was announcing the girlfriend to close relatives, and probably to everyone in the world they had once shared, was startling. He was making it clear that he was moving on, starting over—right away. He was through with Ellen, and it changed everything. Ellen realized she hadn't believed, deep down, that she and Matt were really finished. That was nearly six months ago. Since then she'd dropped a ton of weight—the divorce twenty, her therapist noted. Some people said she never looked better; others said they hardly recognized her. She'd never been heavy, wearing a size ten for years. Now she was down to 119 pounds, a size four, and she knew she looked like hell. A five-foot-six skeleton. Her hollow cheeks and sunken eyes gave her that haunted look, the result of no fat in the upper or lower lids; tiny wrists and fingers couldn't sustain her old rings or watches; her limp hair she changed from ash-blonde to an Irish red and cut short and spiky so it would have some style in lieu of texture and shine.

She was constantly in danger of a sudden meltdown, like the one a couple of days ago. She had been in the hardware store buying a small hammer when, who knows why, she was suddenly exhausted by it and started sobbing, wet stains dripping down the front of her favorite green Club Monaco T-shirt. She couldn't stop crying. She shuffled along, finding herself paying for the hammer, her shirt lightly soaked by the time it was her turn. At the cash register Jake Burnside stumbled all over himself trying to understand what anyone in his store had done to make her cry.

"Nothing. Absolutely nothing," Ellen said, her face like stone, tears dripping off the edge of her nose onto the counter. Jake grimaced as he saw her body fluids dotting his counter. Not wanting to upset her further, he leaned back slightly, looking down under the counter to make sure his Lysol and roll of paper towels were handy. Behind her the people in line bobbed left and right trying to see what was going on. Ellen didn't care if they saw, what they saw, or how they felt about it.

"She all right?" a woman asked. She pushed against the Formica counter, leaning over to get a good look. "What's going on, Jake?" Jake didn't know. He wanted to tell her women were just nuts.

"Not a thing's wrong, Mabel."

He handed Ellen her change, winking and smiling stiffly as he gave her the hammer in a brown paper bag. "We're all checked out now, aren't we?" Ellen hadn't been able to laugh or cry about that crazy incident. It was just who she was now. She couldn't trust herself to behave anymore.

Tired of the bridge, Henry pulled hard on the leash. Ellen turned to let him know she'd pick up the pace and caught sight of a sailboat gliding through the break walls on its way out to the lake. She smiled for the first time in three days. Sailboats were chariots of the gods. Strong and swift, yet so vulnerable to the violent whims of wind and tide. They survived even after capsizing and filling up with water, just by being right-sided and bailed out.

There's a metaphor.

Several weeks ago she'd run into an old high school friend, Elliott Beck, and he told her the twenty-one-foot *Lightning*, the boat that Ellen's Uncle Samuel sailed for years, was now his. She had learned to sail on *Lightning*. She wanted to think it was Elliott now on his way out for an hour's ride, the lake a fickle lover, the need to catch the wind at any moment a discipline and a fearful joy. Lucky Elliott, safe home.

"All right. We're off, sweet Henry. Let's get you some stinky mooneyes, shall we?"

Henry nearly danced across the bridge.

Four

Ellen slid off her corduroys and slipped into her sleeping pants. She had four more pairs of the light cotton flannel bottoms in the drawer, all washed so many times it was like wearing her favorite T-shirt on her legs. She pulled the chocolate-stained white shirt over her head and threw it into the bathroom hamper, then picked up her toothbrush and toothpaste from the drawer by the sink.

You are pathetic.

She pushed at her sunken cheekbones, moving in closer to look at her teeth. Still blazingly white after nights of sleeping with a mouthful of custom molds filled with bleaching agents last year— she was briefly thankful. Her skin was so pale, she wanted to rub her cheeks to bring up some quick color. But she didn't dare; a couple of weeks ago she had done that and small black-and-blue bruises rose up after the pink disappeared. Finishing quickly so she wouldn't have to look at herself anymore, she went into the laundry room and pulled a fresh white long-sleeved shirt from one of the stacks on the dryer. She stared at the three precisely folded piles of short- and long-sleeved white T-shirts. They were almost comical in their sameness, none with any artwork or clever sayings on them, no this-is-where-I-went-to-college or Hard Rock Café London imprint.

I appear to be one amazingly simple woman. Or just a boring old simpleton devoid of taste and style. Then again, maybe I'm looking at the clothes of a woman who knows what she likes and when she finds it, never strays? That's not me. Or perhaps this is the uniform of a woman so tired of life that she has lost her sense of fun. Getting warmer. At any rate, one observation is unmistakable: I only buy the best. Only soft, thin-gauged, all-cotton, well-cut, and finely stitched T-shirts from Club Monaco at forty dollars a pop. It hasn't always been true, but I like the fact that I can do it now. When I was raising the boys and paying all kinds of household bills, I knew all about Fruit of the Loom. I was right there with the other moms trolling the racks in Wal-Mart looking for inexpensive underwear for myself, picking up a packet of Hanes Her Way comfort briefs, three for $3.99, a bra for $5.99, and T-shirts, three for $10. Not the end of the world.

It all changed when she hit her fiftieth birthday. Deeply affected by the hard reality that she was in the final phase of her life, with only thirty more years of living if she were really lucky, Ellen had made a sacred pledge to herself on that milestone birthday: only the best underwear and beautifully made soft T-shirts from now on.

More than that, she had decided to use really good luggage. She discarded her $19.99 black carry-on bag with the funny rollers and zippers that failed after a few trips. For her birthday that year she bought a dozen Club Monaco T-shirts, eight pairs of Victoria Secret underpants, six Bali bras she loved, and a full set of Hartmann luggage.

Sitting now on the edge of the bed in her tiny Oswego house, she reached into the nightstand for a Twix bar, unwrapped it quickly, snapped the twin bars in half, and popped one into her mouth, not caring that she had just brushed her teeth. Her nosy neighbor across the street would have a lot to talk about if she ever discovered both the monochromatic T-shirt drawer and this deep drawer stuffed with chocolate bars. Ellen could hear her asking, "What kind of grown woman piles candy bars into the nightstand, eats them in expensive white T-shirts, and stays skinny as a rod?" She wouldn't know what to tell her, except to say the candy bars were the only thing that appealed to her besides milk and V-8 Juice, and the occasional egg and toast. Nothing else worked.

"The diet of the clinically depressed," her therapist said.

She slid off her socks, wriggled her toes free, and tossed the socks across the room, missing the hamper by two feet. The old Ellen would have jumped up to get those socks and put them where they should be, *pronto*. Not today. She fell back on the bed, massaging her temples with long fingers, closing her eyes, feeling the relief of grayness, enjoying the melting chocolate on her tongue. If she wasn't careful she'd fall asleep. She looked at her watch and sat up, running her fingers through her short hair. It was only four thirty, and while the early fall twilight suggested she could give up on today, she knew it would be foolish to tuck into bed at this hour. She'd only wake up around nine, then be wide-eyed and restless the entire night.

"Who wants a treat?" she asked. Henry's ears rose up instantly to point position, his mouth open, grinning as he pulled himself up, tongue out, his eyes boring into hers. "All right, buddy, let's go get you some munchies." Henry sat as still as a Victorian portrait while Ellen pulled the bag of organic snacks from the cupboard. He ate his one meal a day at noon and loved these treats in between. Henry was panting lightly now, anticipating the crunchy oval cookies as well as the long dental stick, which he'd save for last. "Enjoy," she said.

Leaning against the kitchen counter, she watched him snap at those hard cookies, little crumbs spewing out of the sides of his mouth as he chewed. He'd stand up and lick the floor clean when he was finished, never leaving a hint of detritus. She smiled as she watched him hold the dental stick between his front paws, coming in sideways to munch away its semisoft goodness. When he was done, he came over to say thanks.

Ellen snuggled his forehead, her hands rubbing his ears the way he liked it, around the base of the ears in a circle, gently, his big dark eyes never leaving hers. She was surprised when she heard a low growl rising in his throat. He angled his head side to side, his ears peaked, danger detected. An intruder? Not likely. Another UPS truck whining gears down West Fifth Street driving him nuts? A far-off boom of thunder only he could hear, terrifying him again? Henry broke away and slid wildly on the hardwood floor. He raced out of the kitchen, gained his footing as he hit the music room carpet, and charged through the living room until he landed at the front door, barking wildly as if he'd just cornered a cat. Ellen heard the doorbell ring. Moving quickly, she called ahead, telling Henry to quiet down, it was all right, and to stop barking! When she was nearly to the front door she wondered who'd be calling on her. She really didn't know anybody in Oswego anymore—at least, not well enough for someone to just drop by unannounced.

She grabbed Henry's collar and opened the door to see that snoopy neighbor from across the street standing tentatively on the edge of the porch, looking as if she were ready to turn and run down the steps if necessary. In her arms she held what looked like a large bone sitting on a bed of paper towels. Henry pressed his nose against the screen door that separated them, barking hard, spraying spittle on Ellen's pajama pants.

"I thought your dog might like this bone now that I'm finished with the lamb," said Ruby Bainbridge. She pushed back her shoulders and stood spine-straight, her face tight, her eyes never leaving that dog. Saliva ran from Henry's mouth as he continued to bark as if she were the very hound of hell come to call. Pulling hard against Ellen's grip, Ruby wondered if he might break loose.

"Oh. Well, how nice of you," Ellen said. She struggled to hold onto Henry, bending down to speak directly, nose-to-nose. "Stop that barking right now. I mean it!" Henry's barking turned into soft throaty growls as Ellen told him to *stay*. He sat down, panting from the excitement, looking right at Ruby the whole time. He was calmer now, catching the scent of the lamb bone, sniffing toward Ruby, the bone in his viewfinder. "He's really a very friendly dog," Ellen said. Ruby drew back her head as if to say, "Really?" Ellen didn't care if Ruby believed her or not. "Well. It looks as if he's fine now. I was just about to start dinner, or I'd ask you in. But this is very nice of you to think of Henry. Very thoughtful."

As she said it Ellen let go of Henry's collar and opened the screen door just a little, intending to slip outside and talk a minute with the woman, get the bone, and be done with it. What happened next was shocking even to Ellen. Ruby would later say she felt like Charlie Chaplin in that old silent movie *The Tramp*, where he's just strolling along the peaceful country road when a car comes out of nowhere and hurls him into the air, knocking him upside down, topsy-turvy—such a surprise, a total stunner.

"There I was just being a good neighbor and that crazy dog comes out of the front door like a bullet, jumping up hard on me, grabbing that lamb bone, and tossing me down those front steps like a sack of potatoes," Ruby told her old friend, Violet Dohner, who brought homemade raisin toast soaked in butter and wrapped tightly in waxed paper, to keep Ruby strong during her hospital stay.

Ellen's jaw had dropped at the sight of Ruby rolling down those front steps. She wanted to scream but gulped in air instead, hand at her mouth, feeling as if she were seeing one of those terrible *America's Funniest Home Videos* as the horrifying scene unfolded. Seconds after Ruby landed, Ellen raced down the steps. She knelt next to her but didn't move the woman in case she had broken bones. Ruby was dazed but awake, her face bleeding and her wrist dangling at a frightening angle. She lay on her side, her legs piled on top of each other, an anklebone visible where it had popped through the skin. Knowing Ruby might be in shock, Ellen ran back to the porch and grabbed the throw blanket she kept on the Adirondack chair. She gently laid it over Ruby and dialed 911 from her cell phone.

"I need an ambulance! A woman has fallen down my porch steps," Ellen told the dispatcher, giving her the West Fifth Street address.

"I didn't fall," Ruby said, her voice small. "I was pushed down by that horrible dog. Oh-h-h-h, I'm bleeding . . ."

The ambulance arrived in less than five minutes, one of the benefits of living in a small, dying, upstate town. Rush hours were at nine in the morning, and again at five in the afternoon, both lasting less than twenty minutes. "Rust Belt" rush hour, a television newscaster had called it. Ruby's cotton dress twisted around and rode up her thighs as the paramedics pulled out the sheet they would use as a lift to get her onto the gurney. Ellen heard herself offering the obvious salvos. "It's going to be all right, Miss Bainbridge. Don't worry now. The ambulance will get you to the hospital in just a few minutes."

Lifting her head slightly to eyeball the front steps, Ruby tried to sit up. "Just tell me where that crazy dog is," she whispered.

"You're in no danger, Miss Bainbridge," Ellen said. She was relieved to see Henry settled at the far end of the porch, gnawing away on the lamb bone he gripped tightly in his front paws. "He's enjoying the bone you gave him."

The siren screamed as the ambulance pulled away from the curb, and Ruby closed her eyes, overwhelmed by the shock of her fall. She forgot all about the creamy mushroom stew she had left simmering on the back burner of the stove at her house. In her best five-quart soup pan.

Five

Ruby groaned as she stretched her neck to look at the digital glow. Another hour had passed. It was still dark and too early to expect a visit from the nurse. She pressed the self-medicate button twice and waited for the painkiller to take the edge off. It was such a relief not to wait until some magic hour to get the medicine into her veins. Medication autonomy was certainly an improvement over the time she lay screaming in pain from her burst appendix and the surgery that followed. The nurses had acted like Russian border guards with their, "Not until eleven o'clock, Miss Bainbridge. Doctor's orders." As if the pain could tell time.

She lay with her eyes open trying to think about it, trying to get it straight in her mind again. The bone, the dog, the fall, the hospital, and now a cast on her broken ankle, another on her broken wrist, a dislocated left shoulder, and water on her left knee. What was it the doctor had said? She'd have about six to eight weeks in the ankle cast, then physical therapy to restore the range of motion in her ankle. The same with her broken wrist. Right ankle, right wrist, left knee swollen like a softball. How could she get around or use a walker when the right side of her body looked like a rag doll after a back-alley run-in with a cat? Not to mention that the left knee couldn't bear any pressure. On top of that, her dislocated left shoulder, popped back into place in the emergency room, thank God, was as sore as a mouthful of cankers. Good lord, she was one big hot mess. Ruby felt the sting of tears.

Oh, Mother. If I ever needed a bowl of cherry Jell-O, it's now. What I'd give for a big glass of flat ginger ale with Arthur Godfrey's soothing voice coming out of that old fashioned radio, asking questions, playing the ukulele, introducing singers, and telling innocent jokes, keeping me company in those lonely bedridden hours. Oh, sweet Mother, you gave up that kitchen radio so I could have it upstairs in my bedroom every time my colitis flared up, my stomach turning cartwheels, diarrhea racing through me, stuck in bed for two or three days at a time.

The colitis attacks had come every few months for about ten years, from the time she was eleven years old. Her Uncle Sean, the MD married to Mother's sister, said the colitis would go away as Ruby grew up, accepted things, and found a better way to handle the things that bothered her. Nobody talked about "stress" in those days. It was 1950s medicine and Uncle Sean was almost right. The colitis subsided in her early twenties. However, it was replaced by periodic anxiety attacks that ruptured when things got stuffed down deep inside of Ruby. With no wiggle room to rationalize the worries, her anxieties manifested themselves as violent, unpredictable diarrhea attacks, triggered by anticipated events or casual remarks, things that stayed with her for days or weeks, grinding up her insides, pressuring her head to pound, and eventually, her bowels to explode. Ruby felt Mother looked at her as if she were a stranger each time Ruby doubled over in pain. In her calmest voice Mother would ask, "Ruby, what is it? What are you afraid of? What makes you so nervous, sweetheart? Tell me, please. I'm sure I can help."

But there was no help for it and Ruby couldn't explain it to her mother then, nor to herself even now. She only knew that when

Mother described her to people as "a sensitive, nervous little girl who was born to take care of us in our old age," Ruby felt better. She was happy enough to spend her whole life on West Fifth Street in her parents' house, the house her grandfather had built in 1896.

"I think there's something wrong with me sometimes," Ruby told her first real girlfriend, Joanne Cignataro, in the fifth grade. "I saw the lady at the cash register at Castro Giovanni's grocery point me out to a customer yesterday. She said I was a strange girl, an odd sort of kid, with a quick tongue. Stranger still, Joanne, I really didn't mind that description. Don't you think that's weird? I mean, weird that I don't mind her saying that? I kind of liked it when she called me strange."

"You are different," Joanne said, her darling little white teeth all in a row, the front one overlapping just a bit, just enough that you wanted to tell her a good night retainer could work wonders right there. "But you're different in a good way, Ruby. In a creative way, I think. My papa always says I have a quick tongue. I've decided that's just the adult way of saying we tell the truth and they don't like hearing it."

Ruby had lost touch with Joanne in junior high. Nothing dramatic occurred. They just went their separate ways and found new, more interesting friends. They'd wave to each other and smile in the hallways and Ruby always felt a little guilty because in her heart, Ruby knew she had ditched Joanne because she thought Joanne was just, well, boring. Still, they had written forever notes in each other's yearbooks in 1964. "Love with a capital L," Ruby had scrolled with a big flourish in ending hers. Joanne went on to nursing school in Rochester after graduating from Oswego High. She married a doctor and had a big house on the water in Seattle the last time Ruby had news of her. Joanne had told Ruby early on that she would marry her way out of Oswego. Most of the girls Ruby knew in high school felt that way and nearly all of them had succeeded.

After college Ruby had her own thoughts about traveling to Spain and France, of having a husband, a home, and a child. Like the lives of Mother and Mother's sisters, Ruby thought she'd teach a few years until she got married, then become an at-home wife and mother, running the household, planning small cocktail suppers for their friends and her husband's business clients, baking from-scratch brownies for the church bake sale, owning a full length Blackglama mink coat and a nice little Russian Sable fur stole to wear to bridge club. She had pictured herself driving a sleek black Cadillac like Mother, or a saucy convertible like her aunt.

She had had plenty of opportunities for that life, dating some of Oswego's finest prospects: Herbie Swanson, Lester Harris, and Charles Morrison, to name a few. But she never let any of them get to first base. As soon as they kissed her on the lips, she was busy the next time they called. She didn't like all that touching, the smell of their breath, and the idea of their hands on her. Still, when she thought about a married life, Ruby had envisioned having a darling little girl. Her mother wondered aloud how Ruby could ever manage having a child, for heaven's sake: "You're all nerves and dreams at the same time! Not to mention how you hate to be touched, Ruby. Don't you know a child needs to be touched?"

In time the idea of having that kind of life simply faded away. The longer she lived at home, the easier it was to stay. She turned forty and the life her mother and aunts had modeled slipped from Ruby's grasp. She took care of her parents into their old age. Both of them lived at home right up to the end when heart failure finally gripped them within six months of each other, Mother and Father both dying in their late eighties. As expected, she inherited the house and Father's money; she was set for life, assuming she was reasonably careful with things. Of course, she would be, they knew. By the time she was in her early fifties, Ruby had become a happy spinster, a woman who wrapped her home around her and enjoyed the quiet life. At least that's what she'd tell the women at church whenever they asked her to come with them on the bus trip to New York City for a few days of fun, food, and the wonderful tours of the Catacombs, the Cathedral of St. John the Divine, and of course, St. Patrick's Cathedral, where they'd try to guess the value of the solid brass baldachin over the main altar. "We make a game of it," they'd say. "The tour guide tells us what he thinks it's worth, and whoever comes closest to his guess buys the rest of us a drink. It's very exciting!"

"I have enough excitement right here in Oswego," Ruby would say as a caution to them, her tone almost a warning that things outside were far too dangerous for anyone to fool with. She certainly wouldn't. "I have all the drama I need right here at home."

In fact, the thought of leaving Oswego even for a trip to the Upstate Medical Center down in Syracuse forty-five miles away was enough to rile her up. She had heard the doctors talking about it last night as she lay in the emergency room waiting for her X-ray results. They suspected all three of her anklebones had been damaged and some kind of microsurgery was needed. No one on the Oswego Hospital surgical roster had the advanced training necessary, but Upstate had plenty of specialists, they said. Ruby had dozed off before her X-ray results came back but she knew one thing for sure: Syracuse was out of the question. She would heal right on West Fifth Street and no one could make her go to Upstate Medical. No way. Period.

She reached for a Kleenex on the nightstand. This strange room, her broken body, and all this disruption pushed her to tears. She closed her eyes, determined to think about something else. She decided to picture herself resting in her own bed in the roomy front bedroom that used to be Father's. It was the best of the five upstairs bedrooms, with its widow's walk running along the west wall, the lake breeze finding its way through the open windows at night, the curtains fluttering, pounding lightly against the screens like summer waves, rising and falling. She could just feel her lumpy mattress and the soft pillows. The pillows were broken in perfectly even though they had those telltale caramel-colored streaks Oprah said were poop skid marks from dust mites living inside. Oprah had even shown magnified pictures of the mites on TV and, well, they did look nasty. But replace pillows every six months? Oprah had lost touch. Ruby Bainbridge wouldn't be throwing away good money on new pillows when those mites didn't hurt her. Oprah was way too rich for her own good. Let them live in there if they wanted.

She stretched for another Kleenex and noticed the eerie yellow light coming from the street lamp on the corner of Oneida Street. London. Foggy night. Dr. Jeykll and Mr. Hyde. She looked at the digital clock again. Six o'clock. The sun would be up soon. She had trouble settling down. She felt undone, like a ribbon was dangling before her and she couldn't get a grip on it.

There's something I need to think about, but I can't see it. I can't get it into focus. It was as if she had a tiny crack in her mind, a crack lodged somewhere that she couldn't finger. *Oh well, it'll come back to me if it's important.* She took a deep breath and thought some more about what she'd do when she got home.

Tomorrow she'd have breakfast on the back porch since the weather was still decent. A five-minute soft-boiled egg with a piece of crisp rye toast cut into vertical soldiers for dipping, a thin slather of cherry jam on the toast, and a cup of instant coffee, black and hot. She'd top it off with some nice, cold, tart Bluebird canned orange juice in her favorite juice glass with the oranges painted on it, a glass she'd had since childhood.

First thing when I get home today I'll get out that pound of ground round from the freezer. I can watch Judge Judy *while I make a small meatloaf. I've got one more envelope of Lipton's Onion Soup mix that I can add in, and I know I have about a cup of leftover Ragu spaghetti sauce in the fridge. I can pour that on the top and add a little shredded yellow cheddar cheese at the end to melt. That will add nice little crispy bits on top. Just enough. That meatloaf will last me three days. Oh, for a cold meatloaf sandwich right now!*

Her stomach growled. She was hungry and thirsty for something other than tepid water sipped through a childish flexible straw from a plastic cup that the night nurse insisted on refreshing every few hours. It's no wonder she was hungry. She hadn't eaten anything since that hot lamb sandwich yesterday afternoon, for crying out loud. Now it was settled. Meatloaf and onion—mashed potatoes, and gravy for supper with some sautéed mushrooms. She had bought a nice bag of mushrooms at Price Chopper the day before yesterday, thinking they'd be a change from canned vegetables.

"Oh, that's it," she said. Her cheeks filled with saliva just thinking about it. She ran her tongue over her lips. "I'll slice up those button mushrooms and toss them into a couple of tablespoons of butter, salt, pepper, and a shot of Worcestershire sauce so they get that rich, dark color." She took a deep breath and smiled to think about how happy she would be, back in her own kitchen, the radio on, her cozy dining alcove with her favorite chair all soft and roomy, her squirrel friends providing the live entertainment, and a sentimental Turner classic movie on at seven. Maybe she'd slide a cold-hearted Bette Davis film into the DVD player instead. *Dark Victory* was about her favorite, or *Mr. Skeffington*. She loved the way Bette took him on.

Happy now, she closed her eyes, resting. She started to doze off, a tiny whistle sneaking out of her dry nostrils as she breathed deeply, a noisy little snore ready to launch. Then out of nowhere, it hit her.

"Oh my god!" she screamed. Her eyes popped open like fearsome jack-o-lanterns. She gripped that dangling ribbon with all her might. "Mushrooms! I left that mushroom stew on the back burner, simmering on low, simmering with the top off, *yesterday*." She sat up straight, tugging at her hair.

How could I have forgotten? How could I have been so careless? How could I have been so stupid?

Then she caught herself. It wasn't her fault! She had intended her Ellen Varner visit to be just a few minutes of delivering the lamb bone, a nice neighborly moment of simple conversation, and her return home with an invitation for lunch, or tea, or supper at Ellen's at some later date, in a week or two. It would be a thank-you for Ruby's thoughtfulness and Ellen's desire to be neighborly right back. That dog had ruined everything. That vicious, dumb, awful dog. "And Ellen not being able to control him," she spit, a handful of gray hair falling on the blanket.

The bedrail nearly collapsed as she threw herself against it, stretching to get her fingers on the emergency call button built into the side of the bed. Feeling it finally, she pushed and pushed the button, then flopped back down in bed, terrified, as the nurse strolled in.

"Well, good morning, Miss Bainbridge. Are we finally ready to go to the bathroom?"

Six

Ellen watched as the fire truck pulled up across the street. Two firemen in full regalia raced to the back of Ruby's house, pulling hoses as they went. Beeping sounds come from the truck as the firemen moved with an air of determined precision, a don't-even-think-about–bothering-us-now attitude in their work. She went out on the front porch and looked warily at her neighbors who were gathering quickly, the excitement pulling them all outside.

"What in the world?" whispered the woman who lived next door to Ellen, a woman she had only seen once since moving in. Her neighbor was a tall woman who appeared to be in her seventies. She had that cultured look in the genteel pull of her pure white hair into a classic bun at the nape of her neck, her black patent leather flats framing narrow feet, a lovely pale pink cashmere sweater over her shoulders, and a paper-thin diamond watch on her delicate wrist.

"I really don't know," Ellen said, her voice flat and low. It was all just a little much, this trauma drama. She wanted it to go away. She wanted these neighbors to disappear and the singular life of each household to return to isolated normal, beginning with her own. But Ruby Bainbridge seemed determined to bring the world to Ellen's doorstep.

"I heard about Ruby's fall from your veranda," said the neighbor. She moved her thin blue-veined hand over her eyes, shielding them from the sun, squinting as she looked up at Ellen on the porch. "What a terrible thing for you both to endure. Do you still have that naughty little dog?"

Ellen stepped back and edged toward her front door, wanting to escape, not interested in talking with the woman, nor with anyone on West Fifth Street. But she was stuck.

"Of course I still have my dog," she said. "His name is Henry and he is a wonderful animal, a fabulous dog. What happened to Ruby Bainbridge was very unfortunate and I feel very sad about it. But if you come to my front door with a fresh lamb bone in your hands, unannounced and uninvited, I think you take a chance that the dog in the house will go for that bone, don't you?"

"Standing here right this minute, I am understandin' your point," said the neighbor. She moved closer to the porch. "I am so sorry for you both havin' to go through such a terrible trial. I truly am, though I simply cannot take sides. You know that wouldn't be right. Besides, look at me! Am I not just the rudest person you know in our little town? Here I am standin' right before you, realizin' that I have not visited with you even once since you moved to West Fifth! Let me take the opportunity this very minute to introduce myself. I am Frances. Frances O'Reilly." She smiled and extended her hand, forcing Ellen to step down off the porch or be thought of as an impolite, boorish neighbor.

"I'm Ellen Varner. You aren't rude. I haven't been out of the house much except to walk Henry. We haven't had the chance to introduce ourselves." Ellen's social training pushed her forward, although her voice was cold. "How long have you lived next door, Miss O'Reilly?"

"Oh my, you simply must call me Frances! I do insist upon it— and it would be Mrs. O'Reilly, although my dear husband, Alan, departed this life two years ago. To answer your question, I have lived nearly all of my life—my adult life, that is—in Oswego." The lines in her soft white skin were deep and defining, evidence of a long life right there for all to see. "My husband was born and raised in Oswego and we moved here shortly after we were married. I'm an old Georgia peach, as my daddy used to say, a southern transplant in a northern world I could hardly have imagined, even if I had possessed the insight of the Prophets." She explained that she and Alan had met as young people at Vanderbilt University, in Nashville, "a wonderful old southern school. Alan was studyin' law at Vandy, and I was right close by at Peabody College getting my teaching degree," Frances added. "We were married forty-seven years and we lived in this house next to you for every bit of those years. Can you imagine? I hardly can, and I say that sincerely."

Frances was so delightful that Ellen felt guilty about her frosty response. She knew she should be better—and nicer. She should be the welcoming, outgoing person she used to be. It took so much energy. Right now all Ellen could think about was how to get this charming southern belle to go back into her own house and leave her alone.

"Oh! It looks like they're fixin' to leave," Frances said, pointing to the firemen. They watched the men rewind the hoses and prepare to board the truck. "Well, *hallelujah*. It must have been a small fire then. Ruby surely doesn't need anything else to complicate her life."

"Oh, I didn't mean to imply that you were at fault, Ellen, honey," she said. "As you so insightfully noted, a dog and a bone go together like hot biscuits and blackberry jam. I only meant Ruby is a delicate woman and change is just plain hard on her. Do you know her at all?"

Shaking her head, Ellen said, "No. Not even a little. I've seen her in the front windows from time to time, but until yesterday, I'd never actually met her. I assume she lives alone?"

"Oh my, yes. Well, now she lives alone, but she lived with her mama and daddy all of her life. She took care of them until they both died a few years ago. She was born in that very house. She never did marry. A happy spinster, we like to think."

Frances said Ruby's mama was fond of saying Ruby was the "change-of-life baby the good Lord sent" to take care of them in their old age. "I will say to you quietly, however, that I think her mama said it a mite too often," Frances added. "I believe it surely created a self-fulfillin' prophecy, if you know what I mean. Not that Ruby seemed inclined to do anything else. She always seemed content, happily moored to that house and the mama and daddy who loved her."

Ellen tried to imagine it. A whole life lived in one house, where first breaths ebbed into last ones; a life with never-ending parents, in a world of fading couches and chairs, and wallpaper too familiar to be replaced. She had a momentary vision of Ruby Bainbridge moving in and around the twilight rooms, year after year, with their thinning carpets and heavy drapes. She imagined Ruby pausing as she passed by the formal dining room where the table for twelve sat gathering dust like Miss Havisham. It was enough to make Ellen shiver.

"What about you, my dear? What brings you back to Oswego? I was given to understand you were raised here but moved away when you went to college."

There it is. The invasion of privacy. No matter how genuine its intentions, no matter how delicately handled, the basic premise never changed: everybody has to know everybody else's business.

"Gosh, I hope you'll excuse me, Mrs. O'Reilly, but I want to catch the firemen for a minute before they get away." Ellen raced down the sidewalk, waving at the men, leaving Frances standing in the grass, a stricken look on her face as if she had just been slapped. Ellen waited while the fireman acknowledged her before asking what everyone wanted to know.

"How do you think the fire started, and how extensive is the damage?"

The fireman turned and pushed back his big black hat, sweat covering his face, smudges of something gray on his cheek and lips. "There was no fire as it turns out, ma'am. But lots of smoke. *Lots* of smoke. It was pouring out of a big pan of something on the back burner of the kitchen stove. Whatever was in the pan had cooked away to nothing."

He took a long drink of water from his thermos and added, "Miss Bainbridge was lucky. If Mrs. Schmidt hadn't called it in when she heard those smoke alarms going off, it could have been a lot worse." He waved two other firemen toward the truck, signaling they were ready to move out. "Smoke damage is the devil to get out of a house, especially an old house like this one with all of that fancy woodwork and those Oriental carpets," he said to Ellen. "Not to mention the silk drapes. Gets into those things and stays forever. Miss Bainbridge may have to trash a lot of stuff when she gets home. I know that will just about kill her, but I hope she realizes how lucky she's been."

"Everything's out, then? No danger of any smoldering fire?"

"Oh, no danger now. We took special care with our wet-down. We all felt it would be a crying shame for her to lose her house after all the trouble with that crazy dog knocking her on her keister. What a terrible thing to happen to her, ya know?"

Ellen inched backward, smiling, thanking the fireman for the good news. "I know Ruby's friends and neighbors will be relieved to know."

She turned around and walked back across the street, aware that the neighbors were watching her every move. She looked up to see Mrs. O'Reilly sitting in one of the Adirondack chairs on her front porch, waiting for Ellen.

Oh, no. I'll never get rid of her. I'll have to share the news or she'll sit on my porch until I do. On second thought, this can be a good thing. I'll tell Frances what the fireman said, and ask her to spread the news on West Fifth Street, since she knows everyone. Then I can go inside.

She heard Henry barking in the backyard as neighbors returned to their homes. Most of them went around to the rear of their houses for a quick look around, just to make sure all was well and no fire-starter scenarios were hiding in their garages or on their back porches. Ellen knew they were feeling lucky that they were not as careless as Ruby had been; given half the chance, they knew they would be.

"Everything turned out just fine, Mrs. O'Reilly," Ellen said, out of breath as she edged into the other porch chair. "I'll give you the quick version of what he told me."

"Oh, my dear, please call me Frances," she interrupted. She touched Ellen's arm lightly. "Just take a breath and settle down a minute. When you're ready, tell me exactly what the fireman said. You must start from the beginning and don't leave out a thing! Every old woman knows the truth finds its home in the details."

Without warning Ellen started to cry, tears inching out in a weak stream, edging down her cheeks, creating sorry-looking thin wet streaks, like clown makeup gone wrong. She couldn't speak. All she could think about was getting into her bed, pulling up the sheet and soft white blanket, putting her head down on that cool pillow, and closing the blinds. She was drop-dead exhausted.

"Oh, my precious little darlin'. Look at you. And listen to me, pushing you beyond your edges. There now, just let it go, honey, let it go," Frances said softly. Looking away, she gave Ellen the space to be fully and completely inside-out sad.

"I know just how it is to be sorrowful, honey. Haven't I lived in Oswego for forty-nine years? Haven't I felt like putting myself into a big brown paper sack, tying it with a tight cord, and tossin' myself into the Oswego River a least a dozen times?" Frances said.

"Well, certainly, I have. I do believe we all have at one time or another."

Ellen pulled her knees up to her chin, hugging them, rocking slowly.

"Bless your heart," Frances said. She leaned back and closed her eyes. If an ice-cold glass of Chardonnay and a smelly old unfiltered cigarette had suddenly appeared before her, Frances would have grabbed each one with both hands. It was that kind of night.

"That's right, darlin'. Let yourself go all to pieces," she whispered. "Howl at that big old harvest moon."

Seven

Oswego seemed to change overnight from fall to winter. Most people remembered liking it as children, that quick turn-around, the unexpectedness of putting on the new winter coat in late October, the duty of kicking up leaves on the way to school replaced by windblown gutters, barren and clean. The change of seasons always brought hope, the chance for something new. People couldn't exactly put their finger on it, but something good—or at least something different—could happen when the short summer turned into vibrant fall and then rolled into long, insulated winter days.

Maybe it was the surprise element that made the season-change work. One night they'd all go to bed with the window open, the midnight air fresh and cool. "Good sleeping weather," folks would say. In the morning they'd throw off their comforters to discover a heavy frost. Turning on the morning news, they'd wince to see the weatherman all fired up, giddy at the prospect of nasty weather, his importance in their lives suddenly skyrocketing. "Will we see freezing rain and snow tonight?" he'd tease. "I'll be right back after this message with the full report. Stay tuned."

Oh shit, everyone would think. But they didn't leave their bedrooms. They waited for him to come back and tell them what hellish weather was on its way, blowing down from Canada, picking up moisture from the lake, dumping it all on little Oswego before it moved south, its power diluted by the time it got to Fulton just fifteen miles down the road.

The annual rituals of winter preparations finally pushed hard on people then, and they could no longer overlook their get-ready chores. Rakes came out of nowhere, enchanted by the siren song of a last-chance dance to get it done. Seemingly endless leaves were raked into bags and dumped at the curb for the Monday pickup that had been announced right after news of the imminent freeze. Old-time Oswegonians groused at the sight of the stacks of black plastic bags piled on city streets. Whatever happened to a good old week or two of burning leaves in the street, just off the curb in the gutter? Whatever happened to neighbors lending each other a hand, talking casually outside, moving the leaves along into the fire as they exchanged ideas about snow removal, the best insulation to put in the attic, and which tree would be the last to drop its leaves on the block? The time of fall rituals was gone, they'd mumble. Oswego isn't the same anymore, they'd agree.

The porch furniture was cleaned and whisked away to the garage or cellar. Peeling paint was patched up and the front steps were covered with thick, black, non-skid rubber runners, outdoor carpet, or step mats. The four-foot shrubs were clothed in protective circular fences made of wood and wrapped in burlap to stand up to heavy snowdrifts. Hanging baskets were dumped into the trash, their work done for another year—so sad, really, to see the petunias and impatiens still eager to squeak out more blooms, childish in their ignorance of the fundamental shift in things, oblivious to the telltale signs of the coming of the Oswego winter. Women got busy changing out the clothes closets, their suits and coats wearing the sharp fragrance of mothballs for two to three weeks into the new season. Summer wear was replaced by lined wool slacks and blue jeans, crew-neck sweaters and long-sleeved blouses, along with turtlenecks in several colors to brighten up the dark days ahead. Transitional gabardine jackets, quilted vests, and sweatshirts with hoods were lifted from the back to the front of the closet, different weights and textures ready for Indian Summer and the warm-cold shifts in weather before the winter settled in for five long months. Here we go.

Ellen dug around the back of her closet to find the box of winter gear, the gloves, scarves, and hats she had packed together last March in her move from Nashville. She also needed that box of knee-high and ankle-length boots, loafers, and walking sneakers. She wondered if she should buy those strap-on ice walkers she had seen in the L. L. Bean catalogue. Apparently they could be stretched over the bottoms of shoes or boots and their balled rubber edges would grip the ice or packed snow, securing your walk. She'd be out this winter in all kinds of weather with Henry. It was tempting to get them. She'd think about it later. There was still plenty of time to go online and order them.

Max could be right, she thought, pulling one of only two heavy sweaters she owned out of a box. Her older son had sounded very worried when he called her the other night from his home in Atlanta.

"Mom," Max said. "Get out of Oswego before the winter hits. I'm telling you, if you think your life is bad now, it will be a nightmare being stuck inside and snowed in all winter long. You'll be so depressed. Don't you remember how bad it gets up there?"

She did. What Max didn't know was that the idea of being snowed in was very appealing to her. Still, it would be a big change. No more moderate Tennessee climate with spring in February and cool rainy Christmas mornings. No more, "Y'all come back now, y'hear?"

41

Well, that would be a relief. She stacked the sweaters on the bed. Max had been kind to her since the divorce. She had gone to see him a few months ago in Atlanta, when his wife went on a shopping trip to New York City with her girlfriends. They spent the weekend together in Atlanta, just the two of them, walking the winding roads around his suburban home, cooking pasta, sleeping in, watching movies. Max encouraged her to go forward now. "What's done is done, Mom. Learn from it," he said. "Move on."

At thirty his medical career was going well, his marriage was happy, and his life was successful. "I'll never get a divorce," he said. "It's just not worth it." She was glad he felt that way.

His younger brother, Chip, was in Boston, his law practice new and busy, his marriage of two years bringing him joy. Unlike Max, Chip had stopped talking to her when she and Matt had separated. It was too much for him. Since her move to Oswego he was back in her life, thankfully. Reconciling, he had told her to let him know if she needed him. She did, and last month he had flown in to spend a weekend with her. It was the first time in months that she had felt loved and secure. Driving him to the Syracuse airport on Sunday morning, she was desolate once again. She had littered the front seat of her car with used tissues, crying all the way back home.

Ellen pulled out another box, opening it to find good worn jeans and workout clothes. Sliding the jeans on hangers, she wondered if Ruby had finally come home. She saw no sign of her, although she had seen a dark-haired teenage boy cutting the grass and Mrs. Schmidt watering the hanging baskets of green ferns on Ruby's front porch, not wanting to ditch them until Ruby gave permission. A conscientious neighbor, the one who called in the fire alarm, Mrs. Schmidt apparently kept track of things in the neighborhood. Ellen would steer clear of her.

Frances was another matter. She felt a connection with Frances right away. No doubt their Nashville ties had something to do with it. Listening to Frances drag out her vowels and drop letters off the end of her words brought back memories of the many happy years she had spent living in the South. Maybe one day they'd share their Nashville stories, get to know one another better.

For now, Ellen knew Frances stayed in touch with Ruby, who was down in the Sweeney Upstate Rehabilitation Center after her ankle surgery. It had been two weeks since her dive down the front steps, and Ellen lived in limbo. Well, she'd been in limbo for months. Maybe it would be better to say she lived in an agitated state of limbo at this point, wondering what Ruby was going to do to her, wondering if a malicious lawsuit was headed her way.

"Do you have any idea how Ruby feels about me, about this whole episode?" Ellen had asked Frances over the fence in the backyard one morning last week. Ellen was pruning the huge pink morning glories that were climbing up and over the fence after the cool sunny summer. Frances was hanging out wash, a white load of personal items—ankle socks, a full-bib apron with faded teapots embroidered on the pockets, two blue potholders she clipped together with one wooden clothespin, and three Peter Pan–collared blouses with short sleeves. It had been thirty years since Ellen had seen one of those blouses. Gosh, she hadn't realized they still made them.

"I don't trust my drivin' enough to go down to Upstate to visit her, although I surely would like to," Frances said. "Which means I don't know if she's feeling poorly or not. I did telephone her day before yesterday and we had a nice little exchange. She seemed all right. A little cranky, perhaps. That's certainly understandable. She didn't mention you, and of course, I didn't bring it up. Why? Are you givin' yourself a little worry fit, Ellen?"

"Worry fit? No, I wouldn't say that, Frances. You just never know what someone will do. Obviously I don't know Ruby at all, and I wondered what she might be thinking at this point, that's all. I'm not worried so much as I'm, oh, just feeling that I don't have the energy for a fight, if that's what she has in mind."

Frances said she had never known Ruby to choose a fight.

"She's more the type to walk away if she senses things are gettin' real ugly. Of course, I have no idea how she'll feel about the fall, and all the trouble that's caused. I just couldn't say, dear. I imagine she'll be reasonable. She's the reasonable sort. It probably will depend on how you handle it and whether Josh Leighton has gotten hold of her yet. He'd be a real fly the ointment."

"Josh Leighton? Who is he?"

"An attorney. Used to be with the DA's office years ago when my husband was doin' criminal defense work. Josh comes through the courtroom door like a Tennessee Walker. He's straight-standing sure of himself, and proud as they come." Frances stopped hanging wash and looked over at Ellen. "You must realize that the story of Ruby's fall has been all over town, and good old Josh may smell the opportunity to do a little work representin' her. Even after all these years he's still a bit of an ambulance chaser, if you know what I mean."

Oh, great. Isn't that just the nasty little sliver in my heel that I need—an arrogant compensation attorney coming after me.

She put down the trimmers and backed down, sitting on the heels of her feet, out of Frances's sight. She had home insurance but she'd need to check on the limits. She had agreed to the coverage her insurance agent suggested months ago, a basic liability policy of $100,000 each occurrence. She hoped that would be enough. It would depend on the depth of Ruby's anger, or greedy streak if she had one, or both.

Ellen hadn't spoken to Frances since that brief backyard chat. A friendly phone call could be made today without Ellen appearing to be stalking Frances for news, or using her as a conduit. In truth, she wasn't. Frances was the only person Ellen could stand to be around, the only person she felt safe to talk with, if only for ten minutes. She didn't like herself knowing that most people got under her skin these days. She found it nearly impossible to focus, and casual conversations drove her nuts. Despite months of therapy, all she wanted to do was stay with her destructive, looping thoughts.

Instead of moving forward, she was obsessed with reviewing her decisions over and over, questioning Matt's decisions over and over, and picking at the scabs until she was worn out. Was she right to walk away from Matt? Was it fair to resent him for not working the last eight years of their marriage, putting all the burden on her to pay the bills, to keep the lifestyle going? Had it been a mistake to encourage him to go ahead and develop his art instead of finding another job after he lost his to middle-management downsizing? Was she the most cold-hearted bitch in the world for leaving him after encouraging him to follow his passion, draw his pictures, and paint those canvases?

"I don't want you to wonder what might have been *if only*," Ellen had said to him when he waffled between finding traditional work and pursuing his art. "I can support us for a while. Go ahead and grab the time. See what you can do." Unfortunately, that artistic while had turned into years. When she pressed him about it, he took a hard stand.

"You'll have to work, because I can't get a job anymore. I just can't," he said.

Had she been wrong to let the resentment build in her until it had eaten away any respect she felt for him, any feeling at all? She shook her head, remembering the sight of Matt standing in the front doorway of their historic home at 6:15 in the morning in his tan fleece-lined slippers, a mug of tea in his hand, a European cotton shirt tucked into his corduroys. He made it a point to see her off to work every morning, waving his hand as she pulled out of the driveway for another twelve-hour day. "All my love, darling," he'd call out. "Be careful!"

Every single day as she drove down the street she asked herself, "What's wrong with this picture?" She asked Matt the same thing and he just laughed.

"We're not the typical American marriage," he said. "It's just a different picture. Nothing wrong with that!"

But it was wrong in the end. The heavy responsibilities ate at her, sent her into a spin as she began another year, another season of work, another advanced degree, her mind bitter with resentment. She began to think about a different life, one that was miles away from this one, one that took the pressure away. She wanted to toss that teacup out of Matt's hand and smash it on the sidewalk. She wanted another life. She knew Matt was taken by surprise when he discovered the brokenness of their relationship. How had this happened?

"Let's talk about it," he said.

They did, but his message was always the same: "I can't help you with the work issue. You're the one who has the degrees and experience. I am doing what I can, and I can't do any more than this."

Months later she told him she was done. No more histrionics, no more negotiating. She was fifty-one years old and the end of her life was in sight. She would start again and find her own way. It was her turn for a clean canvas.

They were more than fair with each other, splitting things up amicably, packing boxes together for her move to New York. How strange was that? *Very sophisticated we were,* she smiled to herself. Then the news had come about his quick turnaround, the new woman in his life, and while she didn't blame him, it was devastating.

What did you expect, Ellen? You told him to go and be happy. He took your advice. It was just sooner than you expected. Or did you

46

think he would wait forever, broken-hearted, pining for your return? I did think that. How stupid was I?

Backing away from the boxes, she closed the Venetian blinds, dropped the winter hats and gloves on the chair, and climbed onto the bed. She'd have to inquire about that lawn boy to see if he'd work for her, too. She was tired of cutting her grass, weeding the beds. Henry jumped up in one neat pounce to curl up at her feet, moaning softly as he moved into place, this mid-morning nap now a part of their daily routine. Ellen closed her eyes, covering them with her arm, creating the dark. The wind was picking up, the cold front moving in as predicted. She'd call Frances in a little while.

Eight

It took two grown men to get Ruby from the car to the front porch and inside her vestibule.

"I tell you, for such a small woman, it sure did feel like we were moving a wheelbarrow full of wet sand," Mr. Schmidt told Leo, the bartender at the Captain's Riverside Inn. "When the missus asked me to pick up Ruby and get her home, I thought, well, heck, that's easy enough. But hear me good, Leo, she's not as light as she looks.

"More than that," he said, leaning into a low whisper, not wanting the whole bar to hear. "She's pretty ornery, Leo. I mean, I understand with all she's been through why she might be touchy, but getting her out of that rehab place? We saw a side of her I didn't know she had. I mean, she can be real feisty! Know what I mean?"

Ruby would have cringed to think that Joe Schmidt would say anything about her, much less compare her to a wheelbarrow full of wet sand. She would have walked naked all the way home on the interstate, chin to the sky, singing, "I Am Woman, Hear Me Roar," if she had known. What she did know was enough: she was going home. She was finally getting away from the godforsaken rehab center with its fragrance of despair and its smell of death. Sweet Jesus, Mother Mary, and Joseph, how she hated the place.

"One more day of this and I will shoot my way out of here," she had told the rehab therapist.

Her room had been at the very north end of the long hallway, the farthest room from the nurse's station. Immediate help was out of the question. The doors at the end of the hall were never locked so that in case of fire, the non-ambulatory people could escape the building. *Which is all of us*, Ruby noted. To add to the craziness, the back door next to her room opened and closed all night with a great big bang, like timed Fourth of July fireworks, as the night staff went outside for smokes and fresh air and then came back in, letting the door slam shut. It made sleep impossible. Ruby told everyone who would listen that it was simply unbearable, just too much, just way, way, way too much.

"I want to go home. I will never recover here. Never. Let me go."

She realized by the second day that angry complaints weren't going to work. The staff didn't give a hoot if she liked it there or not. They were immune to patient complaints, having heard them in one form or another with each new admission.

"People seem to think a rehab center is a spa," they said to each other.

The staff offered pitiful comfort with silly, bored, fake smiles pasted on their faces. Ruby quickly accepted her reality. *I am just one more pathetic hostage in this drug-induced, semiconscious purgatory. I could die here and no one would be too surprised.* She spent her second night tossing and turning.

"It's time you gave yourself a good talking-to, Ruby Bainbridge," her mother scolded her in a dream. "This nagging and whining aren't getting you anywhere, little girl. Maybe it's time to think it all over and get yourself a plan. Do you think you can do that?"

Even though she had been dead now for more than two years, Mother was a constant part of Ruby's dreams and internal daily life. She felt Mother's aura everywhere and heard Mother's voice as surely as she heard the downtown firehouse whistle blow at noon each day announcing lunchtime, as it had done for more than a century. Mother was Ruby's guiding light, her voice of reason. Ruby had learned a long time ago that Mother was astute about everything. A good talking to herself was exactly what she needed.

She spent a dedicated hour in the middle of the night sitting up in bed creating a Ben Franklin sheet on the back of a get-well card turned vertically in her lap. She drew a line down the center and headed the left side *What I need to do to get home* and the right side *How I will get it done.* It wasn't exactly the model of pros and cons of the original Ben Franklin concept, but the idea was good. On the left she began with, "I need to be able to get around by myself with a walker." How would she get it done? "I will do three times more work than that masochistic physical therapist requires of me." On the left: "I have to show the staff I have an appetite and that I am not dehydrated." The action steps on the right: "Drink all my fluids and ask for more. Eat at least some of the disgusting food they serve; tell them how much I enjoy it and look forward to the next tasty meal."

Lie your brains out, Ruby.

She started her campaign to be released from the Sweeney Upstate Rehabilitation Center on the third morning of her five-day stay. Her dogged efforts paid off as she mastered the art of moving efficiently with that inflexible walker in her ankle cast, ate mushy peas and canned fruit until her plate was clean, and drank more than a human share of water and Diet Coke. She learned to use her left hand instead of her right, which was in a soft cast, and was grateful that her left shoulder was feeling pretty good. Her left knee was almost back to normal thanks to a steroid shot that reduced the fluid, followed by two days of ice and heat. By Friday she was fully hydrated and ambulatory with the walker. Her release was approved. To say that the staff was glad to see her go was not entirely true.

"I am a firm believer that our real nature comes out in difficult situations like the ones we have here at Upstate Rehab," the night nurse said to the physical therapist. "In her case, I think we have a fifty-something woman who is terrified of being away from home. I feel sorry for her, crying her heart out every night, calling out her mother's name. I never took her jabs seriously. And, wow, she may be small, but did you notice? She sure could throw down those cream cakes and Cokes, couldn't she?"

They both laughed, and were relieved when the two men came to take Ruby Bainbridge home, thankful that they wouldn't have to hear her moaning and groaning in her sleep anymore, wouldn't have to wonder what she'd say next, a pointed dagger wrapped inside the sweetness of her words, a hissy fit about to erupt any minute. They were glad that she wouldn't be their responsibility anymore. Which suited Ruby just fine. She couldn't wait to be alone again in her house. As the men lifted her out of the car and set her down carefully inside the vestibule, she quickly sent them away with a dismissive wave the second they got her walker snapped into place.

"You've been more than kind to me," she said. Skillfully maneuvering, she used the walker to block their way into the front hall. The three of them were scrunched together so tightly in the vestibule that the men retreated onto the front porch. "I'll be perfectly fine now, you two. Another big thanks to each of you, and I mean that. Now you go on along home! I know your wives will be looking for you and wondering where you are. Please tell them I'll be in touch in a day or two to say thanks myself, and that I am absolutely all right and just delighted to be home."

The men turned and left feeling like the staff at Upstate, neither glad nor sad. They simply were relieved to get it over with, pleased to be finished now with this funny little surprisingly heavy woman.

No one was more relieved than Ruby. Before the men reached the bottom step of the porch she locked the wooden screen door, and, jogging carefully sideways in her walker, firmly closed the heavy walnut front door behind it, decisively turning the deadbolt into place. She stood a moment, nearly out of breath at the exertion, and leaned her hand against the thick door, grateful for its impenetrable nature, newly pleased that Mother had insisted on the deadbolt after Father died, the two of them alone in the big house with no man around, a fact Mother noted daily. Although when Ruby thought about it, with his wobbly legs and stooped shoulders, her aging father had not been a threat to any would-be intruders for many years. Yet just having him in the house had made them both feel safe. Old habits die hard, as Father liked to say, usually referring to his cigar smoking and just-pour-me-a-small-scotch-on-the-rocks rituals.

Ruby rubbed her hand over the door gently, almost lovingly, thankful for the familiar feel of it. The outside door of the vestibule was original to the house, a beautifully carved walnut piece her grandmother had commissioned in 1895 as the house was being built. The top half of the door held a stunning piece of beveled glass that Ruby found both lovely and unsettling. She admired the clear, clean glass. Its sharp beveled corners reflected the afternoon sunlight like a prism, creating a rainbow effect from time to time. But she found the openness disconcerting. She didn't care for the friendly message it gave. She never knew who would be on the other side of that glass as she responded to the doorbell.

She hated the idea that someone could see her coming, her hair not washed for a day or two, her apron stained with cheese sauce and tomato juice if she couldn't pull it off over her head in time. It was even more annoying when people peered into the glass to see if she were coming, a hand cupped over their eyes, squinting into the front hallway, ringing the bell a second and third time. It unnerved her. She felt exposed, like the feeling she got when she gained a little weight and her bra didn't fit the way it should. She hated the added weight that made her breasts spill over the bra top creating a seductive, sexy look to her otherwise quiet figure. She was no wild woman like Elizabeth Taylor, although she loved Liz in *Cat on a Hot Tin Roof*, and watched with envy as she sashayed around boldly in her white slip, those perfect breasts of hers pushing against each other forming a moist cleavage for Paul Newman to eyeball, even though it turned out that Liz was wasting her time with him. All she knew was, full breasts made her feel flashy and vulnerable, so when the extra weight came on, she'd stop eating desserts right away to get those breasts back into the Playtex minimizer B cups where they belonged.

All right, get yourself under control now, Ruby. Let's go. Get out of this vestibule and into the house. No need to give Ina Schmidt any more stories to tell than she has already.

She moved carefully in the small entry, gathering her strength and courage, straightening up, taking the three or four steps from the front to the inside door of the vestibule. That second door opened into the main hallway of the house, and like the outside door was half glass, although not nearly as old, nor as elegantly appointed. It too was carved walnut but more simply done, decorative pebbled edges the most complicated part of its design. Closing it now, locking it firmly, Ruby was glad that the first thing she had done after Mother died was to have a thick satin-lined burgundy velvet curtain made to cover the glass of this second door. Now when the doorbell rang she could tiptoe up and ever so carefully pull back the side of the curtain, just the tiniest bit, and decide if she was at home, or not, to the caller. If she decided she wasn't at home she would stand to the side against the wall, flat-backed and rigid, quiet as dead dog, and wait until the intruders had gone away before stepping back into the hallway. She thought of herself as being in a Hitchcock film, all terrified like Audrey Hepburn when she hid from Cary Grant in *Charade*, lips pressed tightly together, holding her breath, barely breathing, not moving a muscle until the danger was past and she heard the footsteps fade away. Big sigh of relief. She had won.

I need to get myself settled into the house before another minute passes, before I collapse right here from the demands of this day.

Checking and rechecking that the door was locked, pulling on the brass handle two and three times to be certain, carefully sliding the thick-linked safety chain into place, she was finally satisfied that she was safe. She turned the walker around and began what now seemed to be a long journey to the kitchen. Stepping slowly, she stopped just inside the parlor on her way, then into the library across the hallway to turn on a lamp in each room. In the silence of the large house the *ca-clunk, ca-clunk* of the walker created a steady metal cadence, a marking of every move that at once annoyed and pleased her as she parsed her steps, moving slowly and carefully to avoid a fall—no broken hip, please.

These walker-walks will wear me out. They'll be a daily killer. I'll have to think about what I need to do before I get started each time. I'll need to get good mileage from every effort. Plan ahead, Ruby. Plan ahead. Not your strong suit, but do it until, just do it until—oh, my lord, I'm Dr. Phil.

Moving past the formal dining room with its tall windows and heavy damask drapes, she stopped to blow a kiss at the violin that hung on the wall, the sheet music to Hans Debussy's *The Girl with the Flaxen Hair* fastened flat on the wall under the violin as a sort of artistic frame. Mother's admission recital to the Boston Conservatory required a solo and she had memorized the haunting, long stroked Debussy piece to demonstrate her talent. Mother was accepted that very day and studied at the conservatory for two years. However, she left before graduating to marry Father after he proposed on a Christmas Eve sleigh ride in 1936. Mother loved playing that violin well up into her late seventies. When her fingers couldn't move quickly enough and her playing became labored, sloppy, she decided to stop playing altogether, mounting the violin on the wall as a constant reminder of her first love.

"I know I should put it in the case so it's kept out of the air and light," she told Father the day she decided to stop playing. "But I will miss it terribly. It has been my companion since I was eight years old. How can I say good-bye to it, not see it anymore?"

Father encouraged her to create the wall hanging. In fact, he gave Mother permission to hang his 1880s tenor banjo with its mother-of-pearl neck on the other side of the sideboard to even out the musical décor. She put sheet music behind his instrument, too. She loved it when he hammered out *If You Knew Susie*, his fingers squiggling all over the top of the neck, his right hand picking, flying up and down around the head to the quick beat. Both liked seeing their wall of music, as they called it. Both knew their playing days were over. Nodding a small salute to the banjo as well, Ruby moved on, reaching the kitchen in a dozen labored steps. She stopped and took a breath, nearly limp from the effort.

Oh, Mother, I'm home! I'm home! I honestly didn't know if I'd ever stand here again in our very own kitchen. Oh thank you, Jesus, Mary, and Joseph, thank you. Thank you for bringing me home.

She smiled and looked around, leaning against the kitchen counter, warmed by the sight of her favorite chair and the TV, both still sweetly in their places, the kitchen just the way she had left it, clean and tidy. Ina Schmidt had undoubtedly taken the liberty of cleaning up after the near-fire. Any old excuse to get into her house. She opened the refrigerator and saw a fresh quart of milk and a loaf of Pepperidge Farm cinnamon raisin bread and a pound of butter on the top shelf, a bag of her favorite Macintosh apples on the middle shelf.

Well, thank you, Ina, for providing my breakfast tomorrow.

She had smelled the smoky residue in the Oriental carpet all the way down the hallway, and she was grateful all over again to those firemen. She'd have to make a special contribution at Thanksgiving to Station 112, and that would be just the beginning. This whole smoky mess was going to cost her. She'd have a big cleaning bill to get the drapes and carpets back in shape. She had no idea what she'd do with the smoke-damaged wallpaper. Can they wash grass wallpaper? For certain she was looking at the cost of a new soup pan, and probably a new stove since, as a precaution, the firemen had doused the back burner with foam.

Then there were the medical costs. She had no idea what to expect there, but one of the nurses had warned her, "Hang on to your hat, sweetie. The biggest surprise is yet to come." Whatever that meant. Still, she had felt a shiver go up her spine when the nurse said it. She seemed so sure it would be shocking news.

Regrettably, the biggest debt she had was to Ina Schmidt. *Oh, my sweet heart of Jesus. She is such a pesky woman, such a West Fifth Street gossip, but I have to give credit where credit is due. For once Ina's meddlesome ways had paid off. I can't deny it. If she hadn't called the fire department when she did this house would have been a pile of burning embers, and I'd be out in the street. Oh, I hate to owe anybody anything, and this will be such a debt to pay.*

Ruby started to sweat, her mind racing. This was Ina's big chance to get inside her life at last. She knew Ina. She'd want to collect over and over, in little ways, just once a week coming over to take a good look around the house to be sure everything was all right.

"Just keeping an eye on our Ruby as your mother and father would expect us to do," she'd say, worming her way into the house. "We don't want another little stove fire, do we?"

Ruby's stomach churned. Ina was spoiling her homecoming.

It's just too much to think about, and I have no control over it right now. I will not think about it another minute. I won't spoil this homecoming. Bad thoughts, go away; hide somewhere I cannot find you.

She shuffled over to the window to watch the squirrels at the feeder gripping the dried corncobs, chewing as if they had a bus to catch. She closed her eyes, determined to banish all disagreeable thoughts. She was an old hand at repression, well trained in forcing herself to think of something else, something that would give her a laugh or bring back a happy memory, anything to stop the torturous ideas from nagging at her. She took a deep breath, and with a big imaginary black eraser wiped her mind clean, envisioning it now as a blank white page.

Switch gears, Ruby.

She began to picture the long ride home from rehab, the two men and Ruby locked in that little two-door car, the car stinky from the residue cigarette smoke in the cloth seats and on the men's jackets, the nasty stench on their fingertips and in their hair, and she could only guess about their breath. Disgusting. They had rolled the front windows halfway down trying to dissipate the smell, but all that did was send cold air blasting into her right ear, her hair swirling around like buzzing bees. Smoking was such a horrible habit. "Oh, well. We've all got to die of something," Father used to say, and Ruby supposed he was right about that.

Then she smiled to think about them trying to get her out of the car, diverting their eyes from her private parts as she lifted her legs out of the front, heavily placing her feet down on the sidewalk. Both of the men were a riot to watch, nearly twisting their heads off as each one spun around in a different direction to divert his eyes. If they only knew: they could have looked straight in there all day long and never gotten more than a good look at her thick old black girdle. Hid everything, that girdle. All the way up to her midsection and down to her knees. Ruby had choked back a smile as she pushed herself out of that car, holding onto the roof for traction. Resolved to remain serious, she scowled at the men as they peeked back at her, looking to see if she was safe, trying equally hard to make sure they weren't getting an eyeful. What a scene. She laughed until her eyes closed. For the time being, she managed to Scarlett O'Hara her worries away.

Happier now, she opened her eyes and looked over at her two birdfeeders. They were empty. She'd have to make sure they were filled with sunflower seeds tomorrow. The birds were selecting their winter-feeding stations now that it was fall, and she didn't want them all over in Ina's or Frances's backyards. It looked as if Ina had managed to have Ruby's lawn cut while she was away—thank you, Ina. It would need the final fall cut in another two weeks. She'd heard young Mario Simonson was doing yard work now. She'd telephone him tomorrow and see when he could come.

Turning around, her ankle told her it was time to sit down. As she started her walker-shuffle, she heard a muted police siren screaming in the distance, no doubt in pursuit of someone gone wrong. She saw the dusk turning into early darkness, and she felt calm. Time to snuggle in.

She moved slowly over to her favorite easy chair, dropping down into it with a groan—no ladylike touchdown on the cushion, just a straight drop from the walker. She wasn't taking any chances on not hitting the mark. *No falls, no more broken bones.* Safe and alone at last, Ruby felt her breathing ease, her headache begin, and a piercing pain in her ankle. But none of it mattered. She was home, tucked in safe and sound in her familiar sanctuary, and nobody could touch her now.

Ruby didn't know, of course, that she was the talk of the neighborhood that night and the subject of idle chitchat around the bar at the Captain's Riverside Inn. She didn't know that the recent story of her life and her homecoming would be served up along with scrambled eggs and hard-cooked bacon at the Canal View Café in the morning. All she knew was her happiness at being home again. She took a deep breath of the acrid, smoky air. It was a good smell, one that graciously replaced the pungent, poopy, sick-people, Lysol smell of the rehab center. The nightmare was over. She had survived. She had found her way home.

Just before falling asleep she cleared her mind again, racing past the clouds, stretching her arms faithfully before her, traveling toward the light, shooting up to heaven like a kite in whirlwind pursuit of God. It was another one of her rehearsals, another run at finding God the way the nuns had said she could if she simply practiced hard enough. But she came up empty. She saw no circle of compassion, no warming colors of white or soft yellow to welcome her into the joy of the next dimension. No streets paved with gold. She felt no wave of peace pouring over her. She knew she'd never really get the hang of meditation. Opening her eyes, she stared at the ceiling in her beloved kitchen alcove.

What a funny life I have.

Nine

Ellen paced back and forth, stopping briefly to peer out the window, nervously eyeing Ruby's house, looking for any flutter in the front drapes, any sign that Ruby was back.

"I do believe she'll be comin' along home today," Frances had said earlier this morning in a phone call. "I don't guess she'll be fully ambulatory for several weeks. All things considered, I imagine she'll stay tucked inside her house for the next little while. Until she feels stronger about things."

"Stronger about things? What things do you mean, Frances?"

"Well, just everything, Ellen, dear. Surely you know this situation has been a burden for our darlin' Ruby. The drama of the fall and the ambulance screaming down West Fifth, with everyone snickerin' about the accident for days on end. Then the hospital and that rehabilitation center? My word. Knowing our Ruby, she would have taken a big sip of Clorox before being in the middle of all that! Why, surely you know this?"

"Oh, Frances, of course you're right." Leaning down to snuggle Henry, Ellen put her face right into his, smelling the dense doggy breath, remnants of yesterday's supper lingering in his gums. She was frightened of what Ruby might do to Henry, what vengeance she might seek.

Whatever she does I'm prepared to fight her every inch of the way, buddy. Don't you worry.

"Given her feelings, what do you think I should do, Frances? I want to see her, to make sure she's all right, and certainly to apologize for everything. But I don't want to upset her any more than she already is. What do you think? I really need your help with this."

Frances said she'd been thinking about that, knowing Ellen might ask her for advice.

"I think a nice little supper would be a fine place to start. Would you be up to fixin' something for us to take over and serve to her? Something she could reheat the next day? I'll be happy to put together a chocolate pecan pie. Ruby simply delights in that pie. She thinks it's southern magic when it's really just lots of Karo syrup, pecans, butter, and chocolate. But she just loves it. How would you feel about doing something, too, Ellen? I do realize I'm askin' this without even knowin' if you cook."

Another piece of history would be forced out of Ellen and there was nothing she could do about it.

"Yes, I can cook. I'm actually a pretty good cook, Frances. Tell me, what kind of food does Ruby like to eat, do you know?"

Frances said Ruby liked good, hearty British and Irish food, and German food, and Italian food, and certain kinds of Mexican food. She paused.

"My goodness, perhaps I should begin by telling you what she doesn't like. I know she doesn't care a thing about what she calls California food. She's not particularly fond of salads and fruit as a rule, unless the fruit is under a buttery crumble and the salad has steak and blue cheese dressin' on it, if you get my meanin'. Just as quickly let me say, Ellen, that everyone knows I came out of the land of comfort food, and I love it dearly! I surely do understand Ruby's point of view."

Frances hesitated, clearing her throat. "Let me think a minute now. Oh yes! I know she just adores canned vegetables, particularly whole asparagus, creamed corn, and pickled red beets. And I seem to recall that she's crazy about baked beans. Does that help you any?"

It was just shy of a nightmare, actually. Ellen's joy of cooking included fruits, vegetables, chicken, fish, and good beef. She loved cheese but used it sparingly as a flavor enhancer, not to sell the dish or cover up the lack of well-seasoned flavors. Still, she knew how to create hardy upstate New York cuisine and enjoyed eating it herself. She could serve Ruby her favorite dishes. Those canned vegetables were mind-boggling, but she would make them work.

Already peeling potatoes in her mind for a delicious shepherd's pie with sweet onions, mushrooms, and a nice hint of garlic and Worcestershire sauce in the meat filling, Ellen stood up.

"That helps a lot, Frances, thank you. I think I know just what to make. If you create that chocolate pecan pie, I'll take care of the rest of the meal. Does that work?"

Frances said that would be just grand. "Just one more tiny detail, Ellen, honey. I don't think I'll let Ruby know we're carryin' her supper to her, if it's all the same to you? I'd feel obliged to tell her you were comin' along with me, and I'd rather not stir up that little nest of vipers, if you know what I mean. Besides, a surprise is so much more fun, don't you think?"

"Of course, however you want to handle it, Frances. You know best. What time should I be ready to go?"

"Let's go on over at six o'clock? I know she likes her *Dr. Phil* and *Oprah*, and then she normally has her supper around six or six thirty. I'll come to your kitchen door and gather you up just before six, shall I?"

"Fine. One more thing! Should I bring a bottle of red wine? It will be cocktail time by then. Does Ruby drink wine?"

Careful not to make Ruby sound like a woman who drinks, Frances said, "That might be a nice idea. When we get together for the holidays she does seem to enjoy a glass of somethin' spirited."

Ellen hung up the phone and considered her next move. She didn't like to think of herself as the kind of person who plans her moves, but there was a lot at stake with Ruby. She had confirmed with the insurance agent that her memory was intact: her policy was written with a $100,000 per occurrence liability provision. When she shared the bare-boned details of what had happened, he said she could be in trouble.

"I'll be honest with you, dogs are a real problem," he said. "Attorneys and judges seem to love to go for pretty big money for dog injuries. The prevailing opinion seems to be that dog owners should keep their animals under control. No excuses. Do you think she'll sue?"

Ellen said she had no reason to think that, and please, this conversation had to be in the strictest confidence. "I don't want talk around town about our conversation. Do we understand each other?" He said he understood, but she didn't trust the loyalty of an old-timer's tongue in a small town. She could only hope that her inquiries didn't reach Ruby or any attorney she might have retained already. She had wanted to ask Frances if that old attorney she mentioned had been hired by Ruby, but it never felt like the right time. *Oh, well. It would all come out soon enough.*

"Come along with me, Henry James Varner. We've got an important dinner to make." He trailed behind her to the small galley kitchen in the back of her five-room house. "We are about to discover if Ruby will pull out my hair by the roots or play nice."

She opened the bottom freezer drawer of the refrigerator and picked up a pound and a half of ground round, dropping it down into the sink. She had bought good beef, hot Italian sausage, loins of pork, a leg of lamb, chicken, and hamburger meat for the freezer a couple of months ago when she thought she'd be entertaining old Oswego friends. The freezer remained full as Ellen learned the golden rule of homecoming relationships: don't move away and come back thirty-two years later expecting the secret handshake from old high school pals.

Running into an old high school friend at the Canalside Coffee Shoppe last week, she understood her place.

"Oh, is that you, Ellen Varner? I heard you'd come back to Oswego," said Christen. "Nice to see you again. How long do you plan to stay?"

Ellen said she'd bought a house. "I'd love to catch up on things. Would you like to have dinner together, just us old Oswego High girls again?"

Christen said that might be nice. "Right now I have my hands full with my kids and family, not to mention my job and trying to keep up with my long-time friendships in town," Christen said, cutting her off, smiling as she waved to the coffee house owner. "See you at lunchtime, Charlie! The blueberry muffins were extra good this morning! Bye, Ellen. Good luck."

Ellen quickly understood she was mistaken if she thought her return would be viewed as testimony to the value she put on life in Oswego, that her coming home was an affirmation of their lives and histories: "See, old friends? I'm back because this is the best spot on earth to be! You were right. I was wrong. Come on, give me a hug." It simply didn't work that way. She chose to tear off into the world; they chose to stay behind. No matter what she said now, she was an outsider.

"So you're back," Jesse Ryan said coolly when she pulled alongside the curb at the city hall. "And driving a BMW, no less. I guess you've done all right, Ellen Varner. What brings you back to our little hometown? Your restless energy all used up?"

Ellen was stung. She looked past the fine lines and graying sideburns into the face of still-handsome Jesse. She saw the eighteen-year-old Jesse, the football star, her old high school boyfriend, the man she once thought she'd spend her life with in Oswego, buying a house on the lake, raising six kids, arguing about whether to send them to Catholic high or public high, gladly hosting the annual clam bake for their family and friends.

"No, Jesse. I just wanted to come home. Back to my roots. I'm glad to see you. I suspect the feeling isn't mutual, is it, Jesse?"

"I wouldn't say that, Ellen. I'm happy you've found your way back, I guess. Well, if I'm honest with you, it doesn't mean much to me one way or another. I don't mean to be cold or anything. I just find it interesting that the people who leave Oswego, then return decades later expecting a warm welcome from those of us who stayed the course, find it unusual that we don't break out the champagne and yell, 'You've come home!'"

He drew his hands through his short hair and leaned into her car. "You see, we know what it's been like to keep Oswego alive through plant closings and recessions, job losses and home foreclosures, fires and deaths, cancers and a nuclear power plant that nearly killed every living thing in our lake before they shut it down. We've fought to keep our Oswego going, and you didn't. That's just the way it is."

Ellen eased out of the car and looked up at Jesse. "I understand, really I do. Believe me, I expect nothing from you, or any of my old friends here. No problem, Jesse."

He stepped back, taking a good look at Ellen.

Ellen wondered what he was thinking, and why he was being so hard on her. Was Jesse angry that she hadn't kept in touch with him in the last thirty-five years? The last time they had seen each other was in 1978 when he had visited her in New York. She had been a stop on his business trip and while they both tried to reconnect, she thought it had been apparent that their once-explosive chemistry couldn't begin to bridge their differences, which were legion. She had married and had two sons; he later married and had two sons.

That was as close as they would ever come to synchronicity. Still, she felt a pang for the old Jesse, seeing him as he stood there looking at her.

"I hear you bought the old Elliot place on West Fifth," he said. Actually what he had heard is that she had walked into Lakeshore Realty and wrote a check for the full asking price the same day she had been shown Mary Elliot's house. "Like she was buying a pack of gum," Kathleen Fogarty said.

However, Jesse knew the Elliot house wasn't in the same league as the imposing turn-of-the-century homes on West Fifth. The Elliot house was modest, in fact. A solid two-story with three bedrooms, it had a small fenced-in backyard with covered back and front porches, horse chestnut trees in front, and a good-looking perennial garden Mary Schiller Elliot had planted over the years. Realtors liked to advertise it as having a seasonal lake view. Jesse knew that meant on tiptoes in the attic window, in the middle of February. Its one-car detached garage in the back had a nice little studio apartment on the second floor where Mary had created colorful acrylic paintings of flowers and sailing ships. Jesse had done some work on that studio years ago. It wasn't a mansion, but the Elliot house was still a fine old house, not cheap.

"Are you planning to retire at your age?" Jesse asked, eyebrows raised. "Or will you be looking for a job?"

"Right now I'm just finding my way, Jesse. I'm not sure what I'll be doing yet."

"Well, I'm happy for you. It must be nice," he said. He didn't even try to hide his sarcasm, echoing what his friends had noted. *She doesn't even have to work.*

She recognized the old Jesse now, heard it in his voice. Boy, he hadn't changed. He was still the guy who smiled and punched at the same time. Especially if he thought fairness was at stake, or his own desires. She remembered his cruelty when he broke up with her the day she came home from college. She had been eager to see him; she had assumed they'd spend the Christmas holidays together having fun, making plans.

"I think it's time we both moved on," he had said. "I'm ready for something new." That was it. No attempt to sandwich the bad news in with gentle reminders of their good times, not a smidgen of empathy in his words. He had just looked past her to the new girl coming his way, a big smile on his face.

Jesse, your mean streak still shows. Ah, well. Old habits, old boyfriends, old scars. Henry is the only male I want in my life now anyway. What a relief.

Preparing now to begin Ruby's meal, she thought more about the reality of her homecoming. She decided she couldn't argue with any of it. *It is what it is.* Besides, the silent treatment gave her some comfort. It relieved her of struggling to renegotiate friendships and navigate the old high school bruises they all felt. She'd survive.

I just hope the town doesn't team up against me as I navigate Miss Ruby Bainbridge and her long history as the faithful, loving, dutiful, responsible daughter who cared for her parents until the day they died in their beds in the big Victorian house on West Fifth.

She'd find out soon enough. Opening the cupboard under the sink, she pulled out a three-pound bag of Yukon Gold potatoes. Thinking she might be cooking more in the days ahead, this morning she had bought food to stock a cook's pantry. It was good to feel the kitchen around her again, adequately supplied for the moment with the staples she was used to having in her life. She had tiny moments of joy when shelving the sharp British marmalade and yeasty Marmite, the good Dijon mustard, stuffed green olives and salty black ones, shelled walnuts and pecans, ginger root, French bread, Gruyere cheese, cured ham, unsalted butter, heavy cream, crisp Braeburn apples, lemons and oranges, celery, sweet onions, heads of garlic, and good wines for cooking.

Now all I need is an appetite. Maybe one day I'll get mine back.

She filled up the large stainless steel pot with water and put it on the stove, then filled another pot with cold water to hold peeled potatoes while they waited for the big pot to boil. Scrimmaging around the largest drawer in the kitchen, she put her hand on the black rubber-handled potato peeler with the sharp blade. It had taken her years to finally discard her old metal one with its annoying, jiggling blade. Cooking was much easier when the tool was right. Moving over to the sink, she rested her hands on the edge and stood still. The hard silence of the kitchen rippled through her. She welcomed the dense quiet as a rule, but it felt mean-spirited today, as if she were being punished by the stillness. *Oh, hell.* She couldn't let the silence drag her down today. She had too much to do and it seemed important, although she felt herself slipping fast into that melancholy of neutral, wondering if anything was worth the effort.

Yes, this little dinner party is worth the effort, Ellen.

She pushed herself forward to the wide windowsill above the sink, turning on the Bose radio. Immediately, comforting sounds filled the air, deep and rich, the dial set to a New Age station. The lonely wind of Celtic flutes and the breaking-glass softness of the harp glissando flooded the kitchen, competing with the desolation of the gray day, joining in at times in the melancholy of it all, creating a warm surround of sympathetic longing. She stood and listened, feeling the pureness of the music, breathing it in. She held onto her life just for a moment.

I can't change what's been done or left undone. It doesn't matter if I am in the middle of this passage or still in the abyss. I have today, and I'm all right. I have enough in me to keep going.

It had been months since she had cooked, but she trusted her skills, her history. Plopping the ground round into a bowl, she turned on the microwave defrost cycle. She hated to microwave anything, but she had no choice. It was already three thirty and she needed to prepare the meal from scratch. The microwave would be her only shortcut. She picked up the eight-inch chef's knife from the wooden cutting board. The fit of the carbon steel knife in her hand was perfect, solid and weighty.

The memories of her days as a chef came flooding back with the warmth of a rich glass of port. Her culinary days had been one of life's detours, one she'd take all over again. After years of trial-and-error training and the help of TV shows and books by Fanny Farmer, Julia Child, Madhur Jaffrey, Marcia Adams, and Jacques Pepin, she wanted to open a small restaurant, the dream of most dedicated cooks. Matt had agreed, and they started looking for a little farmhouse in the Tennessee countryside where she'd cook fresh food daily. It would be a place where people called in the morning to ask, "What are you cooking today, Ellen?" Or they'd call to ask what was coming up that week so they could reserve their table for her French onion soup on Wednesday, and chicken Kiev on Friday night. She'd always have a good steak and nice piece of fish or seafood to offer if they didn't like the day's fare. But mainly, she envisioned a comfortable ten-table back-roads bistro where she cooked great food that people drove into the country to eat.

A few months after her fortieth birthday, Matt found a country place that fit the bill, and Ellen panicked. She sat up in bed for several restless nights eating Tums until her tongue was thick with chalky film. The day before they were to sign a contract to purchase, she acknowledged her fear: I'm about to buy a restaurant and I've never worked in a commercial kitchen before. What in the world am I thinking? They dropped the idea of buying the farmhouse and Ellen searched for a kitchen job. She found one easily and started peeling potatoes, chopping onions, and cleaning carrots with the entry-level kitchen staff.

She learned something new every day watching and working with the executive chef, Hans Bittner. Ordinary pork chops became juicy, elegant sautéed chops topped with paper-thin slices of tart green apples, gently bathed by a delicate maple crème and butter sauce ladled over and around the chop, with a dusting of crumbled toasted pecans. He was inspired when it came to the special occasion themed menus, which he designed with five courses of cuisine from Tuscany, another time Provence, yet others from England and Spain. He showed great patience with Ellen, taking her love of cooking and turning her into a strong part of his team.

Weeks of long hours and challenging work paid off when she was named *sous-chef*, the under-chef, the person charged with running the day-to-day operations of the kitchen for Chef Bittner. She became skillful in orchestrating the work of the pantry and pastry chefs and overseeing the creation of delectable sauces and soups with the sauté chef, but she buckled under the relentless pressure endured by the line cooks. She became a specialist in creating artful hors d'oeuvres spreads on table-length mirrors for large crowds, and easily organized and ran parties and buffet lines for 250 guests. She became Chef Bittner's right hand, and it came with a price. Darkly temperamental, the good-looking chef was a wee-hours-of-the-morning hard drinker given to mood swings that kept everyone on edge. Showing up hours late with a nasty hangover most days, he depended on his *sous-chef* to stay sober, be on time, organize his kitchen, and stay on top of the drama. He didn't realize the kitchen only came alive when he was there. Each day was like walking barefoot on snowballs while they waited for him. When he was really late, they speculated that he had finally dumped his motorcycle in a ditch. When a big party was scheduled, they tried to anticipate his wishes, knowing how harsh he could be if things were not done well, praying he'd show up to help before the dinner crowd slammed the line.

It was a life-changing fourteen months. She fell in love with food and cooking, and kitchens, and Chef Bittner. In the end, as much as she loved all four for a time, fortunately it didn't last. The life was too hard, the hours crazy, the kitchen a honeycomb of intrigue, and the kitchen family overwhelming in its needs, leaving her empty and spent at the end of every day. Ellen realized she didn't want her own restaurant after all. She walked away with a deep respect for the back of the house, a culinary confidence she never thought possible, an armful of caramel-colored scars from hotel pan burns, and a dozen white chef's aprons. It was plenty.

Enough with the reveries. If she wanted to get this meal ready by six o'clock, there could be no more traipsing down memory lane. She had to get moving. Snatching a full head of garlic from the fridge, she swung around to grab a couple of sweet onions from the basket on the floor of the small pantry by the kitchen door. Working quickly over the sink, she wondered if Ruby liked onions. Some people didn't, and if not, it was no small aversion. That would be just her luck. But shepherd's pie was nothing without sweet onions. She'd have to take the chance. Should she mince the onions small enough so that Ruby won't notice them? She'd taste them, but maybe she wouldn't see them. Then again, maybe she loved onions. What to do?

Flavor will win her over, Ellen decided. Pushing down the garlic head with the knife, loosening the cloves, she panicked again. Garlic was in the same love-it-or-hate-it category. "Just cook, Ellen," she told herself. "Don't make yourself crazy."

Twenty minutes later the potatoes were boiling as she moved the now-transparent garlic and onions from the sauté pan to a bowl. She turned up the heat on the pan, added a little more olive oil, and began browning the hamburger, letting it stick just a little, creating a nice crusty bottom to scrap up and give character to the sauce. A small puddle of blood from the meat lay on the counter, oozing out from the plastic bag. Quickly reaching for a paper towel, she scooped it up and wiped it off, rinsed it down. She hated the sight of blood; it made her want to vomit.

She chopped thick wedges of mushrooms and added them to the pan after the meat was browned and drained, hitting the mushrooms with a little good olive oil, salt, and pepper. Tossing them together, she added the garlic and onions, Worcestershire sauce, a dollop of tomato sauce, some organic low-salt beef stock from a carton, a healthy smattering of flour to thicken it up, and a couple of shakes of A-1 sauce. She tasted it, then splashed on a little more pepper, a dash more of the Worcestershire, and another dribble of stock while the flour melted into the sauce. It was coming along nicely, bubbling away, thickening up to a velvety consistency.

Now for her favorite mashed potatoes. *The creamy depth of Yukon Golds can't be topped.* Mashing the potatoes with a long-handled ricer, she sliced off chunks of unsalted butter, cold from the fridge, and swirled them into the hot mixture. Does Ruby like her mashed potatoes lumpy or creamy? People had such strong preferences when it came to food. Well, too late now. She was getting creamy today, the gold standard. Adding salt, pepper and a cup or so of cream to bring the mash together, Ellen whipped in freshly grated white cheddar cheese into the hot potatoes. She'd bet her turquoise cowgirl boots Ruby was a cheese lover.

She looked at the time. Only forty minutes to go. She poured the meat mixture into a buttered soufflé dish, piled on the potatoes, added more cheese and butter on top, and covered the potatoes lightly with buttered aluminum foil. She put the dish in the oven, preheated to 200 degrees. Just before they went over to Ruby's she'd push the heat to broil, crisping the cheese to a bubbly light brown.

"Now for the woman who loves soggy canned vegetables," she said aloud. Henry's ears perked up at the sound of her voice and the smell of the casserole. He got up and moved over to his bowl, alternately looking at Ellen, then at his bowl.

"Sorry, buddy. No food for us in this meal." Grabbing a large Milkbone from the cupboard, she held it steady while he gripped it with his teeth and trotted over to his corner of the kitchen. The very thought of serving canned asparagus made her eyes ache. She just couldn't do it. She had to think of an alternative. *Let's see: Ruby probably had a sweet tooth if she loved chocolate pecan pie. What's sweet and good with almost everything? Of course. Carrots!*

She made her favorite carrots, peeled and cut at an angle in thick wedges with the juice and grated rind of a fresh orange, honey, a little freshly grated ginger, butter, salt, and some white pepper. They would be perfect with the shepherd's pie. Long thick carrots were always in her fridge, and even though she had bought them three weeks ago for those phantom-friend dinners, they were still nice and firm, a rich orange color, no blond hairs growing out of the roots and stems. Perfectly all right. By the time she heard a knock at the kitchen door, Ellen was ready.

"What smells so wonderful in this kitchen?" Frances asked. She sniffed the air as she put her pie on the counter. "Oh my, Ellen, it certainly smells as if you can cook."

Ellen laughed, sliding the buttery, citrus-infused carrots into a covered dish. She pulled her main dish from the oven, the top perfectly brown and crispy, and turned to show it to Frances who leaned in, waving the aroma toward her nose.

"My stars, Ellen, this is marvelous." Frances was proud of her protégé even though she had nothing to do with her success.

You have lots to discover about your interesting next-door neighbor, Frances. I am nothing if not layer upon layer of stuff. "Shall we go while it's all still hot? Let me grab a bottle of wine."

"Of course, my dear, by all means. Ruby is in for such a wonderful surprise. A real treat! I trust she'll be in good form. Let's hope she got a little nap today."

"How do you think she'll feel about my tagging along?" Ellen asked, anxious now, a jump in her stomach, her arms suddenly weak as she picked up the tray of food.

"Oh, I think she'll be just fine, honey, but honestly, who can be sure? Let's just go in forthrightly with all the best thoughts we can muster, and see what happens. Shall we do that, dear?"

Ellen eased the tray back down and opened the drawer at the end of the counter. She reached in for a Snickers bar and slid it into the pocket of her cargo jacket alongside the bottle of red wine.

"Yes, we shall. I'm ready." Watching her step, she trailed behind Frances, thinking Daniel must have felt this way when he marched into the lion's den.

Ten

Ruby slept until nine, which was typical for her although she didn't like to admit it. "I never sleep past seven," she'd tell the ladies at the eleven o'clock Mass on Sundays. "No sense sleeping away the light, as Mother used to say!" But in her heart, she loved to sleep in, especially in the cooler weather.

The fall was coming on fast now, with the night temperatures sliding down to the freezing point. On these cool mornings she liked the luxury of pulling the Hudson Bay blanket up to her chin, stretching her legs down as far as she could to the foot of the bed, and flexing her ankles to feel the muscles pull tight in her calves and thighs. Exercise done, she'd turn over to snuggle in for another hour.

The flexing wasn't as easy today with her right ankle still in the cast. She decided to concentrate on the left foot, pushing the calf muscles twice as hard to make up for the injured right. She couldn't raise both of her arms over her head. The left shoulder throbbed with pain just as soon as the medicine wore off, making movement impossible. As before, she decided to concentrate on the opposite side, raising the right arm up over her head, giving a stretch to her neck and a slight pull to her biceps.

I am still not well. The soreness nags at me like desperate charities at the end of the year. I am simply worn out. I'm taking the day off, even if it is the middle of the week.

The gray day was not unwelcome when she finally pulled back the thick blanket and sat up in bed, looking at the time—10:15 on a blustery early November morning. And she was home. She reached into the nightstand and felt around for the Swiss Army knife she had carried with her since she was a child. As always, it was right where she could get hold of it, like the good friend it was. She put it on top of the nightstand. She slid her legs over the side to stand on her good left foot, reaching for the walker.

"Up you go, Ruby," she said. Inching off the side of the bed, she gripped the walker tightly. She stood up, her flannel nightgown falling to her toes. Her hair was a bedhead mess, and her breath tasted as strong as onions left too long in a dark cupboard. She pulled on her chenille robe, the good arm first, as they had taught her to do in rehab. She reached down for the Swiss Army knife and dropped it into the pocket of her robe. She slowly eased along the thin Oriental carpet, picking up the walker slightly to avoid making carpet creases, which could trip her up and send her sprawling.

Oh, she could smell herself. Her underarms were fragrant with that rubbery smell of rancid sweat. Well, she'd have to be content with sink baths for a while and that's all there was to it. Oh, how she'd love a good hot bath, a long soak in the tub with lots of bubbles up to her ears. With plenty of nice hot water, and more to come as it cools. She didn't like any nonsense when she soaked in the bath. No glass of sherry or magazines, and certainly no candles surrounding the tub. That just seemed foolish. It would unnerve her to balance a glass of sherry on the edge. She'd wind up watching it constantly to be sure it didn't fall into the bubbles. Moreover, who could relax with lighted candles all over the place, not to mention handling a favorite magazine with wet hands? She didn't care for any of that.

It's all simply Madison Avenue nonsense, as Father would say. She just liked a good hot bubble bath with nothing to think about but staying covered up with hot water until her hands wrinkled.

"Well, you won't be having one of those today, or any day soon," she told herself. "It's far too dangerous getting in and out of that bathtub. No taking a shower in the tub either. The very process of getting in, standing, pulling the curtain around and finagling the handheld shower wand? Too many high-risk maneuvers. No, it will have to be good old sink baths for a while."

She moved down the narrow hallway, passing Lizzie's old room with its thin bed quilt of pink roses and the matching drapes lined with white muslin and weighted at the bottom with stiff collar stays sewn into the hems. Next to the single bed was a long oval hand-braided rug of green, blue, and deep pink. Mother had found the rug in a barn sale more than thirty years ago. She'd only paid two dollars for it. It had been a wonderful buy, almost criminal.

"The farmer woman was desperate," Mother said. "She was a widow who couldn't carry the farm anymore. I offered what I thought was a fair price and the widow accepted. If it is worth one hundred times that amount, then it is my good luck. That's all there is to it." *So it goes*, Ruby thought.

Her sister Lizzie had been dead for fourteen years, leukemia taking her in no time at all. She would have been sixty-four this year.

I always thought she'd be around, wanting to hear my small stories about the ladies of the Altar Guild and what I was cooking for Father and Mother's supper. Lizzie thought I was a good cook. She had asked for my recipe for Spanish rice saying she admired its daring ingredients of garlic, red and green peppers, and that zippy paprika. I miss you every day, Lizzie.

"Try to remember that Lizzie had a full life, even if she was only fifty when she died," Father told Ruby when she was sad. He was probably right. Lizzie was married to a successful architect and they had three talented daughters, all of whom were graduated from the College of St. Elizabeth in Convent Station, New Jersey.

"Sadly for us, each one of them moved out of town after Lizzie's death," Father said. He liked to note that not only did Lizzie have the biggest house on West Fifth facing the lake, but her husband had built a seven-bedroom lakeside summer cottage as well. They took trips to Europe on the Cunard Line, and Lizzie drove a sleek black Mercedes when she went to her Daughters of the American Revolution meetings. She had married into her DAR status. Her husband's great-great-great-uncle had served in the New York State Militia against the British.

"She did very well," Father said. "What life she was given, she lived fully and well. That's all we can ask."

It nearly broke Mother's heart when Lizzie died, but she began to accept it after a time, warning Ruby to be careful of vodka. Mother said she had a sneaking suspicion that Lizzie's daily penchant for two or three large vodka-and-tonics was the real culprit behind that cancer. Ruby never touched strong drink. Why take the chance? Besides, she didn't think sherry was in the same category. It couldn't be. It was wine; *fortified* wine in fact, which certainly implied added benefits for good health.

Ruby loved her daily sherry, which she poured into her grandmother's cut crystal juice glass, one of only two left from that beautiful set of six, the mouth small and round. It made her feel sophisticated just holding it in her hand. It was the perfect size for keeping the fragrance of the sherry at bay in the bottom so that it remained full and strong, the thin glass elegant with its curvy sides. Raising the glass at five o'clock every day while she watched *Oprah*, Ruby was glad for the medicinal value of the sherry. She had read all about it in the newspaper.

"Look at the French," the reporter wrote. "They drink wine like water, practically, and from an early age. The result? They don't have as much cancer or as many heart attacks as Americans do."

Ruby kept the newspaper clipping of that story in a white envelope in the kitchen drawer in case anyone asked her why she drank a glass or two of sherry every day. The fact that the piece was written about red wine was not important. Wine was wine. Unfortunately, Mother had died not knowing about wine's medicinal aspects. Ruby wondered if Mother's life might have been a little sweeter if she'd been able to sip a glass of sherry in the afternoon.

Ruby went limp in the doorway. A wave of loneliness for Mother and Lizzie nearly took her breath away.

Oh, Lizzie, where are you? I need you, my wonderful older sister. You were so good to me. You never expected me to get a job or use my college degree, like Phillip did. He was such a big, fat pain of a brother, always needling me: "Get out of this old Victorian house and create a life, why don't you?"

"Don't you know that Mother and Father can take care of themselves?" Phillip had insisted. "If they need a live-in caretaker they can afford to hire one, Ruby. Don't waste your life on them. Go and get a life for yourself!"

Ruby curled her hand around the Swiss Army knife in her pocket.

"Well, Phillip, maybe I stayed here because I am happy just the way things are and I loved my parents. I am not you, and you are not me." She might as well have been talking to a pile of bricks. He never acknowledged her life as having any value whatsoever.

"You might as well go and hide in a convent with all those other women who are terrified of life," he had said. "At least they admit their fear."

Ruby burped, a sour taste filling her mouth. Phillip had been dead to her for more than four decades, really. He hadn't even come home for Mother or Father's funerals. He was too busy in California with that marketing executive he married and with his career as a venture capitalist, whatever that was. He did send birth announcements celebrating each of his two children and a Christmas card with his perfect family gathered around a California redwood tree one year. In the end, his children grew up without ever meeting their grandparents or their Aunt Ruby. Honestly, it was a shame. Yet no matter how long he stayed away, Mother never allowed a harsh word about her Phillip. He could do no wrong.

"He's a man, Ruby. He has to make his way in the world. I don't expect him to pander to his mother now that he's grown. Don't blame him so much. He's out in the world and he seems to have a full life. Let's be happy for him."

Blinking, Ruby shook her head, an angry knot of resentment forming in her temples. Hating Phillip would do her no good now. She'd ignore him as she had for the last forty-one years. "Bad thoughts, be gone. Good riddance," she said. Another hot burp rose in her throat. She swallowed several times to get rid of it, jiggling her right foot frantically, the soft cast heavy on her ankle. She took a deep breath and leaned into her walker again.

As much as she didn't want to, she paused to take a good look into Phillip's old bedroom, the second-best of the upstairs five, really. Located at the end of the hallway next to the bathroom in the back of the house, its floor-to-ceiling windows allowed a wide vista into the backyards of the homes behind them, the houses along West Sixth Street. She had coveted this room as a young child.

Phillip went wild whenever he caught her in there, but she was careful, plotting times to sneak in when he was gone. Once safely inside, she loved to sit on the floor by the tall windows and pretend she could see right through the walls of her neighbors' houses. Their kitchen windows and back porches offered fine openings for her imaginary telescope. She envisioned herself floating into their houses through the small laundry room window or the bigger one in the attic. She'd glide through their living rooms and bedrooms, her life taking on the petty details and big ideas of theirs, as she decided on a place to light. Once settled, she'd listen to their life stories, picking up the threads of their conversations, joining in, relaxing to the sounds and smells of their lives, feeling so welcome.

One day it would be the Fogartys with their five messy children and hardly a spot of grass in their muddy backyard. Such hodge-podge kids in their mismatched argyle socks, wonderfully loud plaid pants, and striped shirts, running in between the clothes lines, the sheets pale gray from weekly washings and not enough money for bleach. She liked to pretend to race around the backyard with them, yelling at the top of her lungs, throwing things at each other, tripping over rusty bicycles and a swing set with only one swing left, getting dirty and pulling each other's hair.

All this time Mrs. Fogarty would be hiding in the house, not having the energy to take control, letting them go, hoping for the best every afternoon as she made supper, the boiled cabbage and hamburger meat on the stove, pungent smells seeping out of the kitchen window, the pale yellow-green cabbage water saved for soup the next day. Life at the Fogartys' was enchantingly dangerous. Rough and ready with not enough of anything to go around.

The next day she might become an Altdorfer, unlocking their backyard gate and pricking her finger on the trailing roses all along the wooden fence between her house and theirs. She could smell the lunch they'd have, Mr. Altdorfer coming home at noon sharp every day from his store downtown, the twenty-minute walk giving him a big appetite. They'd feast on a platter of crispy thin-skinned pork sausages with good grainy brown mustard and yeasty hard rolls with soft butter, the smell of sauerkraut making her eyes water, the music of Wagner filling the air with booming kettledrums as she settled into the dark dining room with its big furniture and heavy damask drapes, closed now during lunch, for privacy.

For dessert they'd have thick slices of moist, dense fruitcake that Mrs. Altdorfer made at Christmas each year and meted out carefully during the winter. She always added a dollop of stiff creamy hard sauce on the side, a sauce with the fragrance of brandy or something like that in it, something exotic-smelling and alcoholic. After lunch Mr. Altdorfer would rest in his burgundy leather recliner for thirty minutes before returning to work. While he napped, Ruby would snuggle into the big stuffed chair by the fireplace, quietly reading the horrifying tales of the Brothers Grimm.

She liked thinking about being an Altdorfer. They were successful in life. "Theirs was a life of hard work," Father said. Mr. Altdorfer's furniture store was the biggest in town, his carved German grandfather clocks finding a spot in the center halls of all the big houses in Oswego. Women knew their husbands were a success when the Altdorfer truck pulled into the driveway with a delivery. With windows open to catch a breeze on warm summer nights, those beautiful clocks could be heard chiming the hours, keeping life on track; especially in the middle of the night when women lay awake, restless, wondering if it would be too hot to play golf at ten after the men got through, or if they'd have time to push the gift cart around at the Oswego Hospital for a couple of hours in the afternoon. They'd listen without moving, waiting for the *ding-ding* of the quarter-hour chime, time closing in on another night, another day fifteen minutes closer.

Ruby snorted, shaking her head. Invariably, right in the middle of the best parts of her daydreams, Phillip would barge into the room and claim his space, pushing her out in a loud voice, arms flailing—self-righteousness personified—slamming the door after her. Ruby would cry, hating him for making her let the families down by leaving early, the tea not finished, the sausages half-eaten, the laundry freezing on the line.

How silly she had been, she sniffed, moving again, heading for the bathroom. She could have taken over Phillip's room when he left, of course, but she didn't. By then it was much too late for daydreams, and somehow the room always smelled like him even though she washed the woodwork with Lysol and sprayed lemon juice into the air every week for a full year. No matter what she did, the room retained his cold arrogance.

She preferred Father's old bedroom now anyway. Mother had suggested she move into it after he died because it was three times the size of her small room across from Lizzie's. Father's room was in the very front of the house with four tall bay windows that faced West Fifth, giving her light and access to neighborhood comings and goings, especially when she could keep the windows open at night. Inside the bedroom was a door leading to a small covered balcony on the side of the house where she could settle into the chaise lounge and not be seen from the street, a thirty-foot fir tree screening her from Mattie and Tom Hannigan's house next door.

She even could keep track of things from her bed. She heard the night sounds of a car door slamming, or being carefully closed. She could tell if the Fitzhugh girls got home by midnight or not, and she could peek through the partially opened blinds to watch their dates pressing against them on the front porch, working hard to make a kiss more exciting than it was. She was sadly anxious during the week by the urgency of Mary Downer's *clickety-clack* heels as she walked home quickly after closing the library at nine o'clock, frightened of the dark, terrified that the tall beefy man would step out again from behind one of the big oak trees, opening his coat to her, naked, revealing his thing, thrilling himself and sending Mary to her bed for three days, exhausted by all that white, flabby flesh, that thing pointing straight at her. Mary told Ruby she couldn't bring herself to tell the police; the very thought of describing him gave her stomachaches for a month.

Ruby groaned just thinking about it. Good Lord, she could write a book. *View from the Bedroom*, she'd call it. She certainly had all the drama, all the terror, and all the sexy she could handle right here. Too bad she wasn't a reader, or a writer.

"Don't you ever read books?" Phillip had asked her, eager to talk about the latest John Irving novel back in the sixties.

"I have no need for books, Mr. *New York Times* best sellers list. I don't need to read about anybody else's life. My life is plenty interesting enough." He had rolled his eyes and looked at her as if she were a bad smell. But he shut up and never asked her about books again.

She shuffled past Phillip's room to the bathroom. It was time to clean herself up for the day. She was hungry and the twenty-five-minute stop-and-start fanny walk down the front staircase was the only thing standing between her and a plate of toast with butter and sweet orange marmalade. She might even treat herself to some of that Swiss hot chocolate mix and float a marshmallow on top. She hummed and pushed the walker as fast as she could. The struggle with the sink bath was exhausting.

It was forty minutes before she could ease into her pale blue blouse and her favorite cream-colored cardigan sweater. She stepped into a mid-calf jersey skirt that wouldn't trip her up with the walker and slid her good foot into a Weejun penny loafer. Just before leaving the front bedroom she transferred the Swiss Army knife into her skirt pocket, then turned to open the red leather jewelry box on the tall dresser. She pulled out a string of pearls, the long ones she could slide over her head. She wore them often. Pearls were good with everything, Mother had insisted. She also had maintained that dressing in a nice outfit every day was essential.

"The slippery slide into eccentricity begins with not bathing and dressing well every day, Ruby. Always look your best, even if you don't expect to see anyone. You never know what the day will bring. Be ready."

Ruby agreed and complied easily with Mother's advice, except after her death, Ruby incorporated her own every-other-day-or-maybe-two-days rule for showering and washing her hair. She felt a little defiant doing it the first few times, but she got over it. The dressing part she kept holy. She only wished other women in Oswego had the advantage of Mother's rules. When Ruby saw how women dressed today, it disturbed her. How could they run around in those skinny jeans with sweaters pulled tight so that they showed the rolls around their waists as if they were something to see? *Sweet Mary, Mother of Jesus.* "Cover it up," she wanted to scream.

Carefully and painfully she managed to ease herself down the stairs. She collapsed the walker and slid down a step at a time, regretting the jersey skirt, which kept riding up with every fanny-based movement, no doubt picking up lint and carpet crumbs as she went. She held onto the railing with her good left hand. What if that crazy dog had managed to break both of her wrists? And the bigger question: Did Ellen still have the dog? Oh, sure she did. That dog seemed to be her world. Ruby imagined he was the only friend that woman had in Oswego. She'd never get rid of him.

But he should not be allowed to hurt someone else. She supposed she'd have to see to that. She hated to think of what that might entail. Ruby had always been fond of dogs. When she was twelve, her constant companion, Cinnamon, a rangy Irish Setter, died. It felt as if someone had cut out her heart. It hurt so much, she had cried for months.

"I'll never have another dog," Ruby told her mother. "Never again. What's more, I will never love anything or anyone like that again. I won't let myself. It just isn't worth it." Mother didn't comment, but the look on her face told Ruby she was troubled.

I never could understand why she was upset about my saying that. I still don't understand her worrying about it. I was only being smart. Surely she could see that?

At last, the bottom of the staircase was under her feet. Ruby snapped her walker together, making her way down the long hallway to the kitchen. The smoky smell was everywhere, but she was immune to it already. She'd have to start thinking about repairs and cleaning projects soon, however. With all this chair time ahead of her, the thought of projects appealed to her. She could supervisor closely when the workmen came, sitting right in the room with them because of her immobile state. It was perfect.

"Idle hands are the devil's workshop," Mother always said. "Get busy with something, Ruby. You can't sit and stare out that window all day."

She'd start a post-fire repair list today during the commercials on *The Price Is Right*.

Everything was taking longer to do. Instead of grabbing a loaf of bread and popping two slices into the toaster, she had to rest on the walker, balance herself securely, and then open the breadbox. Using her left hand, she awkwardly managed to get the slices of raisin bread into the toaster and push down the handle. Unfortunately the kitchen was not designed for chefs with the efficient work triangle design: sink, to stove, to refrigerator. Ruby's refrigerator was at the far end of the kitchen in an alcove, and the stove was at the opposite end. She needed to get out butter and marmalade. She began her shuffle to the alcove.

The toast smelled wonderful. Nothing compared to it, really. What was it Kirsty Alley had said to Oprah a few years ago when she showed the world her weight loss by marching around in a bikini? Kirsty said she'd never do the popular no-carb diets; any diet that didn't let you have toast was off her list, she said. Ruby loved Kirsty for sharing the joy of toast. Pulling the hot slices out, Ruby carefully placed three thin pats of butter on one slice, and then put the second slice on top to help it melt. This was a good way to stretch the butter from one piece to another. *Tricks of the careful person's trade,* she smiled. If her right wrist had not been injured, she would have winked and touched her finger to her nose to underscore this particular cook's secret for the Food Network television camera she imagined was focused on her.

She pulled the measuring spoons out of the utility drawer, opened the jar of sweet marmalade, and scooped out a level tablespoon, plopping it onto the warm toast, again covering one piece with the other and pressing them lightly together so the butter and jam could transfer. She decided it was too much work to make hot chocolate. She grabbed the canned Blue Bird Orange Juice as she returned the butter to the fridge and stood at the sink to drink her juice and eat her toast.

She savored every bite, making it last, wondering if she'd have the stamina to make a decent supper. The freezer was nearly bare, a small Banquet frozen entrée sitting alone in the center. Its dinner for one contained a single meat patty with a serving of dry mashed potatoes and peas. She supposed that would be all right. She loved peas. And she did have those apples in the fridge. Tossing her soiled paper napkin into the garbage can, she eased over to her favorite chair.

She checked to be sure her shopping pad with the attached pencil on a string was in the magazine basket by her chair before plopping down. All set. She could start her project list just as soon as she was ready. *Ohhhhhhh.* It was good to sit down in something comfortable again. She put her feet up on the ottoman and rested her eyes a minute, the morning's exertions catching up with her.

The blue jay was back. She could hear him bullying the sparrows at the feeder, pushing them out only to discover empty sunflower seed shells on the rim. She'd have to get that filled before dark or there would be hell to pay tomorrow morning. As she drifted off, a small smile puffed up her cheeks. The words on the spare tire cover of the Jeep driving in front of her last summer on the way to the lake flashed across her mind.

Life is good, it said.

Eleven

Ruby was startled awake by the roar of her snore.

"Oh! All right! What is it?" she asked the room, still snoozy, her eyelids sticky with gunk. "Ahhhhhhh. OK. All right. Here I am. Here I am." Shaking herself, a chill sneaking down her spine as she sat up, she eased forward squinting at her watch. "Oh my good Lord, it's three o'clock already."

Grabbing the remote control, she pushed the power button on, just in time to join the audience for Dr. Phil's entrance. She was relieved that she hadn't missed a minute, even though she knew the show was automatically recording. If the show was particularly good, she might watch it again at night. She preferred to watch it live, and hated coming in a minute or two late because it made her feel she wasn't part of the full experience somehow, that she wasn't a good team player. She was just in time. She smiled and relaxed, wiggling back into her warm chair.

Dr. Phil looks good this year, she thought. Tailored suits—fancier suits—with his pink, burgundy, turquoise, and purple ties, each one with a small matching silk handkerchief peeking out of his chest pocket. Sometimes no tie at all, just an expensive sports coat with his shirt collar open. That was his informal look. Phil was in gray pinstripes today with an interesting green tie. Nice. Not only was his wardrobe more dramatic, but also the stage this year was pure Las Vegas with its huge columns, mahogany and glass everywhere. It was a big showy set. Robin's hand was behind these changes, she felt certain. That woman was a princess, but Ruby liked her well enough anyway. *The only time Dr. Phil disappoints is when he tells the audience he would never say or do anything disrespectful or demeaning to Robin, God forbid.*

"You better believe I wouldn't cross my wife!" Phil would sputter, aghast, acting all scared of her when he said it, his hand on his heart like he felt faint. Meanwhile Robin would sit there grinning. "That's right," she'd say while her head bobbed up and down like one of those spring-loaded Cupie dolls. Robin and her perfect husband, perfect kids, perfect grandbaby, and her petite-perfect big life. Well, maybe it was all true. Ruby hoped so. She really did.

Whatever fantasy they're living, Phil deserved all the happiness and extravagant suits and stage sets the world has to offer. After all, look at the crazy people he deals with to make it all happen. Ruby shuddered thinking about that woman a couple of weeks ago who sat right up on that stage and told Dr. Phil she was dating a much younger man while her husband stayed home with their five children, all under the age of ten. She was slick as black ice saying it, no guilt whatsoever. Worse yet, right in front of her own husband, she said she had no intention of giving up the man or staying home at night. Dr. Phil had a field day with that one. He called her a cougar. That may be the clever way to describe her, but if Mother had been here she would have summed up that woman as nothing more than a tramp.

"You can dress it up, wrap it in mink, comb the hair, and lipstick the smile, but it just doesn't matter," Mother liked to point out. "In the end, the tramp comes through. You can't buy good breeding, and you can't hide a bad seed, Ruby. It's really that simple."

Ruby shifted in her chair, the pain in her ankle relentless. She'd have to get up at the next big break and take some pills. *Phil's back. This should be good.*

Phil had a couple of smarty-pants teenagers on stage today with their I'll-do-exactly-as-I-please attitudes. One had been pregnant twice already at seventeen and the other had tattoos from her chin to her toenails and was the head girl of something called the Skull Molls, a female motorcycle gang in Detroit. Phil was his charming self, asking them questions, trying to determine, "What were you thinking?" She loved it when he said that. She also giggled every time he pretended to be amazed at people who went down the same path of destruction, over and over, making one bad choice after another, ending up with the same disastrous results.

"So how's that working for ya?" he'd explode, hands up, that incredulous wide grin on his face, all the while knowing the answer, of course. He was something.

The two strumpets just sat there and smirked at Phil, showing no respect for his position and extensive knowledge. Their sullen responses were infuriating. Ruby wanted to reach right into that TV and slap their faces. On second thought, and in all fairness, she knew those young girls weren't born that way, all defiant and mean. Somebody must have taught them it was all right to behave like that. *Oh, the world these kids grow up in today. Parents and schools don't have any idea about discipline any more. They don't have nuns with rulers in their hands ready to teach children painful lessons about respect. For heaven's sake, even Catholics want to talk back these days. Pity the Holy Father. Pity Dr. Phil with these two harlots.* Ruby was enjoying this.

During the commercial break she looked out to see the darkness coming in fast. She loved twilight time, although the Channel 4 Action News Team said it was the most dangerous time for car accidents. Her stomach growled as she waited for the commercials to end, five of them in a row. Dr. Phil did seem to have a lot more of those this year. Well, she supposed they paid him a good salary, not to mention Robin's expensive clothes that she changed every single day. She had never worn the same thing twice in all the years Ruby had been watching the show. Who lived like that?

Then Phil was back, grilling a man about giving his drug-addict son an apartment by the ocean and a new sports car to drive. Was he nuts? "No," the clueless dad explained. "I just want my son safe and off the streets when he's high so he doesn't get killed." *Oh boy, hang on mister. Dr. Phil is turning purple. Turn up the volume.*

Ruby was in a good mood by the time Phil was recapping the show and striding offstage to pick up Robin. Life was getting back to normal. *Thank you, Jesus, Mary and Joseph, for protecting me.*

Oprah was next, but she had a couple of those new age guests, Wayne Dyer and Deepak Chopra. That Dyer fellow turned Ruby off. A PhD, he always insisted on everyone using the "doctor" before his written and spoken name, and then talked forever about not having an ego. He just didn't ring true to Ruby. Chopra might have had some good ideas, but Ruby couldn't understand what he was saying half the time. He had that Indian accent that was difficult for her to get past, especially when he was examining such big concepts as metaphysical life and the cosmos. Oprah gushed, smiling, nodding her consent, and agreeing with just about everything they said, especially when they went on and on about being intentional in our lives. Oprah loved all that nonsense about the universe holding every single thing we could possibly want. All we have to do is move forward in the direction of our dreams and doors will open for us, one after the other, like intentional magic. *What pap*, Ruby thought.

"The Lord helps those who help themselves," was Father's mantra, spoken repeatedly to Ruby when she crossed her fingers or prayed for something to happen. "Nothing beats hard work and preparation." His own father proved the rule; he had shown the way. Arriving as an infant émigré from northern Germany with his parents and two brothers in 1851, Grampa Bainbridge had worked smart and hard all his life. When he died in 1942, thanks to careful investments and his wife's world-class frugality, he left $950,000 in cash, a thriving business, and no debt, of course.

Father followed in his footsteps and when he died, both Ruby and Mother were financially independent, although they never changed their simple, frugal habits one iota. Ruby still washed plastic sandwich bags for reuse, and Mother never gave up her instructions to scrape every bit of the leftovers out of the serving bowls in preparation for a clean-out-the-fridge night at the end of the week. Those tablespoons added up, producing a veritable cup-of-this, two-cups-of-that smorgasbord, which always was accompanied by a fresh dessert to make the supper seem less used.

Listening closely, Ruby could tell Oprah wasn't a Baptist anymore. She wondered what had happened to turn Oprah away from her religious roots. Baptists weren't anywhere near the true faith like Catholics, of course, but they feared God and took communion once a month; at least that's what Irene McTavish had told her. Ruby sensed that Oprah was out there now with that new age crowd and their "divine intelligence" mumbo-jumbo. She decided to pray for Oprah tonight and ask God to straighten her out. *Here come the credits.* She was relieved that today's show was over. With any luck Oprah would get back on track tomorrow. She loved that Oprah.

Massaging her ankle, which was feeling much better now that the pain pills were taking effect, she started to push herself out of the chair when she sensed movement in the backyard. Her heartbeat quickened. Who would be in her backyard at this time of day, in the dark? She sat still as death, hardly breathing as she waited for what came next. She hadn't put on the back porch light yet, so she couldn't see well. But she was certain that she saw figures, people moving, and then she heard soft voices. She gripped the Swiss Army knife and froze in place.

"Ruby, darlin'? Are you all right? Can you see me? It's Frances! Will you put on the light and open the kitchen door, dear? Don't be alarmed. It's Frances."

Oh, piddle it all to hell. Company. And I can't escape. Here I am, big as life for all the world to see, sitting in the glow of the TV, the Tiffany lamp on the end table lighting me up like a red carpet moment. No pretending I'm upstairs or hiding in the corner until they give up and go home. She waved at the window.

"I'm coming," she shouted. As she stood up the Swiss Army knife slid out of her pocket. Grabbing hold of her walker, she reached down to pick it up, the blood rushing to her head. She stood still and took a deep breath. "It'll take me a minute. Hold on, I'm coming as fast as I can."

Moving past the window she saw someone tailing along with Frances. Ellen? Did Frances bring that Ellen Varner right to her door? Oh, that just wasn't possible. Even for peacemaker Frances.

The minute they came through the back door Ruby smelled something heavenly. Her stomach tightened at the fragrance of meat and cheese and something . . . buttery? Well, at least they didn't come empty-handed, or with silly flowers that wilt and drop leaves all over the place in three days.

"What are you up to, Frances?" She squinted at Ellen who stood hiding behind her friend. "Is that you, Ellen Varner? I have to say I am surprised to see you. But come in, come in. The heat's going out the door faster than I can pay the oil bill. Come into the kitchen and shut the door behind you, please."

"We brought you supper, Ruby, dear," Frances said. Teetering on the top step, she nearly dropped the pie, she was that unsettled. "Ellen made it just for you, and I think you'll discover, just as I did, that she is a wonderful cook!"

Ruby staged a smile, her nostrils wide open, inhaling the fragrance. "What's that? Do I see a chocolate pecan pie, Frances? You sweet woman. How kind of you to go to all the trouble of making my favorite pie." Ellen stood still, her hands very warm from holding the casserole dish of carrots with the shepherd's pie perched on top. She wanted to ask if she could put them down, but she waited to see how Ruby was going to handle her.

Ruby moved slowly backward into the kitchen.

"Well, come on in for heaven's sake. What are you going to do with those hot dishes, Ellen? Do you want to put them on the counter, or should I stick them in the oven?"

"Oh, they're ready to eat right now, Ruby. Shall I fix you a plate? Are you hungry?"

Ruby said she'd like to know what was on the menu.

"Oh, certainly. Sorry for not telling you right away. You have shepherd's pie and citrus carrots tossed in butter with a hint of ginger and honey." Her smile vanished at the look on Ruby's face. Oh, no! Had she completely misjudged Ruby's palate? "The carrots are really great. My favorite recipe. Do you like carrots?"

"Not particularly." Ruby stared at Ellen, a dull look in her eyes. "Carrots were my brother Phillip's favorite. He always had a raw carrot in his mouth, it seemed. He liked them any way he could get them."

"Well, I guarantee he would love them this way. I love carrots. I guess your brother and I have something in common!"

"Oh, you may have more in common than you know, Ellen. You and Phillip might be soul mates, in fact. I suspect you're both the same type, now that I think about it." Ellen warmed to the happy connection. Ruby started to move toward her chair, needing to get off her ankle.

"Let me get your TV tray table," Frances said. "Will you eat right where you are, Ruby dear?"

"Oh, yes. I'll have to eat in my chair. My whole life changed when that dog pushed me down those steps," she said, raising her voice to reach Frances in the hallway. "I don't know that I will ever be the same. And that rehab center! One day I'll tell you what a nightmare that was, Frances. I have been to hell and back—well, not quite all the way back. However, 'bloody, but unbowed,' as Mother used to say."

Ellen moved into Ruby's space, slowly and quietly. She knelt down alongside Ruby's chair and held onto the walker as she looked up into Ruby's face. Ruby flinched, her shoulder moving into a defensive position up to her ear. She instinctively drew back from Ellen. Ruby would have done the same thing if anyone had gotten that close, that intimate, invading Ruby's circle of personal space.

"What in the world? Ellen, what are you up to?"

"Oh, Ruby. I feel so sad that you've gone through so much because of that terrible fall. I wouldn't have wanted that to happen to anybody, and certainly not to you, my neighbor, who was only being kind to us. Truly."

Ruby readjusted herself, staring straight ahead at the black TV. Ellen tried again.

"I am giving you my heartfelt apology, Ruby. I am very, very sorry the accident happened. I know it's asking a whole lot, but do you think you could forgive me? And Henry?"

Ruby turned her head very slowly and gave Ellen a piercing look. "I have been in touch with my attorney to explore my options, Ellen Varner. I suspect that's what you really want to know. Now you do."

Frances let out a soft sigh, then inched in closer, motioning to Ellen to move away so she could put the tray table in place. "Would you prepare a plate for Miss Ruby, please, Ellen?"

A wonderful fragrance filled the air as Ellen piled shepherd's pie in the center of the plate and spooned mounds of the carrots in a semi-circle around it. *If the Food Network cooks are right and presentation is half the battle, then Ellen is well on her way to winning the war,* Ruby thought, eyeing the plateful of food in Ellen's hands.

Frances leaned down to Ruby. "What will you have to drink, honey? We brought a nice bottle of red wine, if you'd like a taste of Merlot?"

"I'll have a cold glass of milk, thank you. I need to build up my bones to help my ankle and wrist heal."

Ruby didn't look down as Ellen served the steaming plate of food. The strong smell of the beef made her want to scream. She was famished. Unable to resist, she eyed at the cheesy crust, broiled like a crispy golden cloud on top of the mashed potatoes; it nearly made her faint with pleasure. If she were alone now, she would scrape it right off and eat it plain. It was the first really good food she'd seen in weeks. The trick now was to get the two of them to go on home and leave her in peace. "Get out!" she wanted to shout. But she didn't. If she had, she knew Mother would have reached down all the way from heaven and pulled her daughter's hair right out by the roots. Ladies never, ever shout, as Mother would say.

"Well, Ellen . . . despite our . . . difficulties, I have to say that I . . . appreciate your cooking this meal." Ruby chose her words carefully. She didn't want to give the dog-mother any kind of hope. "Of course, your baking that pie, Frances, is just the best gift. It was very thoughtful of you . . . both. Now please forgive me for what I am about to say, but it must be said."

She told them she was both hungry and exhausted. Even as she said it, she could hear Mother scolding her. "The truth is, I want to eat this now, and then I want to rest. I would ask you to join me, but I just do not have the strength to entertain company right now. Do you understand, or do you think I am the most ungrateful person you know?"

"Oh, we didn't expect to stay," Frances said. "My word, no. We knew you'd be as tired as overbeaten egg whites today, Ruby. We wouldn't dream of doin' anything other than just exactly what you want. I believe I speak for us both when I say we are simply thrilled to hear you speak your mind in such a kind way, dear. But tell us, would it be any sort of help to you if we kept you company while you eat your supper? Then we'd be on hand to help you to get back upstairs?"

Ruby said no, she was fine. "I'll enjoy this meal, then maybe watch the news, and after that wind my way upstairs for the night. But thank you for the offer." She did ask that Frances cut her a nice, big piece of that chocolate pecan pie before she left. "Then I'll be in good shape, and you two can just go on home and leave me in peace. This supper really does look and smell good enough to eat!" She said it all without ever glancing in Ellen's direction.

Ellen put a nice big wedge of pie on the tray as she headed for the door. She turned with a small wave to Ruby. *"Bon appetit!"* she said.

Ruby waited until she no longer heard their footsteps, then dug into the meal. The meat pie was savory and juicy, the potatoes buttery and creamy. They practically melted in her mouth. But the showstopper was that potato topping! She scraped it all off and ate it in one big bite, chewing the crispy cheese like a big round fireball. Even the carrots were delicious with the touch of orange flavor and that honey and ginger. Who would think to put that kind of thing in carrots? She ate everything on her plate and wrestled with the idea of getting another spoonful.

Don't be greedy, Ruby Bainbridge. That casserole can be supper for the next four days, if you're careful.

What a relief it was to know she had cooked food in the house again, not to mention her favorite dessert. She shuddered at the rich taste of the pie, dragging small bites away from the slice, dense buttery chocolate and chewy pecans a teaspoon at a time, making it last, savoring the joy. *Ohhhh, thank you, Frances.*

It took her only a few minutes to clear up her dishes. She went over to the fridge to check if Frances had fully covered the leftover shepherd's pie; she didn't want it to dry out. Frances had, of course. Frances was careful and delicate in all things, Ruby thought. Walking slowly back to her chair, she settled down again, hands on her warm, full stomach. She decided Ellen had done well with her peace offering. It's too bad they wouldn't be able to share a meal from time to time. It would be nice to have a neighbor her own age as a real friend, one who puts grated orange rind in her carrots.

She laughed, thinking of Ellen's attempt at strategic maneuvering. It reminded her of the time before Lizzie's marriage. Mother felt it was every woman's responsibility to serve delicious meals to her husband and family. Mother was worried that Lizzie showed no interest in learning to cook. When she gave Lizzie a gift of Haviland Limoges china, service for twenty, Mother included a handwritten note that said,

The way to a man's heart is through his stomach. May you always fill these plates with wonderful food for your husband. Love, Mother.

"*Bon appetit,* my foot," Ruby said, pushing the power button on the remote control. "I'm not a fool. I know what you're up to, Ellen Varner."

Snug as those dust mites in her bedroom pillows, she was asleep before the first weather report, a tiny smile on her lips, a bit of caramelized onion stuck between her front teeth. Just before drifting off, she realized she had neglected to fill the birdfeeder. That blue jay would raise Cain in the morning.

Twelve

Ellen woke up to the sound of the wind battering the windows. For a minute she thought she was back in Nashville, back in the land of tornados that tore mobile homes from their roots, smashing them into the ground like busy flyswatters. She leaned over to look at the digital clock: 1:27 a.m.

Henry snuggled up alongside her. He normally slept at the bottom of the bed, enjoying his own space and leaving her hers. *He must be frightened by the wind and pounding rain.* She lay on her back listening to the storm. She loved changes in the weather. Big, howling thunderstorms; soft, heavy snowfalls covering the ground in minutes; blustery winds that made you feel lucky to be safe inside. Oddly enough, the sunny, clear days were her least favorite. Matt used to say she was just ornery.

"Only you would prefer black clouds over blue skies," he'd say. "Melancholy is your middle name." When did he stop finding that charming? When did she stop caring if he did? The gal Matt dated two weeks after their divorce was anything but moody, he'd said in a late-night phone call. They had stayed in touch by phone once a month or more, the habit of checking on each other ingrained after such a long marriage. The fact that the divorce had been amicable, thanks to Matt's determination to make it that way, set the stage for a warm post-divorce relationship.

"She's so much fun, Ellen! She's like a warm, sweet child in many ways. But she's all woman. And Ellen? She waits on me hand and foot, and loves to do it. Can you imagine? She says it's her job." Matt was talking fast, clearly enjoying the fact that he was rubbing it in. "To top it off, she loves to have sex. She has no hang-ups at all. She finds porn films exciting, and she tells me all the time what a great lover I am. For the first time in my life, I know it's true.

"Most of all, Ellen, she really needs me to take care of her," he said. She noticed his voice had dropped to a whisper for emphasis, the slapstick gone now, a serious Matt talking to her. "You never did, that's for sure. I really like the fact that I can be the hero in Treasure's life."

"Treasure? Is that her real name?"

"I know," Matt said. "Yes, it is. Actually, it fits. I call her Treas."

"How adorable," Ellen said.

Three months later Matt had called again. Listening carefully, Ellen sensed that this was not one of their just-checking-in monthly phone calls. He seemed anxious. Knowing him as well as she did, it was clear that he was leading up to something. Ellen waited to hear what it was. After a few minutes he took a big breath, and told her the news. He had asked Treasure to marry him.

"Here's what you need to understand, Ellen. Treas said she would only accept my proposal if I promised absolutely never to have any kind of contact with you again. I need you to understand that I'm going to honor that pledge because I want to marry her." Ellen was stunned.

"Don't you think her request shows she's a little, I don't know, insecure?" she said. "I mean, we spent nearly all of our adult lives together, Matt. We raised two children together. We've both adjusted to the divorce and wouldn't go back. We only talk occasionally now, and who knows when we'll be face-to-face again? But completely out of each other's life, never to communicate again? Do you think that's fair? *Never* any contact?"

"Never. And fair or unfair," Matt said, "I am going to honor it. It's that simple."

The next thing Ellen knew, Matt had sold the home he and Ellen had lived in for two decades, cashing out major equity to build one of those big, southern, palladium-windowed houses in a small development on a cul-de-sac in an up-and-coming high-rent area of a growing town outside of Nashville. The brick house was on a postage-stamp no-maintenance lot, the kind Matt liked, with a customized separate wing and fenced play area for Treasure's three beloved dogs. Matt hated dogs. Ellen knew their exclusion from the main house must have been Treasure's concession to wedded compromise. "You keep the dogs out of my life, and I'll keep the former wife out of yours. That's the deal." She could hear Matt saying it.

We are all expendable, Ellen had thought.

Now all these months later, she was glad they were happy together. Matt was the knight in Jaguar armor for Treas, and she was the sweet-hearted lady who needed him. Not a bad ending to the story. For Ellen, too. Treasure had been right. Out of sight, and eventually, out of mind. Matt could never have been fully hers if Ellen was lurking around in his life, and vice versa. In the end, it was the right thing to do. Most of all, Ellen didn't have to feel guilty about leaving Matt anymore.

Thank you, Treas.

A flash of white lightning lit up the bedroom, followed quickly by a thunderous boom that seemed to shake the very foundation of the house. Henry bolted off the bed and hustled over to the walk-in closet, tail between his legs. He dragged the closet door open with his front paw and eased into the dark space. Ellen looked to see if he had pulled the door closed as a final defense against the storm. He hadn't. She eased out of bed and closed the door halfway, so he could get out later. Fully awake now, she pulled on her long cable-knit sweater with the hood, tucked her feet into fleece socks, and quietly tiptoed down the narrow staircase, hoping Henry wouldn't feel the need to follow.

The wind and rain were pounding the horse chestnut tree in the front yard, tossing it crazily around in a kind of wild native dance, forcing it to twist and whirl with abandon, shaking it to its core. She could almost hear the tree scream its frightened delight. Tree limbs would be all over town in the morning, maybe even uprooted trees, the result of too much recklessness, too much freedom. This storm was a beaut. She passed by the front door and looked across to Ruby's house. The light was on in the second floor bedroom that faced the street. She assumed it was Ruby's bedroom because it was the only light on in the whole huge house.

The mail today had brought a formal letter from an attorney representing Ruby. She had hired Larry Robinson. He was an old high school classmate of Ellen's, a good-looking fellow and smart as all get-out. *Oh, Ruby.* When Ellen opened the letter, she caught her breath as nice-guy Larry tossed out the first salvo in a lawsuit against her. His language was somewhat friendly, indicating that this was the formal notification that Ruby Bainbridge was seeking damages against Ellen Varner for the vicious attack on her by Ellen Varner's dog, Henry. It was hoped, Larry wrote, that this matter could be settled quickly and as amicably as possible, and would Miss Varner and her representatives work with his office to arrange an initial meeting in the next two weeks? Please call the office to set up an appointment.

On a normal day in Ellen's past life, she would have been livid. Today she couldn't conjure up even a decent cry about it. Ruby's aggression was just one more rusty nail in her path. She put the letter by the phone as a reminder to call her insurance agent tomorrow. For now, she'd go back to the wildness of the storm and try to put the potential lawsuit out of her mind.

Looking up, she wondered if Ruby had a TV in her bedroom. From what Frances had said, Ruby was painstakingly frugal, the well-trained child of her mother and grandmother. Saving money was almost a religion to the three of them, apparently. Frances said she was in awe of Ruby and her late mother's ability to deny themselves so much. What Frances didn't tell Ellen was that Ruby could afford almost anything that struck her fancy. Quite simply, she was rich. Not Hollywood rich-and-famous rich, but solidly upstate-New-York rich. Several-million-by-now rich.

Ellen suspected Ruby might think a second TV in her bedroom would be an unwarranted extravagance, a violation of the ethics of sound money management. One was plenty. Two would be lavish, and lavishness does not share a cab with frugality. Her current TV set looked ancient. In fact, Ellen had been pleasantly surprised yesterday to see that it had a remote control. Still, she guessed it was at least fifteen years old.

"If you wipe me out, I hope you at least buy yourself a new TV," she called to Ruby's upstairs window. "Get yourself a great big fancy one in bold, pushy high-definition 3-D. I want life to come charging right out of that screen and grab you like a hawk on a rabbit!"

Just then Ruby's light went out. The large house was completely dark now, the storm swirling around it like a giant hairnet. "Sleep well, Ruby," she said.

Ellen turned toward the kitchen, shivering, feeling the cold and damp, her depression blanketing her like an energy field, a black aura that weakened her like a low-grade fever. She was always on the brink of crashing into full-blown despair. Fighting it sapped her energy; it didn't take much to nudge her into the pit.

She cringed thinking about her trip to the Acme supermarket a couple of days ago. She had gone in to pick up her usual list: candy bars, milk, French bread, eggs, dry and canned dog food. She was moving along the aisles packed with great-looking displays, wondering if she would ever have a real appetite again. She remembered when food shopping had been her favorite part of the week. What was fresh? How good would Indian Butter Chicken taste tonight? Ahhh, that pork loin roast will be great this weekend. She had loved it all once. Now it only made her sad. Then a couple came up behind her, their cart nearly full.

"Jamie's crazy about those Baby Ruth bars," the woman said. "Grab a bag of those when we see them, will you, sweetie?" They were fortyish, a good looking couple both dressed in business clothes, obviously on their way home from work. They were easy together, warm and used to each other, nice. As they passed her, the man put his arm around his wife's waist and snuggled close to her hair.

Rubbing her back playfully, he whispered, "I bet I can guess what you want tonight."

"Oh, you can, can you?" She laughed, facing him directly, stealing a little kiss. "And what would that be, Mr. Smithson?"

He jerked his arm around from the back of his coat and produced a big gold bag of Hershey's Kisses, which he held up to her chest. "Kisses, kisses, and more kisses," he said.

"Oh, you!" she said, taking the bag, tossing it carefully on top of the groceries. "You are just too much."

The kindness of the simple exchange, the sweetness of their easy banter, their intimacy so boldly on display sent Ellen plummeting. She knew what a relationship like that was all about; she had had one. Her legs were like lead as she pushed her cart to the checkout. She considered abandoning the purchases, but Henry was out of canned food and he deserved his supper. She checked out in record time and nearly ran to her car.

Well, that's just how it is.

All I want for Christmas is a hot cup of tea, she thought, shuffling along the hallway, quick tears spritzing her face, settling into places where wrinkles gave them puddle room. Turning on the electric teapot, she grabbed a cup, reached for the honey, and opened a bag of green tea. The pure solitude of being up in the middle of the night, oddly awake when everyone else was sleeping, comforted her. Night-owling was one of the major rewards of not having a job; another was not fighting the weather and traffic.

Leaning on the counter, she savored this reprieve from the pending morning rush hour. Those demanding commuter workdays were hell, and she was glad they were over, at least for now. She'd have to get a job in a few months or she'd go broke, eventually, regardless of how things turned out with Ruby. The good news was the worst rush hour in Oswego was like a Sunday drive anywhere else. But she was probably out of step with the Oswego culture on that point, too. She cut a lemon in half, squeezing its juice into the teacup. Last week she'd watched a man wave half a tuna sub in the air at the Lakeside Café, incensed about the traffic on Bridge Street. It had taken him fifteen minutes to get home from work the night before. Standing up at one point, he had challenged the wary diners to consider if this was the Oswego they wanted to live in.

"Our development-crazy politicians are pushing us to become a Syracuse while you sleep," he said. "But is that what we want? Do we ever think about what comes with all this growth?"

She smiled at the memory. Rush hour, indeed—not to mention the worry that Oswego would turn into a booming metro area. It would take a twenty-first-century miracle for that to happen. Sadly, it seemed to her that rusty old upstate New York was very short on miracles these days.

The cold air hit her as she opened the door to the back porch, which was enclosed by full-length storm windows in the winter, full screens in the summer. It was her favorite part of the house. She didn't bother to turn on the table lamp or the electric baseboard heat, preferring to stay in the dark as she covered up in a down quilt, pulling it up to her shoulders, settling into the faded, chilly, upholstered chaise lounge. The relentless energy of the storm calmed her.

She had so much to figure out; but not right now. She closed her eyes and listened to the black as the thunder boomed again and again, partnering with the wind, pushing tree limbs against the house in a kind of scrappy cacophony, an unpredictable lake-effect symphony: Light. *Boom. Crash. Thrash.* Wind. *Scrape, scrape.* Soft light. Bright light. Fast-rolling thunder. *Boom, boom. Slap, slap. Howl. Crash.* Helpless rooted nature bending to the conductor's baton-frenzy.

"Carry on, carry on," she said. Feeling the energy, she sat up, gently conducting, waving her arms in time with the blasts of wind, calling in the thunder in Mississippi cadence just after the light, the trees like brush drumsticks percolating rhythmic patterns, insistent baselines for the unpredictable violence. "Bravo!" she shouted silently. "Bravo!" She was drained and exhilarated, flopping back down under the comforter, pulling it over her head, feeling the warmth of her own breath, wide awake now.

She stuck her foot into the center and made a tent. It was like old times when she was a child. Hearing the lights-out ultimatum, not tired yet, wondering what Nancy Drew was up to, she would pull up the covers and cross her legs in the air, creating the tent, then read by flashlight, enjoying the danger of it all, sticking her head out to get fresh air every few minutes. Now her toes hurt from the pressure of the comforter and a calf cramp was getting ready to strike. She collapsed the tent and folded the comforter over at her neck, her eyes closed. The sadness was easing now. She was profoundly tired of living on the edge every minute.

Let it go. Find neutral.

She was glad when Henry scratched hard at the porch door, his high-pitched whines urging her to pay attention. She got up and let him in. He waited while she got back in place on the chaise. She lifted the cover. He dove in, head first, aligning his warm body against hers, and resting his head on her ankles. "My bodyguard," she said, softly. The storm pressed on with no signs of letting up. She reached into her pocket for a candy bar, pulling out a Three Musketeers. Happy in the moment, she took her first small chocolaty-chewy bite. The rich milk chocolate oozed onto her tongue, melting as it lay there, the light chocolate nougat creamy in her cheeks. *Delicious.* She rested in the flavor, settled into the sweetness.

She had been forbidden to eat candy bars as a child. They were bad for the skin and anathema to the discipline of a good diet, her Aunt Eleanor had said. But Ellen loved chocolate. She would save her leaf-raking money and her small chores allowance, sneak up to Al's Store, a front-room store in a small house on West Fifth, and buy a candy bar once every two weeks. She would dream of the outing for days in advance, knowing she had to be brave—bold, in fact—as she made the decision to disobey, to take a huge chance at being caught, chocolate on her breath and fingers, telltale spots on her blouse or jacket. Despite the danger, she would go forward every time she had enough extra money. She believed the candy bars were magical, powerful.

Ellen shut her eyes. Those candy bar trips had been intense. She would select a Saturday, then wait until Aunt Eleanor was taking her afternoon nap. She'd sneak out and walk quickly along the short block to Al's, crossing the street, carefully looking both ways before entering the store, hoping her tattletale cousin Gloria wasn't lurking around somewhere. Once inside, even though she had thought of little else for days, it would take her ten to fifteen minutes to decide on a purchase. When one of the dozens of choices was picked, she'd put the Fifth Avenue, or Mallow Cup, or Skybar in her pocket, and slip around the corner of Al's Store, crossing the street again to the First Presbyterian Church where she squeezed into the narrow crevice between the church and its church hall. Safe in this hiding place, she'd slowly unwrap the candy bar, leaning against the stone wall.

Stretching out the moments, taking the tiniest bites, she savored each nibble, imagining the melting chocolate seeping inside her tongue, giving it power, oozing into her blood, her legs, coating her insides all over, giving her superhero strength. She made every second count, looking at the candy bar, tapping it lovingly with the tips of her fingers while she chewed, knowing another bite would come off the end, one more dose of chocolate serum on its way.

The intensity both strengthened and drained her so that when the bitter end came, the agonizing last bite, she had to sit down. It would feel like forever before she could do it again. "Until then," she told herself. "I am strong. I am Ellen Varner, a chocolate-powered force running in my mother's stead. I am full of super powers. I will stay sane. My mind will not play tricks on me. I will be the smartest, strongest, sanest person you know. Chocolate fills my veins. I can do anything."

Ellen shook off the memory, uncomfortable with its implications, afraid to examine it carefully. Childhood was such a crazy place to be. "What a goofy little girl I was," she said.

She turned her attention back to the storm, listening for the sound of thunder, licking her fingers carefully, finished now with the Three Musketeers bar. She was stunned by a brilliant blaze of lightning as it flashed violently across the treetops, followed instantly by more bright lights shimmering in waves of aftershock. Her arms twitched at her sides with each flicker. Henry inched around and stuck his head out, then laid it back down on her stomach, his muscular body trembling.

Ellen sat up tall and looked out to the end of her garden. She watched, horrified, as a fiery lightning bolt split the stately maple tree in half, slicing it lengthwise like a thick head of broccoli. That maple tree had been the anchor of the small backyard for more than a century, giving shade and shelter, nesting spots for cardinals and flickers, and a strong arm for the old tire swing. Every fall the tree's branches tossed fiery red and crimson leaves down like dandruff, and afterward, dressed in nothing but snow and ice, neighbors paused to marvel at its stark power.

A string of black chokeberry bushes grew in the morning sun under it, sprawling along the fence, their thick green leaves claiming light and space, the six-foot bushes tall and full, one after the other, a testament to their persistence. In late summer those bushes produced clusters of juicy black berries that fed the squirrels. As a child playing in her grandparents' backyard with its large black chokeberry bush, Ellen had been mesmerized as she watched unwary birds peck away at the luscious berries only to find themselves drunk on the bitter juice, flopping down around the bushes like weakened pansies after a rainstorm.

She reached down under the duvet to pet Henry, telling him the lightning seemed to be easing up a little, then leaned forward to get a good look at the chokeberry bushes to see if they were all right. As far as she could tell, the heavy maple branches smothered them. She hoped they wouldn't be crushed. She started to count slowly, "One Mississippi; two Mississippi; three Missi—" The thunder came quickly behind the lightning, pounding the air again and again, the sky a row of overhead cannons. Terrified now, Henry slid out of the bed and threw all his weight against the porch door. He escaped into the kitchen where he hid under the table, whiny growls covering his fear. Ellen held her breath, waiting for the lightning to tee up again.

"Oh, please, stop. Please," she said. Even as the words were spoken, she knew it was hopeless. Everything was fair game tonight.

The random wheels of nature were in motion, fierce in their power, taking prayer requests from no one. She stood up to take a good look into the backyard. The tree had landed on her garage, smashing into the roof like an ax on dry wood, splitting it open in an instant, pulling the electric wires down with it, big tree branches flopping loudly as the giant mess came to rest on the lustrous silver 5-Series BMW parked inside.

"What in the world?" she screamed, her fingers pressed against the window. "Damn it all to blazing hell! This can't be true. This just can't be true."

The destructive blitz had taken less than forty-five seconds. She stood absolutely still, the howling winds violent, the flailing trees along West Fourth Street taking a beating. It was as if she were watching it in slow motion, like the early days of film when pages of slightly changing images were piled on top of each other, and then flipped quickly to create quirky discernable animation. An illusion of time and space when moving, deadly silent at the last page as if to say, "All done now. Go back to what you were doing."

Ellen pulled her sweater tight around her waist. The lightning highlighted the morbid mass on her garage, the skinny end-branches of the tree pressing upward, blowing in the wind, a macabre sight, the gnarled mess twisting in the pouring rain.

Am I dreaming? Is this real?

The frantic scream of her car alarm gave her the answer.

Thirteen

Oh, dear. Now that was a terrible crash. Something got hit.

Frances slid out of bed and went to the window. Her hand flew to her mouth at the sight of the enormous tree on top of Ellen's garage, that darling car smashed under the weight of it.

"Have mercy on us in the dark of night," she said. "Look at you, my majestic old friend. Just look at what you've done!" She began to cry, pulling a tissue out of the sleeve of her nightgown. She dabbed at her nose then held the tissue to her mouth to stop any more ugly accusations from sneaking out.

I swear to you, sweet Jesus, on all that is holy and true, I am down to my last fingernail with you. I mean it now. You are floggin' a dead horse. I simply cannot take another disaster.

The lightning was frightening. Her first instinct was to get away from the window, out of its striking path, but she couldn't move. Staring at that weather-beaten tree, she leaned her head against the cold window, wishing the rain could pour right through the glass, hit her in the face and soak her hair right down to its roots. This was just too much. *It's been one thing right after another, now, this catastrophe for poor Ellen. As if she didn't have her hands full already.*

"I am tired of it all," she declared. Her face puffed up as she gave way, for the first time in months, to the anger she felt. In the last three years she had been tossed around by one loss right after another. First it was Alan, then Ruby's mother and father, then Frances's sister Suzanne and brother Martin, and then—saddest of all—her teenaged niece Ellis. All of them gone, whisked away by illness and death, disappearing from her life like ice on a rainy day. Alan had started the string of sorrows when he was diagnosed with lung cancer five years ago.

For forty-nine years she had never known him without a cigarette in his hand or on his lips, the telltale yellowish-brown nicotine staining the top of his small mustache and the hard pack of Marlboros outlining the inside pocket of his suit coat. She had begged him to stop a hundred times, and he had tried twice in earnest. Anxious to encourage him when he tried to stop, she would inquire how he was doing. She wanted to cheer him on. But he'd turn on her like bad egg salad.

"I will not have you asking me if I am or am not smoking, Frances," he'd say. "I told you I have stopped and that is the end of it. Do not ask me about it again."

Invariably she would smell it on his clothes in a couple of weeks even though he would deny smoking. Then he'd give up the pretense and just smoke openly, no excuses, no apologies, and no conversation, letting her know it wasn't any of her business. When he turned sixty she decided to spark him one last time. She carefully initiated a conversation as they sipped their Manhattans by the fire after his successful day in court. As was so often the case, Alan had been masterful that day in creating just enough reasonable doubt for the jury to avoid bringing back a guilty verdict. He was pleased, pulling on the stem of the Manhattan's maraschino cherry, munching its rubbery vermouth-laced sweetness, smiling at Frances.

"You are just a brilliant man, Alan, darlin'," she said. "I do believe your clients are the luckiest people in this world, and I mean that, sincerely. I am so proud of you, honey." She got up to pass him the small tray of extra-sharp Vermont white cheddar cheese with his favorite Wheatsworth crackers. He dabbed a bit of Nance's hot mustard on top and popped one in his mouth. Picking up her cocktail and smiling carefully at her husband, Frances settled into her chair again, crossing her legs at the ankles, knees together, the way good southern girls were taught to do.

"Now, I am mighty hesitant to bring this up since we are so happily enjoying our cocktails, Alan. But I feel I must clear my mind once and for all. Do you think you could bear with me for just the smallest minute? You won't like the topic, and I know that going in, but I need you to help me understand somethin', once and for all."

Alan stiffened. "What is it, Frances?"

"Oh, darlin' of my world, you are not going to like it. It's that nasty old hornet: your smoking. I am simply terrified that your health is going to be completely ruined if you don't stop smoking now that you're sixty, sweetheart. Of course the good news is, you're only sixty. If you stop now, I'm told the damage can be substantially reversed. It's frightenin' to see you still smoking. I love you so, and you know it."

Alan put his Manhattan down and inched forward in his chair, hands on his knees, his eyes cold. He looked at Frances as if she were Josh Leighton, that old buffoon attorney.

"Not this again," he said.

"Unfortunately, yes. I wish it weren't the case, but I have a need to talk about it for my own understandin'. Let me say, right away, that I am not askin' you to take a pledge or even to give me an answer right now about stopping. What I need to understand is why you keep smokin', Alan, honey. I know about nicotine addiction, and I know you've cleared the nicotine out of your system several times in the past. So we both know you can do the physical part. What keeps me starin' at the ceiling at night is not knowing what keeps you hooked? I guess that is my heartfelt question, Alan: Do you know—I mean *really* know—why you can't stop, darlin?"

He had taken nearly a full minute to think about it. She wanted him to take all the time he needed. She knew it was the first time she had asked him that question in just those words. Finally, with a look of total honesty she knew well, he looked at her and said, "Cigarettes are my best friend, Frances. Since I was twelve years old. I cannot imagine my life without my best friend."

There it was. She never mentioned it to him again, not even when she had to walk behind the oxygen tank caddy, which he had to pull around with him everywhere. Not even when she hooked him up to the permanent tank in their bedroom every night for the last fourteen months of his life. She didn't even mention it when he unhooked himself from the tank and sat on the back porch and had one cigarette, then another, until he gasped for breath and at the last minute hooked himself back up. She was neither saint nor martyr. She never mentioned it because she was not about to compete with his best friend. That would be foolhardy, Daddy had told her, a big cigar in his mouth right up to the day when he could no longer pull himself up in bed and light it himself. She knew he was right.

Instead, she made a habit of loving Alan, cigarettes and all, and prayed daily for his health. She prayed that he would be one of those lucky men, like Daddy, who smoked cigars and drank good bourbon right into their late eighties. Night after night she asked her sweet love, Jesus, to keep His eye on the sparrow, to protect Alan from the wages of his addiction, and to take pity on His poor servant, Frances, who loved them both with nearly equal abandon.

In the end, it was too much to ask for. Alan died at seventy-one of lung cancer. She was a widow at sixty-eight, stuck in this isolated northern icebox, a city where black-tie was considered appropriate dress at late-morning weddings, women coming down church aisles in formal evening gowns and beaded handbags, the sun shining colorfully through the stained glass windows. She was stuck in a city with no symphony and not one marginally elegant restaurant or hotel. She was stuck in stifling monthly meetings of the DAR and boring weekly stints at the Oswego Hospital overseeing the young Candy Stripers and wearing one of those Pepto-Bismol-pink aprons as she manned the gift shop. When she couldn't get down to Syracuse, she was stuck shopping for what she needed in the only two big stores left in her dying city by the lake: Wal-Mart and JC Penney. An afternoon in Nordstrom's was a distant memory; with Daddy gone, she no longer had a reason to travel to Atlanta.

When he was still healthy, before his cancer diagnosis, she had begged Alan to buy a roomy condo in Florida, in St. Petersburg, right on the bay, a civilized place where they could retire in peace and enjoy some warm weather. He wouldn't hear of it. His law practice was his life, he'd tell her in that voice he used with judges.

"Surely you know work is what I live for, and will live for, until the day I die," he said. He offered no apologies, telling Frances he thought she had understood that's how things were from the very beginning—or had he misjudged her?

"No," she'd answered. "I have always understood how important the law is to you, Alan. I have understood that for thirty-eight years, my dear."

"Then no more talk about condos in Florida," he said. "Besides, you know we'd miss all of our friends, Frances. We have such great friends, lifelong friends, a circle anyone would envy. Who could we trust in Florida? What would you do if you wound up alone in St. Petersburg, if something happened to me? Who would you call for help and be assured you'd get it? Think about all that we have right here, Frances."

She did think about it, briefly. They were reasonable questions to consider. But she wasted no time fooling with them because the bottom line was this: Alan was never going to leave Oswego. She knew it, and he knew it. He was born and raised in Oswego, as were his father and mother, his grandfather and grandmother, and his great-grandfather and great-grandmother. A native son, he cherished his Lake Ontario roots. If by some fluke every single one of their friends relocated to St. Pete, he would find some other reason to stay here. He loved his law practice, Oswego, and Frances. In precisely that order. She had known exactly where she stood with Alan for years now, and it was all right.

Life isn't perfect, Daddy had warned her. "If you can get 85 percent of what you want, take the deal," he said. Good old Daddy. He was seldom wrong.

Frances picked up her white wool bathrobe and put it on. All that rain banging against the windows made her want to go to the bathroom. As she turned to leave another shocking bolt of lightning spotlighted the fallen tree, Ellen's garage, and that sad little BMW.

"On my Daddy's grave, I swear that car is completely ruined," she said. She shook her head, alarmed by the destruction. "I do hope Ellen paid up her house insurance. Surely she has." Just as she was sincere in her compassion for Ellen, the sight of that gorgeous old maple tree split into pieces equally grieved her.

My dear old friend, you have stood strong and tall as a Tennessee Rebel, a testament to determination, a picture of faith. You never gave up. You never complained. You have been my friend, reassuring me that just as surely as the winter beats us down, the spring comes to lift us up again, your leaves sweet with small blossoms, your new growth red with promise. Now look at you. I trusted you to stand with me, to help me live out my days in this place, and now you will be cut down to a stump, no doubt to suffer the indignity of a pot of petunias on your head next summer.

She wanted to weep until her eyes ran dry, but that annoying car alarm kept screaming, *woo-wooing*, its lights flashing in the broken shelter, eerie, frantic. She wondered how Ellen stood the noise, only fifty feet from her back door.

She moved closer to the window. She looked to see if Ellen was in the back, but the porch was dark. More than that, she realized the street was dark as well. No yellow streetlights shone onto the front lawns of houses behind them on West Fourth Street. Well, of course, the tree must have taken down the electric wires when it fell. She wondered if that meant she was without electricity? She slipped into her lambskin slippers. Fingers crossed, she went over and tried the light by her bed. It worked.

"Thank you, Jesus, for small miracles," she said. How it was possible that she had light when Ellen apparently didn't was a mystery to her, but she welcomed the phenomenon, glad to be spared the trial of a house without power. She returned to the window, wondering if Ellen's house was dark because she was still sound asleep. It seemed unlikely, but stranger things had happened. She ruled out a drunken stupor. Ellen didn't seem to be a drinker—a glass or two of wine, perhaps? Maybe she had taken sleeping pills? Frances suspected Ellen was suffering from depression; her moods were so often flat, their little talks quickly ended if the conversation took a turn that irritated Ellen.

Oh, fiddle, what am I saying? I don't know a blessed thing about what Ellen Varner does behind those closed doors. She could be a roaring drunk or she might just read herself to sleep every night with a glass of warm milk. You're getting to be a silly old woman, Frances. Alan was right. You invent things.

"You just love to pretend people's lives into being, making them more interesting than they really are," he told her often. "Your southern roots show every time you get started—Eudora Welty to William Faulkner, and everything in between. What an imagination you have, my funny Frances, my frustrated little storyteller."

Alan wasn't far off the mark with his patronizing observations. She had thought of herself as a writer when she was young. Teachers told her she had a gift, something rare to be cherished and developed. They told her she could write better than anyone in her class, in the whole school even. They entered her essays in state and national writing contests in her junior and senior years of high school. She came in second twice in a row. She won the English prize at graduation and headed off to Nashville to become educated as an English teacher, thinking she'd write books on the side.

Her sophomore year she met Alan, a handsome first-year law student at Vanderbilt. The writer's life was no match for the security of a brilliant husband who wanted her as his wife—his dutiful, traditional wife and homemaker. Grabbing the chance as if it were a Pulitzer, she married him at the end of her senior year at Peabody Teachers College and wound up never teaching school a day in her life, nor writing even a short story. From time to time, on a blue day, she did wonder what she might have done differently, what chances she might have taken, what interesting work she might have accomplished if she had been more disciplined, more courageous. But she had no real regrets, no honest longings for a life other than the one she had chosen at nineteen.

"You have caught yourself a prince," Daddy had told her. "I am mighty proud of you, sister. Mighty proud. Now you go on along with him and show those northern women how a real southern lady behaves. Make him a home he wants to come to every night. Make him the happiest fellow north of Virginia. I mean that, honey. That's the biggest job a woman has." She had believed him with all her heart.

She could still hear that car alarm. It was so insistent, so annoying. Knowing she could do nothing about it, she decided to get back into bed. Surveying the scene one last time, she caught sight of something in Ellen's backyard. Focusing hard now, she saw Ellen standing, so tiny in the pouring rain, pointing at the garage, something in her hand, pumping her wrist at the stricken BMW.

Oh, of course, Frances thought, as the car alarm was silenced. *Her car keys. Ellen was out there in all this mess getting that pesky little alarm to stop screaming.* Frances sighed with relief, *Thank you.* She waited at the window, wanting to be sure Ellen got safely inside again. But she stayed right where she was in the middle of the yard. "What in Sam Hill is going on?" she said. "Why doesn't she get herself inside now? Oh Ellen, dear, go back to bed." For as long as she lived Frances would remember every bit of what happened next.

She watched in horror as Ellen slid off her long sweater and stood exposed in her underpants and a short-sleeved white T-shirt, stretching her arms straight up over her head, the rain pounding down on her, the wind pushing at her like a tsunami, the lightning striking every few minutes spotlighting her tiny presence, tree limbs scattered around her ankle socks. Frances gasped as Ellen dropped limply to the ground, legs and arms moving slowly, a lunatic snow angel in the rain running on low batteries.

What in the world? Frances banged hard on the window to get Ellen's attention. *Oh, you foolish old woman, she can't hear you in all this commotion. You'll have to go down there. Oh, Ellen, please get on back into the house and stop this foolishness! Please pull yourself together.*

She waited and watched another minute, then knew she'd have to go.

Daddy would have told her to stay out of it, to stay safe and dry in her own house.

"You've got no dog in this fight," Daddy would say. Frances would have had to tell him he was wrong.

"We have to take care of each other, especially when we get the crazies," Frances said out loud so that Daddy could hear her all the way up in heaven. "Our men are all gone, Daddy. We're on our own."

Fourteen

She pulled the covers up to Ellen's chin, fluffed the pillows a little, and watched as Henry jumped up on the bed, settling down into what must be his regular sleeping place at the foot of the bed.

"I'm fine now, Frances. Please go home and take care of yourself," Ellen said. "I'm so upset seeing you in those wet clothes, and your feet all damp, your slippers soaked right through. You need to go on home and change or you'll be getting sick. That would make me feel absolutely terrible."

Frances smiled and agreed. "I do think a good hot bath is in order for me," she said. Her wet stringy hair fell down on her face. "I admit, I feel positively chilled to the bone. But I've got nothing wrong with me that a good soak with Epsom salts won't cure." Frances said she would not leave, however, until Ellen promised she would stay in bed.

"You need a good long sleep, the whole day in bed," Frances told her, even pointing her finger at Ellen for emphasis. "Unless you promise me that you'll stay put, I won't leave." Ellen swore she'd stay under the covers until she felt rested again.

Wriggling her fingers back at Frances, Ellen tried to shoo her along, giving her a small smile in the hope that Frances would feel all right about leaving her. "Now go on home and call me later, if you want," she said.

"All right then, dear. I will go if you're sure you're all right now. Is there anything I can get you before I leave?"

Ellen shook her head no. "I'll get up later and make some tea if I want some. Please don't worry, Frances. You have been wonderful. My only worry now is that you are still standing here, chilled to the bone. Please go home and get dry and warm!"

Frances waved as she stepped into the hallway and moved carefully down the stairs.

"Everything will be just fine, Ellen. You'll see," she called back. "Just don't worry about a thing right now. There's nothing to be done, so rest and sleep, my dear. I'll call you later."

Frances's hands shook as she took the key from under the mat and locked the porch door for Ellen's safety. She was clammy all over in her drenched nightgown and robe. Her slippers squished as she walked, the insides cold as ice against her bunions. She could feel her heart beating, her blood pushing hard now, every step an effort.

Just get me home, Daddy. Just get me home.

Pushing the gate open into her backyard, she was surprised to see the utility truck on Fourth Street already. The storm had finally blown itself south to Fulton, but just barely. Undoubtedly Niagara Mohawk had been getting calls from frightened neighbors, people terrified of the dark and no TVs to give them news. She understood those feelings. She wondered again why she still had power when others didn't. Maybe it was the new line she had been forced to install when she upgraded the electrical system last year? It didn't matter, and she was too tired to think about it.

Home again, she shook all over as she shed her robe and night-gown in the mudroom, which also doubled as the laundry room. Shoving the wet clothes into the washer, she pulled off her slippers and dropped them in on top. She always kept a wool sweater-coat in the ironing closet by the back door in case she had to run outside. She reached in and took it off the hook. It felt good, heavy and soft, long and warm against her goose-bumpy skin. She started to pick up the scoop from the box of detergent, then thought better of it. She'd leave the wash until later so she didn't tax the electricity just yet; she'd wait until she was sure everyone had power again. Shivering like a child too long in the lake, she turned to leave the mudroom, longing for her flannel nightgown and thick wooly socks.

"And underpants," she said, coughing until it hurt. "Nice, dry underpants."

Passing slowly through the big kitchen, the butler's pantry, and down the long center hallway that led to the front hall, she stood at the foot of the staircase. She held the banister tight for balance, feeling a bit woozy and lightheaded. Exhausted, she stopped before taking the first step up the stairs. She had forgotten to lock the back door.

Steady pulsing pain gripped her temples in what she imagined would be the beginnings of a migraine headache, if she got migraine headaches, which she did not. "I'll tell you what," she said out loud. "If you want to come in and rob me tonight, come along, dear hearts. I will give you anything you want. Take it all. As for me, I am goin' upstairs to bed. Lock the door on your way out, please."

She smiled a little at herself, at her recklessness, looking around to the Altdorfer grandfather clock as it struck the three o'clock hour. "I know, my old friend. It's the middle of the night. I'm going back to bed, just as fast as I can. Ohhh, that pain is sharp." She flinched, pushing the palm of her hand against her right eye, hoping to ease the pressure, intense stabs cutting into her temple.

Never mind. Keep going, Frances. Get up into your bed.

Stopping momentarily for another painful round of coughing, she climbed the first level of stairs slowly and sat down on the landing for a short rest. Her neck felt stiff. The pain was extreme now, targeting her right eye with the precision of a laser beam.

Just another five steps and I'll be all the way up.

She held the banister like a ski tow, standing up to face the stairs. Dizzy, she barely caught herself as she stumbled. Her neck was hard and knotted as if someone were screwing it with a vice, forcing her head to sit bolt upright. She dropped down again on the stairs, her head spinning. The pain in her eye was excruciating. She suspected she was having some kind of stroke.

Oh, Daddy, darlin', I need you to help me.

Too lightheaded to stand again, she dragged herself up by the elbows, pulling her limp body to the top of the stairs. She focused on the bedroom just ahead, only ten feet across the upstairs center hall, a thousand miles away.

I will not take ill on this floor. I simply will not. Then dig in, Frances. Keep goin' and get to that bed, or they'll find you here, naked under this ragged old sweater-coat, saggin' skin hanging out, a white-haired wrinkled old woman, exposed for all the world to see. C'mon now, Daddy, help me get to that bed. Your darlin' Georgia peach is not havin' this as her final snapshot.

On her stomach it took everything she had, and three or four precious minutes, to press through the pain, dragging her worn-out body across the hallway. Inside the bedroom she scraped along the carpet and managed to sidle up to the bed frame, slumping against it, barely breathing, half-sitting.

Help me hang on, Daddy, we're almost done.

Her right arm felt weak, almost numb, as she reached up for the telephone. She couldn't get to it. She'd have to get up on her knees.

"Ahhhh . . . noooo, ohhhh, my sweet Jesus almighty," she howled. Rising up on her knees, sensing she had only one chance to get to the phone before she lost consciousness, she threw herself against the nightstand and pulled the phone to her chest. Her fingers tingling, almost numb, she pushed 911, then dropped the phone on the bed, laying her head over it so that it pressed against her ear. She covered the mouthpiece with her lips.

"Nine-one-one. What is your emergency?" the dispatcher said.

"I . . . am Fracis O'Reilly Wes Fiii Stree . . . come now . . . badoorooopen . . . stroook."

"I'm having trouble understanding you, ma'am. Did you say Frances O'Reilly on West Fifth? Is that you, Mrs. O'Reilly?"

Frances collapsed to the sound the Altdorfer clock *ding-dinging* the quarter-hour. She slid to the floor like a silk scarf falling off a hanger, hitting her head on the nightstand on her way down. The sweater coat folded in on itself, graciously covering her up before she landed on her side. Blood puddled into the beige carpet, leaving a trail on her cheek and mouth. A nasty hematoma was already forming above her eye.

Fifteen

Ruby and Ellen heard the ambulance at the same time. Ruby lay stiffly in bed and automatically began to recite the silent prayer Mother had taught her as a young child.

"When you hear the ambulance siren, just close your eyes and say to heaven, 'Jesus, Mary, and Joseph, please protect the people they're going after. Let them be safe, and get them the help they need.' Do you think you can remember that, Ruby?"

Ruby had remembered it all of her life, and was grateful to think that, in her small way, she had been part of several hundred rescues. She sat up in bed as the siren got closer, much louder now, the ambulance charging down West Fifth at top speed. It sounded as if it were coming right to the front door. She panicked, pulling back the covers, wanting to run to the window, knowing it would take her a few minutes to get that walker going good. Ellen was already at her bedroom window by the time Ruby got to hers. They both watched, wide-eyed, not seeing each other, as the emergency technicians jumped out of the ambulance and split up, one to the front door, and one to the back.

Ruby panicked. "Oh no, it's Frances!" She could see the paramedic had no luck with the front door. In a few seconds the other fellow called him around back. That was strange. Ruby knew that Frances never left her back door open at night. Maybe they're breaking in? Just then the lights in the front hallway went on followed by the one in the big front bedroom upstairs. They were with her now.

Ruby would give anything to know what was going on in there. What could be the matter with Frances? She was never sick. In fact, she never complained about not feeling well or having health problems. Quite the opposite. She was very proud that she took no prescription drugs, having only to swallow a low-dose Aspirin and some of that arthritis-strength Tylenol every day, along with fish oil and her vitamins, C, E and D. How old would she be now? In her seventies? She was about twenty-five years younger than Mother, although they seemed like contemporaries when Mother was alive. Frances used to say Mother was the nicest person in the world to her when she came to Oswego as a young bride, a southern belle in a hard-working northern town. It was like a foreign country to Frances until Mother introduced her to the DAR women and the Oswego Hospital Candy Stripers, which Frances loved, running the gift shop for the last eighteen years. Of course, Frances had been welcomed into the Second Thursday Bridge Club, the Oswego Country Club, and the exclusive Fort Nightly Club by virtue of marrying Alan O'Reilly. He was old money here.

But it was Mother who had taken her on, smoothing the way for Frances, introducing her to the best people, giving her an important stamp of approval. While Mother grew to genuinely love Frances, she never quite forgave Alan for not marrying Agnes O'Brien or Marilyn Schaeffer, both of whom were beautiful Oswego girls from solid Catholic families. Anyone could see they had mad crushes on Alan. Mother was convinced that if Alan's mother had taken care of that cold before it turned into the awful pneumonia that killed her, she would have seen to it that he married one of them.

But Alan's determination to go his own way was evident from the get-go, Ruby felt, starting with his choice of a college no one had particularly heard of, down south in Nashville, a school that was supposed to be pretty good, but who knew for sure? Vanderbilt? Who went to Vanderbilt? Why didn't Alan go to Cornell or Yale or Syracuse? His brothers had gone there and had loved those schools. Ruby had long suspected that Alan was determined to run away from home after his mother's death. His father was too deep into his own loss to care one way or another about Alan's college choice, frankly. His only requirement was that Alan go to a top law school to become a third-generation lawyer in the O'Reilly clan. He had left it to Alan to figure it out.

Seven years later Alan had brought Frances home for the Christmas cotillion, introducing her as his fiancée. She was delicately stunning, beautifully mannered, and when asked, Frances said she was a Baptist. Whatever that meant. Ruby had never even heard of that religion. After they were married, Frances attended the Catholic church with Alan, since Oswego was a town with six ethnically associated Catholic churches (Irish, German, Polish, Italian); one small Episcopal church ("Black Protestants," Mother called them); one good-sized Presbyterian church where Ruby and her family went every year for the best pancake supper to kick off Lent on Shrove Tuesday; a little Methodist church; a growing Lutheran church; and one tiny synagogue. There was no Baptist church.

If she felt strange, Frances never let on. She learned to genuflect, stand, sit, and kneel, responding to rote prayers right along with the parish family, even sometimes translating the old Latin in the back of the holy Mass missal. She had taken several years of Latin in high school and college. Frances did say once that she missed being part of a Bible study group, something all Baptists did, apparently. Another time she asked why there were no Bibles in the church pews. She had said she wanted to read the Gospel and the daily readings herself. Alan had winked at her like she had just burped out loud.

"It's not necessary," he said.

Frances converted, formally, to Catholicism after five years of marriage and six months of classes with Father Flynn. Mother struggled with how to celebrate the occasion since she'd never known a convert before. She checked with Father Flynn and finally decided to host an intimate luncheon after the private church service. About thirty family members and close friends dined that afternoon on oyster stew, broiled haddock with a lemon-butter dill sauce, fresh asparagus wrapped in puff pastry, and for dessert, a white coconut cake, which symbolically covered two important bases: the clean, unblemished whiteness of Frances's soul now and the southern tradition of coconut cakes as a celebratory confection. Alan had raised his champagne glass to give the toast, smiling at his adorable wife.

"The family that prays together, stays together," he said. Later, thanking Mother and Ruby for the fine luncheon, he told them how relieved he was that he'd never have to listen to another story about what the Baptists do.

In the end, Frances was a good out-of-town choice. Adding up the years, Ruby decided Frances must be in her early seventies now. It was hard to imagine. Ruby always thought of Frances as a contemporary, the twenty or so years separating them just a matter of birth certificates. She couldn't imagine that Frances had anything seriously wrong with her. She probably just fell and twisted her ankle and called 911 for help. Ruby hoped she didn't hit her head or break a hip. Those broken hips could be death traps for people over seventy, Mother always said. She shivered just thinking about it.

Don't let your imagination run away with you, Ruby Bainbridge. You don't know what's going on over there.

Her eyes were glued to the house across the street. *Oh!* She spotted movement at the front door. They were coming out.

"All right, Frances, hang on." Ruby quickly closed her eyes and pleaded with the Holy Triumvirate to do its job right now, her left foot jiggling impatiently, her prayers more of a demand than a plea to the holy family: *Jesus, Mary and Joseph, please come to our aid now, in the time of our need.*

Spotting Ruby in the window, Ellen stepped aside, letting the curtain fall into place. She was still waterlogged from her backyard breakdown and shivered as she pulled on her jeans and a turtleneck sweater, grabbing a brush and whipping it through her damp hair. Moving quickly downstairs, she made her way to the kitchen door where her boots sat waiting. Henry followed her, tail wagging, excited to think he'd have a walk this time of night as Ellen zipped up her boots and grabbed her peacoat.

Leaning down and rubbing his ears with one hand and unlocking the door with the other, she looked him in the eyes. "Not now, Henry," she said. "I'll be back as soon as I can and then we'll walk. Go back to bed now, you lucky dog."

When she got to the front yard the paramedics were carefully easing the gurney down the front steps. Frances had a bloody bump on her forehead and looked frail under those white sheets, her skin bluish, her hair still wet and matted from rescuing Ellen. The left side of her face was slack, droopy, her mouth funny, almost like a cartoon mouth drawn all wavy and misshapen.

"What have I done to you, Frances?" Ellen whispered, her hand at her mouth. "What has my selfishness done now?" A woman stood by the open doors of the ambulance, ready to jump in and pull back the gurney. Ellen went over quickly, ahead of the gurney.

"Do you know what's happened to Frances? What's wrong with her? What happened?"

"Ma'am, I cannot talk with you right now," the paramedic said. "Please move away from the ambulance so we can do our job. I'm sorry, but that's just the way it is right now."

Ellen asked if she could ride in the ambulance with Frances.

"Are you next of kin?"

"No, but she doesn't have any kin in this town now. She's a widow, all on her own. I'm her neighbor and we're very close. We look after each other."

"Well, I'll let you ride, but not in the back. You have to ride up in the cab with the driver. Now either get in the cab or get away from the ambulance right now. You're in the way."

Ellen hiked herself up into the cab's passenger seat. "The paramedic said I could ride up here with you. My name is Ellen. I'm a close friend of the patient."

"OK," he answered idly. His eyes were glued to the rearview mirror, waiting for the signal from the crew to move out. Ten seconds later they were on their way, a police escort ahead of them, blue lights flashing, the sirens at top volume, every house on West Fifth Street lit up now.

Ellen looked up at Ruby's window as they pulled away. She was still standing there, her forehead resting on her arm against the window, her face partially covered. "She must be frightened," Ellen said to herself. "And once again, it's all because of me."

The hospital ER staff was ready for Frances when they wheeled her in. It took about an hour before a nurse came out to give Ellen an update.

"She's in stable condition and not in danger at this point," she said. "I cannot tell you more because, as I understand it, you are not a relative? Is that right?"

Ellen confirmed that she was just a neighbor and friend, and asked how information works when the patient has no relatives left.

"I may be the one to take care of her when she goes home. Will

I get information at some point?" She could hardly believe she had just said that, made that care commitment. But there it was.

"Mrs. O'Reilly will designate who will be privy to information about her health. It hasn't happened so far, but we expect to get that information from her just as soon as she can make an informed decision. It's all part of the federal HIPPA regs. The patient privacy act? We have to be pretty careful nowadays. All I can tell you now is that she is doing fine and we have admitted her. Would you like to see her for a few moments before she goes up to her room?"

Ellen's heart sank at the sight of Frances. She looked more fragile than usual, her matted hair framing her beautiful pale face like a cheap mantilla. She looked older and smaller all at once. Ellen picked up her hand and squeezed it. Frances squeezed back just a little, then dropped her hand back down to her side. Most of her strength seemed to be used up in that gentle response.

"Seeeems I haaa stroooo," she managed to say, her lips loose and frozen at the same time. "Beee allll riiiisooooooo."

Ellen shushed her.

"Don't talk now," she said, looking into her eyes, realizing for the first time that Frances had gorgeous bright blue eyes. She ran her fingers softly down Frances's forehead like mothers do with sick children. "You and I will be pruning your rose beds in no time, Frances. You'll be fine with some rest. They're going to let you stay here for a day or two, and I'll be here with you nearly all of that time. You won't be alone. Is that all right with you?"

Frances blinked and nodded slightly, tapping a finger just once into Ellen's skin. She closed her eyes and was asleep before Ellen could tell her not to worry. When they took Frances to her room, Ellen told the nurse she would be staying day and night with Mrs. O'Reilly.

"Visitors can come and go as they like, as long as they don't disturb the patient. I'll let the doctor know you want to stay and see what he says."

Ellen called a cab to get home. She wanted to shower and change clothes, walk Henry, and gather up things for the hospital vigil. She also needed to see Ruby, who was probably frantic by now. The sun was rising as the taxi driver pulled up to the curb in front of her house.

"Some storm last night, huh?" he said. He pulled out his wallet to get change for the twenty-dollar bill she had given him. "I would rate that one a perfect ten. It had everything. Now it looks as if we're gonna have a pretty decent day today. At least it's supposed to be sunny and nice. In the high fifties. We'll see, huh? It's all crazy weather these days. Must be that global warming. Who knows, huh?" He handed her fourteen dollars in ones and she gave him back two.

Henry nearly knocked her down from excitement when she came in the front door. He trailed behind her to the mudroom where she grabbed his leash and two pooper-scooper bags. They headed out the back door. It did look like it was going to be a nice day. How was that possible when just a few hours ago the world was exploding? She stared at her garage, at the ghoulish BMW smashed in like one of Gallagher's pumpkins. She saw the spot where she had collapsed, where Frances had found her flying in the rain. It all seemed like days ago.

Sixteen

Ruby saw Ellen coming but waited for her to ring the bell twice. Ruby didn't want to give the impression that she was just hanging around the front door waiting for news from Ellen Varner, of all people.

Of course, she'd already heard from Ina Schmidt, who had raced across the street like a house afire as soon as the ambulance pulled away from the curb. Ruby was not prepared to drag herself down the front stairs to deal with Ina, who would undoubtedly ring the brass off the front doorbell trying to get information. Instead Ruby went out onto her bedroom porch and called, "I-na! Oh, I-na! I'm over here! Upstairs, on the porch!"

Ina had rushed around the side of the house, her big bathrobe flapping in the wind, her hair in giant blue rollers. "What's going on, Ruby, do you know? What's the matter with Frances?" Ruby told her she had no idea what had happened.

"All I know is you need to get yourself back in your house before you catch pneumonia, Ina. We'll all find out soon enough what's going on with Frances. There's no point getting all worked up about it now. None of us knows a thing."

Ina had left, but not before asking Ruby four or five more questions in a desperate attempt at discovery.

"I saw just what you saw, Ina. Nothing more and nothing less. Go home now and we'll see what we learn later this morning. The important thing is that Frances is being cared for. That's all we know, and it's the only thing we can say for sure."

Ina begged Ruby to call her when she had more facts, something Ruby had no intention of doing. She had learned years ago that you could say something very clearly to Ina Schmidt and in the retelling it came out entirely different. She wanted no part of having her name associated with that kind of tangled mess. Unlike Ina, Ruby had seen Ellen crawl up into the front of the ambulance last night. She didn't know what to make of that, really. On the one hand, she was glad Frances had someone watching out for her at the hospital; on the other, she was appalled to think that their dear sweet Frances only had Ellen at her side. How did Ellen Varner manage to worm her way into their lives so fast?

The sun was shining as Ruby opened the door, stepping aside so that Ellen could move through the vestibule. She motioned her into the foyer.

"You've had quite a night, Ellen," Ruby said. "I saw you get into the ambulance with Frances. That was very good of you. Had Frances called you when she fell ill?"

"No, not at all, Ruby. I had no idea Frances was ill until I saw the ambulance arrive. If she had been able to contact friends, I'm sure she would have called you. You have a much closer relationship with her than I do. I'm guessing that she was lucky to reach 911. But tell me, did she say anything to you recently about not feeling well?"

Ruby led Ellen into the front parlor where a humble fire burned in the grate, its red-embered warmth working hard to take away the morning chill in the big room.

"Please sit down, Ellen. Yes, by the fire if you'd like. No, Frances said nothing to me, nothing at all. Just tell me if you would, what is going on with her? Do you know?"

Ellen briefly explained the hospital's policy on confidentiality. She rubbed her hands together, nervous to be sitting in Ruby's parlor, happy for the distraction of the fireplace.

"I don't have any real facts yet," she said. "All I do know is that she appeared to have had a stroke, and now she has stabilized. More than that—the extent of the stroke, any damage she suffered, how her recovery will work—those are all questions without answers at this point. For now, they have admitted her to the hospital for observation and rest."

"I see. Well, thank you for that much information at least. I feel so helpless with this walker and my inability to move around freely. I don't know what I can do for Frances at this point, but I want to do something."

"Right now I don't know what anybody can do, except wait for the doctors to tell us how she is and what happens next. I'll be in and out of the hospital, checking on things. Do you want me to keep you informed about what's happening?"

Ruby stood up and went over to the bay window. She looked across to Frances's house and wondered how her dear friend would fare in that big house, particularly now that Alan was dead. This was the first time a serious illness had struck Frances. *She isn't used to being alone,* she thought.

"Does she have a telephone in her hospital room, do you know?"

"I don't know, Ruby. I imagine she will have one. I only saw her for a few minutes after they got her into a room. She was very weak and fell asleep right away. But I'll find out what her phone number is, and call you. Is that good?"

Ruby demurred. That meant she'd have to give Ellen her phone number. Not that Ellen couldn't call information to get it, but giving it to her was a different matter. It implied something. Friendship, a kind of intimacy.

"Let me think about that," Ruby said. "Thank you for the offer.

I know most of the nurses at the hospital. I feel certain I can get connected to Frances if she has a phone."

Recognizing the falseness of Ruby's smile, Ellen stood up quickly. Grabbing her purse, she reached inside for her wallet. "Well, I've got to be getting along," she said. "I promised Frances I'd stay with her at the hospital as much as possible. You'll see me back and forth. If you need me for anything, here's my card with my cell phone number on it. Feel free to call me if you wish."

Ruby took the card and slipped it into her sweater pocket, not looking at it, not giving it any purchase. She shuffled behind Ellen to the front door.

"Thank you for coming, Ellen. And, thank you again for that dinner last night. I really enjoyed it, and look forward to more of it tonight. It was nice of you to go to all that trouble."

"No trouble, Ruby. We were glad to do it. Have a good day and be careful with that walker."

"Oh, I will. Tell Frances I'll be in touch with her just as soon as I can." Ruby closed the door quickly, hoping Ellen could get back to her house without being hailed down by other neighbors. She knew Ina would be in her dining room window watching what there was to see of Ellen's visit. She locked the outside door and headed for the inner door. She wanted to pull those velvet curtains together tightly so that Ina wouldn't be able to see light, much less any movement inside the front hallway.

Moving down the front steps, Ellen automatically reached for her car keys. She heard the second door close behind her, then the deadbolt engage. She stopped, momentarily, thinking she heard a thump, or the sound of a heavy thud. She stayed still, listening, thinking she heard a little shriek. Then it was quiet.

What now? Did Ruby fall or something in there? She stood

perfectly still, listening intently again. No sound, no calls for help. Would Ruby even call if something happened, knowing Ellen would be the first responder?

Oh, don't be so full of yourself, Ellen, of course she would. She doesn't hate you. She thinks you're silly, even frivolous, an interloper in this tight circle of West Fifth Street. But not interesting enough for hate. Surely not.

She went back up to the front door to peek in, to look for signs of trouble. The inside door was covered with dark curtains. She couldn't see a thing. Should she ring the bell, or call out? Or just go on with her business and let Ruby get on with hers, whatever that was right now? Crud, crud, crud. Piss, piss, piss. How did she get involved in all this? All she wanted to do was go home and fall into bed, cover herself up, and let all of this stuff just go away.

Instead, she rang the doorbell and waited. No response. She rang it again and went over to the front window. With its blinds partially open she could peek in a little, see the general arrangement of the parlor. But she couldn't see into the front hall from that spot. She knew Ruby should have answered the door by now, even with her walker.

"What is it?" Ruby yelled through the front door. "Is that you, Ellen?"

"Just checking to see that you're all right. I thought I heard a noise, that maybe you had fallen. Are you all right, Ruby?"

"Yes, of course, I'm fine. I was halfway to the kitchen when you rang the bell again. Go on. Get to the hospital and take care of Frances. Don't worry about me, for heaven's sake."

How Ruby could have been halfway to the kitchen in such a short time was mind-boggling. *But I will happily believe that lie today, Ruby Bainbridge.* Ellen nearly skipped down the porch steps, car keys pressed into her hand.

"Oh, shit," she cried. She looked at the keys. "I can't drive to the hospital. I don't have a car." Instantly she wondered if Ruby would let her use her car; just as quickly she dismissed the thought as outrageous. Ruby wouldn't let Ellen touch her car, much less drive it. *I can't even imagine asking.* Ten minutes later a cab drew up in front of Ellen's house. "Together again?" the driver said, smiling. He was the same driver who had brought her home a few hours before. "What will the neighbors think?"

"The neighbors think all kinds of things," Ellen said. "Just drive, please, and let's not worry too much about anything except getting to the Oswego Hospital. I'm not in a chatty mood today. Sorry."

"Fine by me. But tell me something? Don't you have a car?"

Ellen explained the lightning strike during the storm last night, and the subsequent damage to the maple tree and her BMW. "At this very moment my car is resting in peace in my shattered garage."

He said he knew a great mechanic for her, if she wanted help with that.

"Will they lift the garage off the car and tow it, and keep the car for a week or so while I get my insurance agent to have the damage appraised, and get estimates for fixing it?"

Sure, he said. They'll do that. Here's their card. Tell them Ben said to give you a good deal.

"Oh, well, that's really nice . . . Ben. Thank you very much. This is the first break I've had in weeks. You wouldn't be fooling me now about these guys, would you? Because, honestly, I don't need any more crazy trouble in my life right now."

"They're legit and good, honest guys," he said. "If anyone can help you and get you a fair deal, they will. I wouldn't kid you. Promise."

Ellen settled back in the cab and rested her eyes, already weary of the new day. She heard the sound of a lawnmower and looked out to see that dark-haired young man cutting Ina Schmidt's lawn. She'd have to remember to get his name and call him later today. He seemed to do everyone's yard work on West Fifth. That was good to know.

Just before the cab pulled away, Ruby had managed to struggle to her knees to watch Ellen slide into the back seat. She wondered why Ellen didn't take her own car, that expensive sporty one that Ina said cost "at least $48,000 for sure, my cousin Jake said." Ellen seemed to have no worries whatsoever about money or wasting money. A cab was probably just more convenient. *Foolish Ellen*, she thought, pulling herself up from the floor, holding onto the righted walker.

Hold on a minute, take a look at who's casting stones! Ruby Bainbridge, you are just as foolish for not being careful, for rushing when you know you shouldn't.

Her knees were sore from scraping them along the hardwood floor. Her good ankle was already swelling up.

Oh Lord, don't let it be sprained or broken. How foolish can I be, trying to spin around with this walker as if I could erase Ellen Varner from the foyer by getting away fast. You are a silly woman. Yes, you are. Thank God Mother isn't here to see you fail like this. Or Father. Oh my word, not Father. May the angels cover their eyes.

She felt ashamed to think of them in heaven, looking down at her life right now, seeing the drama and conversations that awaited her with the pending lawsuit, and the publicness of all that was to come. She felt like the bad witch in *The Wizard of Oz,* pinned down by Dorothy's house, her spirit crushed by forces so much bigger than herself. With no small effort she dragged herself over to the big burgundy velvet chair, Mother's chair, by the front windows. She was sure her good ankle was sprained. Her hairpins came loose as she dropped into the chair, her bun falling out of place against the velvet. Her hair tumbled down to her shoulders, messy, all gray and white, making her look older than her years.

I'll just sit here a minute and rest. See what's going on West Fifth, and calm down a little.

She immediately felt better nestled into what had been Mother's throne the last twelve years of her life. Every day Mother sat in this deep rose-colored chair, newspapers and books around her feet, her glasses on a pearl string around her neck and Blackjack gum in her sweater pocket, ready to freshen her breath. Even when she was reading Mother had managed somehow to keep her eyes on West Fifth Street the whole time. Ruby smiled thinking of the hundreds of times she had pulled up the tray table to serve Mother her breakfast, lunch, and dinner right here in her chair. Mother was always appreciative of her meals. She loved the foods that made the main dish more interesting and delicious: fresh beefsteak tomatoes in summer, crunchy Macintosh apples every autumn, homemade cold slaw with the Friday fish fry, and the boiled vegetables surrounding the Sunday afternoon roasts. Ruby rested, visualizing Mother's sweet face, a face not unlike the Virgin Mother Mary herself.

"When Irish eyes are smi-ling, sure 'tis like a morn in Spring; in the lilt of Irish laughter, you can hear the Angels sing; when Irish eyes are hap-py, all the world seems bright and gay; and when Irish eyes are smi-i-i-iling sure they steal your heart a-a-a-way."

How many nights Ruby had fallen asleep to Mother's sweet voice, each gentle sound smiling at her, telling her things would be all right when the sun came up in the morning. If only she could have those times back. How nice life had been with Father strong and busy, her sister and brother banging in and out of the house asking if they could play tennis or golf, or if they could stay out a little longer at Patty Jensen's party Friday night. Days when Mother, perched gracefully at the piano, pulled back the keyboard cover and played her favorite, "Alice Blue Gown," calling them all in to dance . . . *"In my sweet lit-tle Alice blue gown . . .* feel the music! *. . . when I first wan-dered down in-to town . . .* mind your manners! *. . . I was so proud in-side, as I felt every eye . . .* pick up your feet, Ruby! *. . . and in every shop win-dow, I primped pas-sing by . . ."*

Ruby wanted to get up and dance right now, but here she was, stuck in medical hell, hounded by sprained and broken bones, aching muscles, bruises, and fermenting scars. She knew this was the beginning of the inevitable slide into old age, the waltz toward death. She had watched it happen to Mother.

Mother had been fine until those bleeding ulcers couldn't be contained anymore by a soft diet. Father sent her for surgery at the Lahey Clinic near Boston. Ruby had accompanied Mother, of course. It was 1987 and the first time in her thirty-eight years that Ruby had been outside of Oswego for any length of time. Father called an old law-school friend who lived in Boston and asked him to find a suitable hotel for Ruby—emphasis on suitable, since she would be staying alone while Mother was in the hospital for three weeks. His friend found Ruby a lovely old hotel that had a wonderful dining room with those little lamps on each white-clothed table, soft and heavy hotel sterling service, and wide brown paneling in the captain's quarters with junior lights perched on the top of the thick frames of paintings that were arranged in a kind of seafaring gallery-in-the-round.

Ruby was all right at breakfast every day, but when she returned in the evening for dinner she found it excruciating to eat alone, being a youngish woman, attractive if she did say so herself, and without a wedding ring on her finger. She wasn't a reader but she brought the evening paper with her every night, although she rarely read it at the table. It was awkward, and her fingers picked up that nasty black printer's ink when she did. She closed her eyes now remembering that quaint hotel, and wished she had a daughter who would listen to the story of how she had protected herself against the disgusting, creepy man at the table across from hers. What an interesting story it was, and she was sure her daughter would love to hear it over and over. Ruby practiced how she would tell it to her.

I was sitting in the beautiful, quiet dining room at the table they reserved for me during my entire stay, she'd tell her daughter. I had ordered shrimp cocktail and a nice cold scotch on the rocks. Father always said to drink scotch when I was out. "You won't like the taste enough to get drunk," he said. "but if you do have too much to drink, you won't have a hangover the next morning." I also ordered a plate of olives on the side. I love olives and they go nicely with Scotch, believe it or not. Besides, they help to sop up the alcohol. You never want to drink without eating something at the same time, honey.

Anyway, it had been a terrible day. Your grandmother's surgery had gone well, they told me, but it had taken six hours and I was nearly frantic by the time someone came out to let me know she was in the recovery room. It was a long morning and afternoon, and by the time I got back to the hotel and freshened up for dinner, I was exhausted. All I wanted was a nice meal and a cold, strong drink. I ordered that large shrimp cocktail to be followed by butterflied rainbow trout, broiled, with lemon-parsley butter, and Boston baked beans in a crock. They love to eat beans that way in New England. It's almost a religion.

There I was, settling in, enjoying my drink after a terrible day. I began to look around the dining room, casually, politely, only to realize that the man who sat two tables away was staring straight at me! It wasn't just a nice momentary glance. It was a great big intentional stare. He smiled and raised his drink to me. *Oh my god,* I thought. He's trying to pick me up. My mind was racing and I knew I had to do something quickly or he'd be out of his seat and over to my table before I could say *drop dead.*

Panicked, I did the only thing I could think of. Looking straight back at him, I put my finger up my nose, waaay into that nostril, and dug around, picking my nose, lifting up the side, stretching it out all I could. I had a field day in there. Needless to say, he turned right around in his seat and never bothered me again.

Now I tell you this story, my daughter, because you may find yourself in a similar situation one day and your quick action can change the whole scene for you. Just remember this: sometimes you have to take drastic measures that go against everything you've ever been taught to do, in order to save yourself.

Shifting in the velvet chair, Ruby was proud of herself all over again. How lucky she had been to be such a fast thinker, to be so unafraid of embarrassing herself in front of that disgusting man. The next morning the breakfast waitress had told Ruby the funny story about a nose-picking young woman at dinner last night, not realizing it had been Ruby. The waitress said the story had circulated throughout the staff, and eventually, to the tables of men who dined alone.

"They're on the lookout for our nose-picking guest!" Ruby had laughed. That was just fine.

The rest of her solo dining experiences had been without incident. A month after her Lahey Clinic excursion, Mother celebrated her seventy-sixth birthday and although she fully recovered from the surgery, she was never the same. Helplessly, Ruby watched her adapt to old age. She made the best of things and never complained to Ruby. But Mother grew old before her very eyes.

"My legs just won't work," she would say, defeat in her sigh.

Because of those legs and the steep front and back staircases, Mother made her way downstairs just once a day. She stayed by the window, or on the front porch, or in the screened-in back porch when the weather was warm, living out the day settled on the main floor until it was time to take on those stairs again at bedtime. Ruby wanted to cry remembering how her elegant Mother was brought low by simple bodily functions. With just one bathroom in the house, upstairs at the end of the long hallway, Mother was forced to improvise. Two or three times a day Ruby would cover the blue velvet couch with fresh terry cloth bath towels before bringing in the enamel chamber pot so that Mother could sit on it and empty her bowels. Nearly every day Ruby watched Father flee the room, pushed out by Mother's incontinence, calling for Ruby to bring the vinegar and water in a bowl to seep up the urine from her chair. Ruby also brought some thicker towels, layered, to allow Mother access to her chair without her having to sit in dampness. Ruby was doing three loads of towels a day in the cellar laundry room.

She remembered the awkward moments as she changed Mother's flowery silk dresses, working like a robot, quickly and efficiently, to shorten the minutes Mother felt violated and immodest as she stood holding on to the chair in her slip, her stockings rolled up at the knees for comfort, her thick black shoes sometimes sprayed with dried-on pin-like flecks of morning diarrhea. Ruby had agreed when Father insisted that they needed to put a small bathroom downstairs, just off the butler's pantry, nothing fancy, just a commode and a sink. Unfortunately, Mother wouldn't hear of it. All that commotion in the house to get it done, all those workmen making a mess? The very thought of it terrified her. What if she had to sit on the couch commode while they were working? What if they heard her inevitable flatulence as she got up to move around every couple of hours so she wouldn't get chair sores? No, she would make do with this arrangement, she told Father.

"Besides, Ruby doesn't mind taking care of me. She is a wonderful daughter, such a late baby, a gift from God for our old age."

Father gave up the battle, knowing Mother would have her way. Besides, his legs worked fine and he could go out to the pantry and pour three good fingers of Johnny Walker Black and have a quiet drink until Ruby gave him the signal that Mother was cleaned up and resettled in her chair. Difficult as those days had been, she'd have them back right now if she could.

Tears started to fall and Ruby let go, tired of pretending, tired of being strong and independent, tied of being good. She vented in the privacy of her parlor, sitting just to the side of the bay window, far enough back so no one could see her from the street.

The days ahead frightened her.

I don't want to sue Ellen Varner for what that silly dog did. I know Ellen wasn't really at fault. I know Ellen didn't intend for me to fall down and hurt myself. God knows, if I hadn't been Miss Nosy, I never would have been on that front porch with that bone. Why not just forgive and forget? Why can't I just let it all go?

"Because you're in the right according to the law," Larry Robinson had said. "Even more, you almost have a responsibility to sue, Ruby. You have to show other dog owners that they can't get away with hurting people, causing them to suffer in hospitals and rehab centers, making them push a walker for months like you're having to do. I am giving you the same advice your father would give you about this. Remember, you are the victim. You deserve justice in this case, which means compensation for all of your trouble and your pain. There's a whole lot of money waiting for you when you win this, Ruby. Honestly, I think it's fair to say you'll never have to worry about money again."

The whole idea of a judge and jury, of appearing in court and getting up on the stand to testify, looking at Ellen in court, knowing how their personal business would be spread all over town the next day, reporters picking at every detail, blabbing about it in the *Oswego Palladium Times*. It was impossible. If that weren't enough, the idea that people would think she was doing it for the money, that she needed to sue Ellen in order to pay her own bills? It was a nightmare. No one would ever look at her in the same way again, even if they agreed with her, even if they knew she didn't need a dime of Ellen Varner's money, which they didn't know. Every purchase she made they'd think, "Oh, that's easy for her to buy. She got all that money from the dogsuit. She got lucky."

How I wish Larry hadn't been insistent on sending that letter to Ellen so fast. I told him I needed to think about it a little more, but Larry had mailed it out anyway.

"We need to move on this right away. Hit her hard," he argued. "I want the jury to see what that dog did to you. I want them to know the kind of pain you're in. It won't be the same if you appear in court all healed up and looking strong, Ruby. Besides, the sooner we get moving, the sooner we'll be done."

It was all insane, a train racing down the track, her face slapping again and again against the wind as she tried to see where her life was headed. *I'm in the middle of something I don't know how to stop.*

She closed her eyes, weary from the early morning trouble, worried about Frances and her stroke, and undecided about whether Ellen Varner was the good person she appeared to be or not. She gripped the Swiss Army knife in her sweater pocket, slowly turning it over and over in her hand, settling down. Her stomach began to rumble.

Well, I haven't eaten since supper last night and here it is late morning already, she sighed, looking at her watch. *All that nice food in the fridge and I can't even get to it on this sprained ankle. Look at it! Swollen up like a basketball. You are such a klutz, Ruby Bainbridge.*

She put her other hand in front of her mouth. She'd forgotten to brush her teeth this morning and that shepherd's pie had made her breath smell. Ellen must have put garlic in there. Garlic always did that to her. She pulled Mother's burgundy wool lap blanket over her thighs and closed her eyes again, concentrating on her breathing, focusing hard now on her breath and how it moved in and around her chest. In . . . and out . . . in . . . and out . . . in . . . and out . . . nice and calm now . . . in . . . and. . . .

Gonna take a sen-ti-men-tal jour-ney . . . da da da da . . . sen-ti-men-tal jour-ney home . . . da da da da da . . . gonna take a sen-ti-men-tal jour-ney . . . da da da da . . . sen-ti-men-tal jour-r-r-r-ney home.

Her ankle would need ice soon. Stomach gurgling, she fell asleep.

Seventeen

Ellen fluffed up the pillows behind Frances.

"Are you comfortable?" she asked.

Frances shook her head yes.

"Why are you still . . . hanging around . . . here? Why don't you go home . . . and get some rest? I . . . will be fine, El-len," she said.

"I just want to talk with your doctor once more today, on his five o'clock rounds. I promise, I will go home and rest right after that."

Frances's speech was still slow, but overall very good. Every now and then a word would rumble around in her cheeks like a tiny golf ball, until she managed to spit it out. Her neurologist, Dr. Ireland, said it appeared the stroke had done only mild damage to her language center. All things considered, she was very lucky. "The excellent response time and the quickness of the medical treatment she received are the main reasons she's in such good shape."

She did have some paralysis in her right arm and foot, and was slow to chew and eat, indicating some damage to the nerves that allowed her to swallow. "With no further episodes, she should show a full recovery if she continues her rehabilitation work," he said. The hospital staff had started her rehab work already, just twenty-four hours after her admission. He had said this morning that she might

147

be ready to go home in the next day or two, if arrangements could be made. Ellen wanted to know if Dr. Ireland had decided on a firm release date yet.

"Mrs. O'Reilly has indicated that she wants to go home, which is certainly possible so long as she is not alone. She can complete her rehabilitation work from home, with help. Her social worker will make the arrangements."

"I'll be caring for her at home," Ellen heard herself say once again. "I can get her anywhere she needs to go for follow-up appointments. That's not a problem."

In truth the entire arrangement would be a problem, but that didn't matter. Ellen would have to find a way to care for Henry, secure reliable transportation, change her life by staying day and night with Frances, and keep her mind from sinking into the depths of despair so that she was not a drag on Frances. To do that, she would have to create private time. She needed her own space so she could get under the covers and read herself into another life. She didn't know how it would work living with Frances.

"Whaaat . . . do you hear . . . from Ru-by?" Frances asked. "Is she awww right?"

Ellen said she hadn't been to see Ruby in the last two days since she had spent most of her time here. "I don't want to disturb her at night when I get home. However, I haven't stopped thinking about her, Frances. I intend to see her when I leave here today. I know she is very concerned about you and will want to know when you are coming home. May I give her a message from you?"

"Tell her I ammm fine. Not to wor-ry."

"Will do," Ellen said. She checked the tray table for fluids and discovered that Frances was out of pop. "I'll just go and get you a Sprite before I leave. Be right back."

The nurses had encouraged her to supply Frances with sodas from the mini refrigerator whenever she wanted them. Ellen spotted Dr. Ireland as she entered the small kitchen across from the nurses' station.

"Hello, Dr. Ireland," she said. "I'm so glad to see you. Do you have a couple of minutes? I'm anxious to know what you are thinking about a discharge date for Mrs. O'Reilly. I have a great deal to do before she comes home. I could use all the advanced warning I can get."

A good-looking man with dark blue eyes, dense dark brown hair, and wonderful strong hands, Mike Ireland added half-and-half to his coffee and sat down, motioning her to join him. "I think she could go home tomorrow if the arrangements can be made. Have you spoken to her social worker yet?"

Ellen said she had an appointment with Miss Yunger this afternoon.

"Well, if you two can work things out, I see no reason why Mrs. O'Reilly can't go home tomorrow. She is doing very well and the sooner we can get her back into her home and her routines, the better her recovery will be. Are you ready for what it will take to care for her?"

Ellen said she would be by tomorrow. "We'll bring in a home health care rehab specialist for her workouts, and in time I can learn to work with her, if I need to. I certainly can bathe her, cook, and hire a housekeeper to come in once a week. I think that about covers it. Am I missing something?"

"That all sounds about right," Dr. Ireland said. "but the social worker will know exactly what needs to be in place, so take good notes in that meeting today. Is there anything else you need from me?" He stood up and looked at his cell phone. "I have appointments starting in ten minutes."

Pushing back her chair, Ellen said she'd take copious notes. "I'll be happy when Frances is home. Thanks for all you have done for her, Dr. Ireland. I know she trusts you completely and is very grateful. I'll see that she gets to her follow-up appointments."

The social worker had given Ellen a standard list of things to prepare. Ellen ordered the hospital bed to be delivered to Frances's house by late afternoon. She had a dozen errands to do, things to buy, items to gather up and arrange if she was going to be ready tomorrow. Knowing the paperwork involved in the hospital discharge process, she suspected it would be lunchtime by the time Frances actually arrived, but she wanted to be ready by nine o'clock, just in case.

"She'll pretty much need full-time care for the first few days at home," the social worker said. "Are you going to have someone come in at night to relieve you?"

Finding a relief caregiver was number one on Ellen's to-do list. She had thought about asking Ina Schmidt if she knew anyone who did that kind of work, but then changed her mind. Ina seemed like a nice woman, but a woman who wanted to get in the middle of things. More than that, she seemed to enjoy passing along the details of everyone's business. At least that's what Frances had implied when Ellen brought up her name.

Frances was the queen of understatement, which meant her mild caution was a strong warning. Ellen didn't want any news about Frances's recovery bandied about over the back fences of West Fifth Street. Ina's Monday morning wash would be nothing more than clean laundry on the line, if Ellen could manage it. Who else could she ask? Well, there was Ruby. Ruby would know who was reliable enough for the overnight shift. She needed to check on Ruby anyway since she hadn't heard from her since her last visit. She hated to go over there, but she'd have to.

She gathered up her rental car keys. She had nearly kissed her agent when he told her the insurance covered a rental while her BMW was being repaired. Another stroke of good luck came to her when she called in the Oswego Buccaneer Boys Garage and their used car sales team. They had been as honest as Ben's word, arranging for a dumpster to be brought onsite as they worked a full day pulling the roof of the garage off her car and towing the car to their garage. They even tidied up the backyard of debris and left her garage looking picture-perfect, except for one gaping hole and two sidewalls left in tatters. Oh, well. It would all get fixed in time. She'd have to see what the car was going to cost first, then find out what her homeowner's policy would do for the garage—and maybe the car, too? It was way too much to think about now.

Since it was lunchtime, she thought she'd try calling on Ruby from the kitchen door, knowing she was probably settled in her chair, watching TV. Approaching from the side yard, she looked in the window and saw her. Ellen tapped on the window to let her know she was coming to the door. Ruby didn't respond even after Ellen asserted herself, knocking as hard as she could, her knuckles turning white.

"Oh, crud in six colors, what's wrong?" she cried. She ran up the steps to the outside storm door and grabbed the handle, pushing back and forth furiously, trying to get it open. Ellen leaned back and looked again into the window. Ruby still didn't move.

She picked up a large garden rock and threw it wildly against the windowpane in the storm door. After several fierce assaults, the glass cracked into large pieces. Ellen took off her jacket and wrapped it around her right hand and arm, up to her elbow. Quickly she removed shards of glass around the door handle until she could get her arm inside. Wiggling her fingers carefully, she unlocked the storm door. Now she faced the wooden back door behind it.

Please don't be locked. Does luck come in threes? If so, I've got one more stroke left. That's all I need.

The door opened with one easy turn and Ellen nearly went limp from relief. No time to celebrate, she threw off her jacket and rushed over to Ruby. She winced as she got close. Ruby's breath smelled strong, a combination of garlic and ketosis, which meant she must not have eaten anything in a day or more and her body was burning its own fat for fuel. She lifted Ruby's wrist and felt for a pulse. There it was, faint, but sure. Ellen knelt down and cupped Ruby's face with her hand, shaking it a little, her other hand on her shoulder. She shook her lightly.

"Ruby! Ruby! Can you hear me? Can you wake up? It's Ellen! Ellen Varner! Ruby! Wake up!" Ruby moved a little and sputtered awake, lifting her head, smacking her lips open, testing her tongue, which tasted dry, thick, and horribly stale.

"What is it?" she said. "How did you get in here? What time is it?" Ellen explained the open back door, leaving out details of the smashed storm door. She'd get to that later.

"Look me in the eye, Ruby. Tell me how you feel. No! Don't look away. Look me straight in the eyes."

Ruby stuttered nervously, openly annoyed at being told what to do and wondering what she was supposed to say all of a sudden. "I'm fine, Ellen. Really, I am. Just give me a minute. I was sound asleep, for heaven's sake."

Ellen leaned back giving her space. The smell was terrible and Ruby looked sunken, sick. What has happened to her?

"I haven't been up and around much in the past couple of days. Is it Tuesday? I've had issues with getting around, as you might know. My injuries from the fall," Ruby said. With a discernable effort she shifted to a full sitting position. "I do feel dehydrated. A glass of juice would be good. Can you get that from the fridge for me?"

Ellen stood up and pulled at the blanket, which had partially fallen to the floor. As she straightened it over Ruby's legs, she noticed the huge swelling of her left ankle. She looked more closely, trying to see if a bone had popped through the skin.

"Ruby, have you hurt yourself some more?" she asked. "This ankle looks as if it's sprained, or even broken. Have you twisted it recently? Has a doctor looked at it? Are you in pain?"

"So many questions all in a row, Ellen. Give me a chance to think. Yes, I twisted my ankle the other day. I caught my walker on the edge of the hall runner and lost my balance for a minute. It's not broken, I feel certain. Just a nasty sprain. I've been icing it down and taking Advil for the pain. It just needs time to heal."

"How are you getting around on it? I can't imagine how you could move around with your other ankle still in that cast. Are you able to get up and down on it?'

Ruby drank the glass of apple juice in one long gulp like a thirsty desert fox, and asked for a glass of water. Ellen brought a tall plastic pitcher of ice water to her, and tried again.

"Are you able to walk on that foot, Ruby?"

Ruby shifted in her chair, giving Ellen the cold shoulder, looking out at the bird feeder, which was empty. No birds today. Her squirrel family was hissing like mad from the chokeberry bush. She didn't have any corn out and their blueberry seed block was nearly gone.

"I am not able to get around very well, I must admit. But I am not comfortable discussing the details of my life with you, Ellen. You are not my friend. In fact, you are not even an acquaintance of any consequence."

How childish, Ellen thought. *How sadly childish.* "Oh Ruby, please don't view me that way. I know we got off to a poor start, but I am not a bad person. Really, I am not. And I know you aren't a bad person, either. Could we just clean the slate for now and start fresh with each other? We can go back and resolve old issues later. But for now, could we just try to see each other as good people who can help each other?"

Ruby sat expressionless, her arms folded over her chest. But in the corner of her eye a tear pushed itself out, sliding down the side of her face.

"Come on, Ruby, give me a chance," Ellen said softly.

"Well, I haven't had anything to eat in two days and my ankle is killing me and I can't even get up to go to the bathroom and I haven't had even a sink bath or anything and I smell myself and my breath smells from the garlic you put in that shepherd's pie and I have wet myself several times and, oh God, I can hardly say this, but there is bowel movement in those wads of Kleenex in the paper basket by my chair and I am a mess, and I don't want your help but I guess I'll have to trust you because I can't call on Frances who would always help me so now there's only Ina Schmidt to turn to and she'll blab everything all over town and maybe you won't, so I guess I am stuck with you. What do you think of that, Miss Smarty Pants?"

Ellen looked at her, feeling Ruby's terror, trying not to laugh at the stream of consciousness contained in that one long answer.

"Well, let's see. I think we are damn lucky to have each other right now, that's what I think. So let's keep going. Where do we start? I say, let's get you cleaned up a bit and then have that ankle looked at. Does your doctor make house calls?"

Ruby said, "Yes. He'll come if you tell him it's for me."

A few minutes later Ruby sat up as Ellen dipped the washcloth into the large mixing bowl filled with warm soapy water. She had removed her sweater and blouse so Ellen could clean her underarms and neck, chest, arms, elbows, and hands. Ellen was consciously vigilant, quickly putting a fresh towel over Ruby to cover her nakedness when it presented itself. Ruby pulled her hair back so that Ellen could wash her face, closing her lips tightly, hoping her breath wouldn't escape and flatten Ellen. They both had the idea that a capful of Listerine would be a godsend right now.

Brushing Ruby's curly hair gently, pushing the finger waves into place around her face, Ellen held up bobby pins, which she had discovered on Ruby's shoulders.

"Would you like me to put your hair in a bun, or do you want it down?" Ellen asked.

"A bun would be good. It's less trouble."

With her permission, Ellen ran upstairs to get a fresh bra, underpants, blouse, sweater, skirt, and socks from Ruby's bedroom, and a toothbrush, toothpaste, and mouthwash from the small bathroom at the end of the long hallway. While there she grabbed a pair of lamb's wool slippers from the closet and a Hudson Bay blanket from the foot of her bed. She knew it was out of the question for Ruby to sleep upstairs until her ankles healed. More than that, she knew Ruby couldn't stay alone in this big house while she was this helpless. She needed a plan, and one was forming in her mind. But it was almost unthinkable.

No, I can't do it. She hates me, and I am so not crazy about her. All right then, take another look at things. How else can you make it work? What's possible?

Her mind was racing. She kept coming back to the core idea:

Since I'll be caring for Frances anyway, what if I put the two of them together in Frances's house? That way, I could care for them both at once. Frances could have her bed on the first floor in the living room, which opens out to the sun porch giving her the sun and light she craves every day, and a view of her gardens. Ruby could stay in the front parlor, which faces West Fifth Street, giving her a clear vista to her world, her neighborhood. It seems like a plan, one that I feel sure Frances will agree to. Ruby is another matter, and in fact, so am I. In the name of all that is honest and true, I don't wish Ruby any harm. But living with a demanding passive-aggressive vengeful woman I hardly know, much less like, would be a prison sentence. My life as I know it, my quiet, independent, just-Henry-and-me-sorting-things-out-together life, would be over. All for a woman who is suing the pants off me. It doesn't bear thinking about. Besides, I couldn't leave Henry home alone. I won't. This plan is impossible. But what else can I do? Oh, I wish this wasn't on my plate right now.

Ellen carefully put a sock on Ruby's swollen foot.

Why is it up to me? Both of these women have lives and they're not my responsibility. I hardly know either of them past the common pleasantries. Yet here I am and here they are. How could I sit on my front porch and look over at Ruby's house, or hang out laundry and look over the fence at Frances's house, and know that I did nothing to help them? How can I turn my back on them? Particularly when I seem to be the one who caused their troubles in the first place.

"Ruby, let me make a couple of phone calls and I'll be right back. Wait for me to return before you put on that skirt, please. I'll need to help you with that." She dialed Frances's room at the hospital. Twenty minutes later she had the green light from Frances for the combined recovery plan, verification that a second hospital bed and a portable commode could be delivered this afternoon to Frances's house, and confirmation that Ruby's doctor would come for a visit after lunch.

"I think we have it all worked out," Ellen said, as she returned to Ruby's side. "I think our plan will cover all of your needs, and be fun as well!"

Ruby sat stiff as uncooked spaghetti as Ellen explained the plan to move her into Frances's front parlor for the next three or four weeks. "What? Do you think leaving my home is fun, Ellen Varner? Are you crazy?"

Ellen sat still, giving Ruby time to get over the initial shock. She could tell Ruby was giving it some thought. "It makes good sense to do this. You still will be on West Fifth, with a view. You won't lose touch with your neighbors, and you'd be doing me a favor by being there to keep an eye on Frances when I'm not around. Most of all, you won't have to go back to rehab, which I think your doctor will insist on today if you don't have other plans. You just can't stay alone right now, Ruby."

Ruby wanted to know how long Ellen thought she'd have to stay at Frances's house. She also wanted to know if Ellen would arrange for a TV to be brought into the front parlor. She didn't want to miss any of her shows.

"I have no idea how long your recuperation will take until we've talked with your doctor and he tells us about that ankle. However, I can say for sure that I will get a TV for you."

Ruby pulled the Hudson Bay blanket up to her shoulders. She settled the rest of it around her lap and legs. Finally, she looked up at Ellen.

"Well, if I have to live with someone, I can think of no one better than my kind and generous friend Frances. You'll be all right, too, I guess. The good Lord knows, I am tired of starving, and you seem to be a pretty good cook, Ellen." She put her hand around the back of her head, cupping her bun, enjoying the feel of combed hair in place. "OK, I'll do it. It will be hard for me, Ellen, but I do understand I am lucky to have you and Frances to help me. All that being said, I accept with pleasure your kind invitation to take care of me in Frances's front parlor."

Ellen squeezed Ruby's hand. "It's going to be good, you'll see. Now let's get you something to eat before Dr. Davis comes. Could you stand that shepherd's pie one last time?"

She found several cans of Jolly Green Giant whole asparagus in the cupboard and heated one up. Her hand nearly shook scooping it onto her plate. *Get over yourself, you fresh-food snot.* She put the last piece of chocolate pecan pie on a dessert plate and found a can of whipped cream on the fridge door. She pumped cream on the side of the pie and brought it to Ruby.

"I saw apples in the fridge. Would you like some fruit?" she asked as she poured a large glass of ice water for her.

Ruby said no. Maybe later.

Ellen sat on the floor and pulled a Twix bar from her pocket. She peeled off the paper, snapping apart the two bars easily.

"Is that all you're having for lunch?" Ruby asked.

"Uh-huh. It's all I can do right now."

Ruby stared at her. "A cook who eats only candy bars," she said. Licking whipped cream off her fingers, she made a goofy face. "The world is upside down."

More than you know, Ellen smiled, and took a tiny bite of the crunchy Twix.

"As a matter of fact, there's one upside down but significant proviso that you need to understand about these plans, Ruby. It's a critical stipulation, and it is absolutely not negotiable."

"Oh, what now? Really, Ellen, you can be so dramatic."

Bracing herself, Ellen focused on the Twix bar pretending she was not particularly interested in Ruby's reaction.

"Henry will be part of our little Recoup Hotel," she said. "He'll be living with us. He's part of the deal."

Ruby snapped her head up, eyes on Ellen. "Over my dead body."

"Fine. I'll call the rehab center," Ellen said. Standing up, milk chocolate sticking to her bottom lip, she added, "Or would you prefer the West Side Nursing Home?"

Eighteen

Ellen turned the bed to give Frances a view from the west windows. From that angle she could enjoy the warmth of the afternoon sun, which had started to bathe the side of the house. Frances's three-story Victorian home was laid out in the traditional manner of its period. The parlor was in the front, bordered on the south wall by tall pocket doors that opened to the living room just behind it. When company called, the parlor was used. On a daily basis Alan and Frances had used the living room, except for large gatherings when both rooms were opened up.

The kitchen ran long across the back of the house with a butler's pantry separating it from the formal dining room, which was across the center hall from the living room. Off the kitchen, facing the back garden, was a small knotty pine breakfast room with a wall of windows. Frances said she loved this cozy room the best. It was here that she and Alan had shared their daily meals. A library with a mahogany fireplace was in the front of the house, across from the parlor. The library was essentially Alan's room, although he had allowed Frances to join him for a drink, occasionally, when he was reading and listening to music on a winter's evening. Every now and then she would smoke a cigarette with him. "There's nothing wrong with enjoyin' a nasty old vice from time to time," she would tell him.

Ellen had closed the pocket doors to give Frances privacy when she set up the Recoup Hotel, the name they all had agreed was more than appropriate. "Recoup, mecoup," Ruby had said more than once, with a straight face. It made Ellen laugh every time.

"I don't know if I'll ever get used to sleepin' in the living room," Frances said after her first few days. "It seems so wrong. I'm beginning to understand what Mama's life must have been like when she took over the sunroom of our home in Augusta."

"What happened to her?" Ellen asked.

"Nothing terrible, really. She had pulled a muscle in her thigh and couldn't navigate the front stairs. She stayed down in the sunroom for a week or two while she was on the mend. Then, for reasons known only to her, she remained in the sunroom the last eleven years of her life. Daddy carried her bed downstairs, and he had full plantation shutters installed so that she had a wide view of the side yard and back gardens. At night the shutters were shut tight, allowin' Mama complete privacy. She just adored that room."

"Did everyone accept her decision to live there?" Ellen asked, puzzled by the very idea of life in the sunroom.

"Why, of course, yes. The decision was hers to make. Mind you, I don't think she came to it lightly. There's an old southern expression, 'she took to her bed.' Everyone knows what it means. Sometimes it starts with a the death of a child, or a parent, or sometimes it's simply the onset of a small illness, something that sends a woman to bed for a week or a month, and she is tended to and cared for until she recovers.

"But then," Frances said, "before you know it, six months or a year has gone by and the woman is still in the bedroom, choosin' to be confined to the house."

Frances gripped the sides of the bed, raising herself up a little.

She was fascinated by the progress of a big-breasted robin strutting across the grass, clearly making its way to her muddy bed of herbs, which had been devastated by the recent frost. "That robin is late in leavin' us," she told Ellen. "He needs to be headin' south before an early winter storm traps him. I'd surely hate to see him feet-up in the sage one mornin'."

Ellen didn't share Frances's interest in robins, but she looked at the errant bird to please her friend. After a minute she asked, "So what's life like for a woman who sequesters herself like that?"

"Oh! Forgive me, dear. I am easily distracted, aren't I? Well, she stops going out and doin' things like she used to, and rarely receives company or even extended family, unless it's well planned in advance. She reads and sews, watches the television some, takes naps, and listens to the radio. Mama kept track of things talkin' on the telephone with friends and relatives. She ran the house from that sunroom, receivin' visitors now and then, and just enjoyin' the vista she had created. She never was so relaxed as when she took to her bed, Daddy said."

Ellen moved to the foot of the bed to face Frances, hoping to keep her focused. She was intrigued by this peculiar southern tradition.

"Are you telling me your mama just stayed inside the house for the rest of her life?"

"Essentially, yes. It sounds strange to say, but when she took to her bed people didn't worry. It was understood, and graciously accepted, that a sensitive woman in her seventies might decide to settle in and enjoy a simple life in her home."

Ellen couldn't imagine it.

"You're not going to take to your bed, are you?" she said. "We need you up and around, being company and receiving company."

Frances smiled for the first time since coming home two days ago. "My word, no. I'd be out of this bed and in the garden right this second if I could." She laughed. "I have no intentions of shuttin' myself off from the world just yet. This sleepin' in the living room is the strangest thing in the world to me."

Ellen looked up, suddenly annoyed. She could hear the high-pitched ringing of the small bell, the wrist action more frantic with each shake. She had given the bell to Ruby to use in summoning Ellen when Ruby needed something. In one short morning, that bell was in danger of being rung out. Henry got up when Ellen started to move, stretching his hind legs, preparing to follow her anywhere. Ellen had noticed he was sticking to her like peanut butter on a knife these days. Most likely he was afraid she'd leave him behind in this strange old house with its strong smells of two bedridden ladies who couldn't take him for a walk, even if they wanted to.

Ellen went back to the kitchen to get a fresh glass of apple juice for Ruby. Dr. Davis had said she must stay hydrated, telling her to drink eight ounces of juice or water every hour, and Ruby was happy to comply. Coming out of the kitchen, she went through the butler's pantry. She enjoyed making her way to the front of the house through the beautiful dining room.

A museum-quality mantle encased the white marble fireplace in the dining room corner opposite the floor-to-ceiling windows framed by eggshell blue satin drapes, which puddled as they rested on the floor. A chandelier, which Frances had said held 120 crystals, was suspended from the fifteen-foot ceiling. The chandelier was centered perfectly above the round, polished cherry dining table with its twelve pale-blue, rose, and yellow floral-patterned silk seats. Ellen loved the room and hoped someday to eat at that table. With its delicately watermarked silk wallpaper, it was a room that was at once historic and modern in its decoration, a style embraced by Frances throughout her home. *She has impeccable taste*, Ellen thought, delighting in the rich patterns of the deep rose and pale-blue, yellow, and green in the Oriental rug that grounded the room, leaving three feet of lustrous hardwood floors to add warmth.

"Coming, Ruby," she yelled forward. *Please stop that incessant bell ringing.* Ruby's bed was set up in the front parlor, at an odd angle to the bay windows, at her request. She had said she wanted to "see the street, not be part of it, for heaven's sake."

"I feel like all I do is ring this bell," Ruby said now, the bell still poised in her hand. "Can you hear it?"

Ellen attempted her best customer-service smile.

"Yes, I can, Ruby. But it may take me a few minutes to finish up what I am doing with Frances, or projects in the kitchen, or taking care of Henry, before I can get to you. Please be assured, I can hear you from all parts of the house." Taking the bell from her hand, Ellen set it within easy reach on the table, next to the alabaster lamp. "A couple of good shakes will bring me bedside in a minute or two. If you'll have just a smidgen of patience, I'll be here before you know it. I promise. Deal?"

"All right, I've got it," Ruby said, an edge to her voice. She shifted sideways in the bed, flinching as the weight of the blanket momentarily pinned down her ankle. She faced Ellen and took two deep breaths before beginning.

"Now this is why I called you, Ellen, and it is the hardest thing I've ever had to do. What you must understand is that I have no choice."

Ellen braced herself. Ruby had been here less than twenty-four hours and already she was high maintenance personified. What in the world did she want now?

Ruby took another deep breath, blowing it out slowly, her eyes closed.

"Could you help me onto the commode?" she asked. "I've put it off as long as I can, but I think it's time. I would rather do anything than ask you to help me with this, Ellen, but I just can't manage it myself." She opened her eyes and looked up at the ceiling. Exhaling, her cheeks puffed up like well-done beignets.

For the love of Pete, is that all?

"No need to apologize, Ruby, it's fine. That's what I'm here for. I'm glad to help." Ellen turned around and pointed Henry toward the hallway. "Go lie down, please." He headed out of the room. "Good boy. Now stay."

She pushed the wooden stair steps alongside the bed. The steps were wide and secure, with rubber grippers on their feet. Ellen had been glad to discover that both Ruby and Frances could navigate them, with a little help. When searching for equipment she'd need for the Recoup Hotel, she had been amazed to find a large, well-stocked medical supply store right in a prime location on West First and Bridge streets. Home Care at Home took up two storefronts in what she estimated to be about five or six thousand square feet.

"Oswego's demographics are kind of scary when you take a good look at them," the store owner, John Huckenbary, told her. "We're a graying city. We're not attracting young people because there aren't enough good jobs here anymore." He showed her the expansive selection of mobility chairs, canes, bathroom tub and shower supports, swinging table trays to fit his inventory of at-home hospital beds, and row after row of oxygen equipment and diabetic monitors, shoes, socks, and test strips.

"The kids who want to stay here and raise a family have a tough time," he added. "Most of the time they wind up moving away. It's a shame. If it weren't for Oswego State, we'd be turning out the lights altogether. Still," he said, "I can't complain. My business is booming."

She had one of his best customers to deal with now, she thought, as she maneuvered Ruby off the bed. It was interesting to feel how solid she was for such a petite woman. Edging down the steps, Ellen holding her under the arms from the back, Ruby carefully shuffled the few steps over to the commode. It was a wide square wooden box with a lift-up top covering the seat and the bowl that housed the discharge unit down in the middle. Only three feet high, it was designed for easy landings. Someone had painted the commode an antique blue to give it a decorator touch, Mr. Huckenbary had noted.

Ellen helped Ruby center herself, pulling up her nightgown to keep it out of the way. As soon as she was settled, Ruby shooed Ellen away.

"Just leave me the bell, please, and go on along now. I'll let you know when I need you to help me get back in bed."

Ellen exited quickly, hoping to get away before she had to pretend she didn't hear the explosive noises that would inevitably come from Ruby. It would be an embarrassment to them both. Turning to leave, she thought about opening the living room window to let in some fresh air, but she had left it too late. If she did it now, Ruby would be even more ashamed than she already was. Ellen would have to work in the fresh air later that afternoon before the sun set and it got too cold.

She was grateful that it was just Ruby who needed the commode. Frances was able to walk to the downstairs bathroom and use its facilities, particularly its stall shower. Dr. Ireland did not want Frances handling the main stairs yet, but she could easily negotiate the three steps down into that small bathroom, which had been an addition just off the mudroom several decades ago. Unfortunately, neither Ruby nor her wheelchair could get down those steps.

"C'mon, Henry, let's see what's happening outside," Ellen said. He came alongside her before breaking away and racing to the kitchen door. She caught up and opened it quickly. Henry charged out into the large fenced yard while Ellen took a moment to breathe in the beauty of the backyard. Frances had developed gorgeous gardens in the back and alongside the southern side of the house. She had achieved her master gardener designation years ago, and it showed. Fortunately, the terraced back garden was almost a half acre, giving Henry plenty of room to run around without disturbing the flowerbeds. Ellen pulled a pooper-scooper bag from the mudroom shelf and went out to pick up yesterday's deposits. Despite what lazy dog owners say, she knew dog poop was not a good fertilizer.

Henry was wriggling into the grass outside, rolling around for a good back scratch, rubbing the smell of earth onto his fur coat, the sun warming his joints. Ellen went back into the kitchen. When he was ready, the back porch would give him shade, and he would yelp or scratch the door to let her know he was ready to come in. In the meantime he could hear her moving around inside through the screened door, giving him confidence to happily stay outside.

Ellen walked into the wide pantry closet filled with shelves holding Frances's cooking staples and canned goods. The Recoup Hotel guests would need lunch in about an hour, and then a good dinner tonight. Frances's lackluster appetite concerned her. She had only eaten a little cream of wheat, some rye toast, and a few bites of banana every day since coming home four days ago. She was taking fluids regularly, water and juice, and already today she had asked twice for green tea with honey and lemon. But she'd need to eat more than that to regain her strength.

"What sounds good to you?" Ellen had asked her this morning after Frances pushed her oatmeal to the side, the melting pats of butter and the brown sugar sprinkled over the top not enough to make her try it. "Is there anything you can think of that you'd really enjoy eating?"

Apologetically, Frances said nothing came to mind. Then, later on, about an hour after breakfast, she looked shyly at Ellen.

"I've been sitting here thinking about chicken pot pie," she said, "with peas and carrots and celery in a flaky crust, with nice big bites of chicken swimmin' around in a thick creamy sauce. Mama used to make it when she and Daddy were going out to a party or to one of their many charity evenin's. She'd say it was a complete meal in one dish, designed to keep us warm inside until they got home. I always loved that chicken pot pie."

Ellen did, too. She made a list of what she would need. Right now, lunch was the job at hand. Ruby had asked for tomato soup and peanut butter on saltine crackers. She told Ellen it was one of her comfort lunches. Frances, always happy to oblige, said she'd be interested in a little soup, and the saltine crackers sounded good.

"Maybe with a little soft butter, instead of the peanut butter. Either way, don't fuss, Ellen. I can eat the peanut butter if that's easier."

Ellen was fine with both requests. The tomato soup was simple to make, even if she didn't have access to good homegrown tomatoes this time of year in Oswego. Canned ones worked pretty well, their intense flavor not getting lost in the cream, or more precisely, the fat-free cream she served in everything now at the Recoup. With Frances on a heart-healthy diet, she had to be careful. She worried a little that Ruby might not like her homemade tomato soup since her request had been very specific: Campbellstomatosoup, as if it were one word. Ruby would just have to expand her horizons a little.

After they'd eaten, she'd give Henry a run. By the time she had done the food shopping and picked up Ruby's new pain prescription, the whole afternoon would be gone. She was stunned by how quickly her life had changed. She yearned for the days when she could curl up and take a nap, or spend the entire afternoon in bed reading and snoozing. Depression was hell, but it did give her psychological permission to wallow in comfort, piles of books in the bed, digging into the lives of other people for hours at a time, distancing herself from her own. Those days were lost to her now. She felt as she did years ago when she'd thrown away her favorite pleated skirt, not realizing how much she'd miss it, not understanding that they'd never make another one just like that one with its rich plaid wool fabric stitched down exactly right on her hips, the skirt a perfect foil for her best red cardigan.

She finishing the shopping list and put it in her purse. Opening a can of good imported Italian skinless plum tomatoes, she eased their rich redness into a medium saucepan, thankful that Frances had a gas stove. An electric stove would have tipped her sanity scale. She quickly chopped a stalk of celery, a small onion, half a carrot, and a clove of garlic, sautéing them in good olive oil until they were soft. She scraped the vegetables into to the soup along with two cups of low-salt chicken broth and a handful of fresh chopped basil, salt, and pepper.

When the soup was bubbling she took it off the stove and lowered the immersion blender into the middle, pulsing it to create a thick smooth mixture before adding the half-and-half, which lightened it up while creating another layer of flavor and creaminess. She checked the seasonings, added a little more salt and pepper, and decided it was ready.

Cleaning up, she was amused to see that Frances's kitchen was starting to look like her own. Every day another tool, pan, or piece of equipment found its way from Ellen's house so she could cook with her own things. She reached for the two breakfast-in-bed tray tables sitting at the end of the counter. She set each one with a fresh paper placemat, verdant green today, and a knife and soup spoon from the good sterling silver cutlery Frances stored in the butler's pantry. Ellen had surprised them yesterday with the sterling flatware at dinner.

Feeling the weight of the fork in her hand, Frances's eyes had sparkled.

"Why, it feels like Christmas! Am I not eating with the best silver service?" she said gaily. "What a treat this is!"

Frances dipped her fork into the rice with almonds in a theatrical motion, plate to mouth. She carried on with that for another few scoops before she put the fork down with a delicate hand.

"Oh, my," she said. "I've just had a very troublin' thought, Ellen. Here we are enjoyin' ourselves like greedy carpetbaggers and when we're finished, you'll have to wash all of this silver by hand! Oh, honey, that seems like a terrible burden when you have so much to do already."

Ellen liked Frances more every day.

"It's no trouble, really," she said. "I've used mine at home for years. I think it makes a meal taste better, don't you, Frances?"

Frances lifted her fingers to her mouth like a fan, and dropped her chin to her chest. She looked up at Ellen in a perfectly staged southern-gal pose.

"I hate to say this, but yes, I most certainly do agree. Eaten from that lovely silver fork the rice tasted like the most divine concoction, straight out of a Rudyard Kipling story. However, I am startin' to have indigestion thinking about the extra work we have made for you because of our little pleasures."

Ruby had heard enough. She chimed in, telling Ellen she thought it was silly to use the good holiday silver every day.

"If you want to go to all the trouble of hand-washing our cutlery after every meal, then you are welcome to it," Ruby said. "I will say one thing though. Using the good sterling seems wasteful to me. Mother never would have allowed it in our house on such a casual basis. Sterling silver is a privilege, an heirloom to be used with care on special occasions."

She stopped, taken aback by the exasperated look on Ellen's face. Ruby didn't want to make her feel bad; at the same time, someone had to tell Ellen when she was being foolish. Frances would never do it.

"I realize you only want to make our mealtimes a little more lively," Ruby said, in a softer voice. "But honestly, Ellen, silver forks and spoons don't make my food taste any better. I just want you to know that this particular effort is wasted on me."

Ellen had ended that exchange with an exaggerated bow to each of them, one after the other.

"We are a house divided," she proclaimed. "In which case, I will attempt to bring the wisdom of Solomon to our table. Pray for me all you who believe." She had wanted to leave clicking her heels, but she didn't trust herself to land without injury. Instead, she produced an elegant theatrical wave, turning into the hallway singing, "I'm off to see the Wizard, the wonderful Wizard of Oz . . ."

Returning to the lunch trays, Ellen put a generous dollop of softened butter into an eggcup and set it in the center of the lunch plate, surrounding it with saltine crackers. For Ruby's tray she loaded up an eggcup with peanut butter and added twice the amount of saltines. As she turned into the hallway, the sound of the summoning bell filled the parlor.

"Coming, Ruby," Ellen called out softly. She didn't want to wake up Frances, who seemed to nap easily whenever Ellen left her alone. "Nearly there now."

An hour later, she smiled as she cleaned up the lunch dishes. Ruby had said nothing about the tomato soup. Neither a thank-you nor a well-done-ye-good-and-faithful-servant. Perhaps the proof was in the pudding, so to speak. No sign of tomato bits and pieces remained in Ruby's bowl. She must have finger-licked it clean.

Nineteen

Ellen wandered around the Price Chopper aisles pulling items into her cart. The store was new, the anchor for a major shopping center out on County Route 104, on the east side of town. She wondered if such a large store, complete with on-site bakery, florist, and pharmacy, could survive the depressed Oswego economy. Then again, she supposed people would always have to eat, enjoy the promise of fresh flowers on a dreary day, and get their meds. The Chopper was probably one business that was sustainable.

Pressed for time, Ellen was piqued to think that she'd have to go back to Wayne's Drug Store for Ruby's new prescription. The would mean finding a parking spot on Bridge Street and traipsing into another store when she could have taken care of it all right here. Unfortunately, Ruby wouldn't think of getting her meds anywhere but at Wayne's, where Jimmy Brenstetter had served her family for forty-five years.

Dr. Davis had called in the pain prescription yesterday after coming to see Ruby in her new quarters. He said he was 90 percent certain her ankle was badly sprained. "We'll need to have it X-rayed to be sure," he added. Ruby refused.

"I know my own body, Dr. Davis," she said. She looked as if lockjaw had suddenly set in. "What I know for sure is that I have a sprained ankle. I will not be moved to the hospital for tests that are unnecessary. They will only confirm what we both already know."

To Ellen's surprise, but not Frances's, Dr. Davis acquiesced.

"All right. But if you are to stay in this situation, and not go to a rehabilitation center or a nursing home for care and therapy, I insist that you follow my instructions to the letter," he said. "I will come back tomorrow and the next day to check on you, and if you are not doing what I ask, I will call an ambulance and send you to rehab. Agreed?"

With the concentration of a monk in meditation, Ruby looked down at the floor. Barely breathing, she raised her head, coldly looking at the doctor.

"If your instructions are reasonable, I will follow them. For your part, Dr. Davis, I ask you to remember that I am not a child. You cannot force me to go into rehab or to a nursing home against my will. I know that, and you know that. Please don't treat me like an infant. The essential truth is, whether I do as you wish or not, I have no intentions of going anywhere. Agreed?"

Dr. Davis picked up his black bag, his cheeks the color of ripe Braeburn apples.

"You are your father's child," he said. "All right. I've done all I can for now. If you wish to recover fully, please follow my rules." He hesitated in the doorway, then turned around to look at Ruby again.

"I have selfish reasons for wanting to see you heal," he said. "It wouldn't be Christmas if you didn't put us all to shame on the dance floor at the Dickens Ball. Don't disappoint me, do you hear?"

Ruby broke into a wide smile, relieved that their parrying was over. "My dancing shoes are ready," she said.

Ellen found the exchange interesting. Ruby could be strong and sweet, simultaneously. Most of all, she was intractable when she had made up her mind. Ellen filed the observation away for reference in the court-case days ahead.

After loading the last grocery bag into the trunk of her rental car, Ellen slid in and immediately turned off the radio, which had come on when she started the engine. She wanted nothing to do with talk radio or the relentless harangue of music from the rock channels that were programmed into the auto-set buttons; reprogramming them would take a patience she didn't possess. More than that, she had discovered how refreshing a silent car trip could be.

Listen to yourself! Less than a week into this Recoup Hotel gig and you're escaping into a two-door Honda Civic to find peace.

A sharp pang of indigestion stabbed her, the acidic sourness centering in her chest. She scrambled in her purse for a handful of Tums and wondered, not for the first time, what the heck she was doing. What had she gotten herself into? She took no comfort in the only answer she could muster.

Whatever it is, Ellen Varner, you have no choice but to keep going. You're in it for as long as it takes, and there's no going back now. You made the commitment and you have to stick with it. It will only be for a month or maybe a little more, and you can survive that. Buck up and stop whining.

As she pulled into the driveway and drove around back to the kitchen door, she looked to see if she could detect Ruby watching from the parlor window. She couldn't. Ruby was a wild card. She was one of the strangest characters Ellen had ever known. Her quirkiness, while charming at times, was troublesome on many levels. What if something went wrong while she was caring for Ruby? Or Frances, for that matter? Formally and legally they both had declined trained nursing help. Still, the courts were a perilous place when healthcare went awry. Ellen was an educator and a former chef, not a trained caregiver. What was she thinking? Whatever it was, she had crossed the Rubicon. *Alea iacta est.*

On the positive side, Ellen was relieved when Dr. Davis had insisted on a physical therapist three times a week for Ruby. She was equally glad that Frances's doctor had set up her therapy before she left the hospital; she had a less complicated schedule, only twice a week for an hour.

Frances's therapist had made his first visit three days ago. He was a six-foot-four muscle-armed Irishman with an accent to match his wildly curly red hair that flopped all over his head, bouncing down on his shoulders. One of his Converse sneakers was bright green; the other, bright orange. He was almost comic relief, and Ellen greeted him warmly, nodding at his footgear.

"England and Ireland all at once?" she said.

"Ahhhh, I'm a man of peace, aren't I, and I want me father's Ireland to be at peace as well," he said. "The English? I don't love 'em, but I don't hate 'em. Same with yer Orange Protestants. The Irish? I love 'em all." He reached down to his sneakers and, with a flourish, came up clapping his hands above his head, his feet dancing a noiseless jig.

"'Tis Ireland all together now, the English and the Irish, the Catholics and the Protestants," he sang, twirling around. "Green and Orange as one, do ya see?"

Ellen shook her head, laughing, liking this Irish hulk immediately. Then, just as suddenly as it had begun, his dancing came to a halt. Vigorously rubbing his hands together like a man about to tackle a juicy corned beef sandwich, he turned to Frances.

"So, my fine colleen, are we ready to get yer sea legs back, then? C'mon, luv, up we go! There we have it! Such a wee bit of a lass you are, hah? Why, I'll have you dancing in no time a'tall. Easy now, here we go, one step at a time."

Frances seemed to be enjoying herself as much as she could with her wobbly legs and listless arms. Seconds after he left, Ruby rang her call bell frantically.

"Could you please contact someone at the home care service and ask who will be coming to work with me?" she said evenly. "I'd like a woman, if possible. Actually, I insist upon a woman physical therapist. Would you tell them that for me?"

"Why, you can tell them yourself, Ruby," Ellen said. "Let me get my cell phone for you. That way, you can be sure your directions are delivered exactly the way you want."

After the phone call, Ruby relaxed into her pillows, a pleasant look on her face for once.

"It's all taken care of," she told Ellen. "Mrs. Beck starts tomorrow. She's a very nice woman, from an old Oswego family. Her mother was a great baker of pies. We used to get them delivered to us when we were growing up. Chocolate and lemon meringue were her best ones, with the meringue piled high and dripping golden tears from the browned peaks on top."

Ellen wanted to tell Ruby that when the meringue weeps yellow tears, it's overdone. The edges of perfect meringue are tipped light brown from careful broiling. No weeping allowed. But she didn't say a word. She was thrilled that Ruby was happy with her therapist. Every elimination of possible drama was a move in the right direction. Ellen's goal was to keep her two charges safe and well fed until they could take care of themselves. *Just a month or a little longer,* she repeated to herself. Heck, maybe she'd dance at the Dickens Ball herself, free and unencumbered once more. *Nah. Probably not.*

Henry galloped across the yard to greet her, his tail wagging wildly; it looked as if it might snap off.

"I'm home!" she called. As she lugged the eight bags of groceries into the kitchen the plastic bags cut into her bony fingers. She despised plastic bags. Since she was cooking regularly now, she'd have to pick up those recyclable cloth bags for groceries. She stopped to enjoy the afternoon sun, which was spilling through the window over the sink, a lovely glow warming the room. Looking around the pleasant kitchen, updated about ten years ago with Sub-Zero and Viking appliances, Ellen felt she had made the right decision to move in here instead of going back and forth to her home.

She realized it was the only reasonable thing to do after exploring the difficult and complicated process of hiring temporary help. The tedious steps of identifying and interviewing candidates, checking their references and police records, and coming to terms with them on hourly rates and benefits daunted her. It would take days, if not weeks, and she had neither the patience nor the time. She had contacted the only home care service in Oswego and they told her she'd be on a waiting list for two to three months unless something unusual occurred. Rather than advertise in the newspaper, her only other option, she had decided to move in. Besides, she was getting to know the sounds and rumblings of her charges pretty well by now. It was simpler at this point to sleep in Frances's bedroom at the top of the stairs, where she could hear them and respond to them quickly.

"If it gets to be too much for me after a few days," she assured Frances, "then I'll explore the overnight sitters. How's that?"

Grateful, Frances had agreed, saying she would hold Ellen to her promise. "If I see you extendin' yourself, and becomin' more run-down than you already are, I will have to give you leave, my dear. I mean it. I could not bear the idea of you gettin' sick on top of everything else."

A sad outcome of their moving in involved Henry. He was intimidated by the strangeness of the four-poster bed with its towering white canopy. As a result, he had taken to sleeping on the floor instead of on Ellen's bed. It wasn't all bad. He seemed to enjoy the large doggie pillow she had bought to give him comfort on the hardwood floor. Actually, he seemed to love that fleecy bed. Selfishly, she missed his lumpy body around her legs at night, as well as the joy of waking up to him straddling her chest, his eager black eyes boring into hers, willing her to, "Get up, get up! Let me outside. Let's go!"

Everything has a price, she decided, washing the green grapes, wondering if she felt like eating some. Eyeing them in the palm of her hand, gripping a couple with her fingers, she knew she should pop them into her mouth right now. She was beginning to worry about her weight loss. She had read plenty about the pounds divorcees lose as they adjust to their new lives. But she was down to 114 pounds, with no appetite in sight. Without question she was anemic, the big bruise on her thigh and the four bruises on her hands and arms attesting to her deteriorating state. She only had to brush into a cabinet or hit her hand getting out of the car and she was black and blue the next day. She would talk with Dr. Ireland about it. *But not today,* she thought, putting the grapes into a bowl.

Moving easily in Frances's kitchen she put things away where she thought Frances would want them: the canned goods in the pantry, the baking supplies in the cupboards above the deep drawer holding the baking pans, wine in the angled corner cabinet at the end of the counter. She had bought several bottles of wine, hoping a daily glass might do the girls some good, might get Frances's appetite juices flowing a little, as time went on. She'd have to talk with their doctors to determine when and if it would be safe for them to have a drink, given their medications. In the meantime, she'd enjoy a glass of Cabernet Sauvignon herself at the end of these long days.

Finished in the kitchen at last, she walked quickly to the front of the house, checking on Ruby first. She was sitting up, watching *The Price is Right* with its slimmed-down host, Drew Carey. Ellen stopped and stared. *Boy, he looks like a different guy with his eighty-pound weight loss.* She mentioned it to Ruby.

"I liked him when he was heavy, too," Ruby said, coolly. "He's a good person. His weight doesn't matter to me."

Grumpy Gus, aren't we? Don't rise to the occasion, Ellen. She had brought Ruby more apple juice and ice water and set them in front of her after she cleaned up the tray table. "You all set for now?" she asked.

"Yes, fine. Except, since you've been to the Price Chopper I assume you've bought groceries? I was wondering what you're cooking for supper?"

"Homemade chicken pot pies," Ellen answered. "And for dessert, a warm white chocolate sauce over fresh strawberries and blueberries, with a little dribble of cream." She'd omit the white chocolate and use just a little half-and-half on the macerated fruit for Frances. "Does that sound good to you?"

"I love pot pies. I always like that cardboardy crust on the top of the frozen ones. I usually break it up into the pie so it will soften it up and I can chew it with the filling. Your dessert sounds like it could be a good way to make the fruit go down, if you know what I mean."

Ellen moved away from the bed, thankful that Ruby's interest in Drew Carey would abbreviate her interest in this conversation.

"I make a flaky pie crust," she couldn't resist adding. "You'll want to chew it all on its own, I think. At least I hope so. You can tell me later which crust you like better. I'm going to check on Frances now. Ring the bell if you need anything."

Frances was smiling when Ellen walked through the pocket doors.

"It's so much fun listenin' to Ruby's ideas, don't you think?" Frances spoke carefully, trying to read Ellen's face. "She has such an interesting view of things. Mama would say her personality is simply unique!"

"That it is," Ellen replied. Her feet were aching, all that running around finally settling into her emerging bunion. She collapsed into the big cushioned chair by the window. This particular chair made her feel as if she had landed in a natural habitat, its cotton fabric serving as a background for parrots, macaws, and cockatoos, all peacefully perching on tree limbs. She rearranged the two soft pillows embroidered with red and emerald-green hummingbirds feeding on a row of deep pink hibiscus. *Hibisci?* she wondered. She put the pillows side-by-side behind her at the base of her spine and picked up one of the books on the end table.

"*Pontoon*?" she asked. She took her finger and ran it over the cover with its familiar street map of Lake Wobegon. "Are you a fan of Garrison Keillor?"

"Alan and I listened to *A Prairie Home Companion* on Saturday night for, my word, twenty-five years? I still listen. That show is as much a part of my life as the Altdorfer clock in the front hall." Frances took the book from Ellen and rubbed her hand along its spine, enjoying the feel of it, longing to get inside and learn what its characters were getting into this time. She handed it back to Ellen.

"A friend of mine gave me *Pontoon* several years ago and I started readin' it. Something must have taken my attention because I lost track of it," she added. "A couple of weeks ago I came upon it when I was cleanin' out drawers in the guest room. I thought this would be a marvelous time to pick it up again. Garrison always delivers such a fine, funny story. Might break up the tedium. But would you like to read it first, dear? Please take it, if you do."

"Gosh, I read it when it first came out, Frances. When was that? Wait! Here it is: 2007. I love Garrison Keillor. Matt and I used to listen religiously on Saturday nights, too." With her finger she traced the Main Street map from the Our Lady of Perpetual Responsibility Church, past the statute of the Unknown Norwegian, down to the Chatterbox Café. "It's so nice to see this book again. I feel as if I know the people of Lake Wobegon. Keillor certainly knows his Scandinavian Lutherans."

"Oh, more than just them," Frances said. "He seems to understand the most fundamental of human conditions, I think. And is he not just full of hilarious ideas?"

"He is, indeed. Speaking of hilarious ideas, you and I have some time on our hands these next few weeks, Frances. I'd love to read *Pontoon* again." Ellen opened the book to the title page. "Would you like it if I read it out loud? That way we could enjoy it together. Does that appeal to you at all?"

Frances put her head back on the pillow and closed her eyes.

"I love being read to. That would be simply divine, if you truly don't mind."

"I absolutely don't mind. In fact, it would be a pleasure."

Ellen read for about thirty minutes as Frances rested her eyes, her attention evidenced from time to time by a small chuckle or a gentle "uh-huh." They both loved the descriptions of Evelyn and her last night out with her girlfriends, the raucous time they had at the restaurant, and the farewells at her front gate with their promises for next week's get-together. Ellen stopped reading when Evelyn was found dead in her bed the next morning. She and Frances frowned at each other. Moments later they enjoyed the reactions of Evelyn's put-upon daughter, Barbara, when she discovered her mother's cold body, a copy of *A Tale of Two Cities* on the floor, just out of Evelyn's reach, the book apparently dropped when her heart attack struck in the night, her eighty-two years of living no longer lighting up her face. Eyebrows raised, Ellen and Frances smiled at each other when Barbara found the letter from her mother outlining funeral arrangements, along with an introduction to a certain Raoul, Evelyn's boyfriend and secret lover for twelve years.

"Shall we stop there and pick up the letter-shock tomorrow?" Ellen said.

Frances nodded yes. Tired now, she turned on her side facing Ellen, sliding her hands under her pillows, watching as Ellen closed the blinds to the afternoon sun.

"This is going to be such fun," Frances said. Lowering her voice to a whisper, she continued, "I was thinking something as you were readin' so beautifully, Ellen. I do believe we should include Ruby in this little adventure, don't you? I know she's not much of a reader, but I feel sure she would enjoy this time together."

Ellen instantly shook her head no. Ruby in the mix would change everything. Her dour spirit would put a damper on the fun, the lightness of reading *Pontoon*, the joy of its sexy silliness, the humorous fatalism of its Scandinavian characters.

"Let me think about it for a minute," Ellen whispered back. She went across the room to the recessed wall niche and carefully picked up the vase of wilting pink roses Frances had enjoyed since bringing them home from the hospital. They were a gift from the volunteer group there. "Can we talk about it tomorrow? For now, why don't you take a short nap while I work on dinner? It's going to be about six before it's ready. Is that good?"

"Of course it is, dear. Whenever you have it ready is the perfect time for us. Heaven knows, we are simply on our knees in thanksgiving for you. What would we do without you?" Her eyelids drooped as Ellen moved quietly to the door. "We will need to talk about it tomorrow, Ellen. Please give it some thought."

In the kitchen Ellen chopped carrots, onion, garlic, and celery, and put a package of frozen peas in the sink. She slid a small chicken into the big pot and covered it with water, adding bay leaves, a whole onion, skin on, and two stalks of celery snapped in half, two cloves of garlic, and the gizzards and giblets from inside the chicken. She tossed sea salt and ground fresh pepper into the pot, leaving it uncovered. When it came to a full boil she turned down the heat to let it simmer for thirty minutes or so while she made the white sauce and the flaky pie crust Ruby might not like as much as the "cardboardy" kind.

Out of nowhere tears bubbled out, falling into the melting butter in the saucepan, sizzling gently as they hit the heat. *Oh, no. Salty tears.* She'd have to remember to put less salt in the sauce. Alternately wiping her eyes and tossing in tablespoons of flour, she stirred the roux, grinding in pepper and a pinch of salt, then pouring in the fat-free milk, a little at a time, whisking it to a velvety smoothness. More tears found their way into the white sauce. *Damn.* She'd have to start again. She couldn't give them pot pies full of her body fluids. How disgusting. She began to sob, hiccupping with her mouth closed until the hard hiccups turned masochistic and silly; she started to laugh and hiccup, alternately.

Upset by the unusual sounds, Henry got up and started toward her, then changed his mind. He quickly slinked past, ears down, trotting into the dining room where he lay down under the long table, safe from the strangeness. Splashing her hands and face with cold water at the sink, Ellen swayed from side to side, a rhythmic energy nudging her back and forth. The old song was running through her mind like soft taffy, the gooey lyrics oozing out of her sore throat.

"Hear the lone-some whippoorrrrwill . . . He sounds too blue to flyyyy . . . the mid-night train is whiiiining low . . . I'm so lone-some I could cryyyy."

Twenty

Resting with her eyes open, Ruby traced the outline of the tray ceiling for the hundredth time in the past week. She didn't care for the pale yellow color inside the tray molding. It was a soft contrast to the light rose of the larger ceiling, and it looked nice enough. It was just too fancy. White ceilings were all you needed in a house. With any luck she'd be able to maneuver across the street and get back to hers.

She was getting closer to executing her escape plan. It needed more careful thought and a couple of trial runs with the scooter this afternoon. If the day went well, she could be out of Frances's parlor by tomorrow, Dr. Davis be dammed.

She knew she should be grateful for this time with Frances and Ellen. She was, really. "It's simply a matter of wanting different things," she told herself. "I need to be alone. Those two thrive on this cozy camaraderie and the idea of helping each other. I was never the sorority sister type. I need to sleep in my own bed, dance anytime I want, and feed those philandering squirrels. Undoubtedly they all are over in Ina Schmidt's corn feeders by now."

Still, things could be worse, as Mother liked to point out when things got as bad as they could be.

"It's an ill wind that blows no good, Ruby," Mother would say. "Look for the good in every situation. I assure you, the blessing is there."

Well, Dr. Davis's visit yesterday had been a blessing, even if a mixed one. He said the swelling was nearly gone in her left ankle, the sprained one. Stubborn as always, he wouldn't agree to Ruby being alone, or safely ambulatory, for another week at the earliest.

"You'll have to be very careful this time around, Ruby," he had warned. "Your broken ankle will need another four or five weeks to fully heal. That means your left ankle will have to do all the work. So let's be sure it's ready before you ask it to carry you again, all right?"

Certainly, Ruby had said. *Tell him what he wants to hear.*

Another blessing was on its way in this afternoon's supper. Ellen had asked what they'd like to eat and Ruby threw caution to the wind, knowing it could be her last meal from this particular kitchen.

"I'd love a nice pork roast, if that wouldn't be asking too much. It's been ages since I've had a good roast." Ruby put her finger in her cheek, lifted her eyes heavenward, and pretended that something else had just occurred to her. "Gosh, wouldn't some crispy roasted potatoes and onions and carrots go well with that? Oh, that's probably way too complicated for you. And too much work. I suppose a baked potato would be fine."

"The roasted vegetables will be easy and delicious, Ruby. They're not a problem." Smiling, moving closer to the bed, Ellen opened her arms, palms up. "And for dessert?"

"Is there any chance you'd make a bread pudding? With a good sauce on it? It's my favorite and I bet you'd make a great one. I haven't had that in a long time either."

Ellen had made a quick trip to the supermarket and was back home now. Ruby wondered if the bread pudding request had pushed Ellen over the edge. She was hard to read. Ruby had to admit Ellen certainly had been useful in turning out meals. In the past few weeks they had enjoyed delicious pastas, fresh vegetables (she hadn't even known she liked those), homemade soups, chili, chops, hamburgers, shrimp and scallops, broiled fish, and creamy casseroles.

Last night they had feasted on turkey breasts *cordon bleu*, stuffed with garlic, butter, and thin slices of some kind of specialty ham with a good-tasting cheese. Did Ellen say it was *prosciutto* ham? *Gruyere* cheese? Never heard of either one, but it was all very tasty. Cutting into the thinly rolled turkey, the juices and the garlic, along with the cheese and the ham, just ran out of every slice, nice and salty. Frances went wild for the bright green steamed broccoli, with fresh-squeezed lemon juice and diced red onions on top. Ruby noticed that Ellen seemed to go overboard with her insistence on fresh ingredients—no bottled lemon juice for her—but she had to admit, it all tasted pretty good, whatever she did.

Through it all, Ruby guessed the greatest breakthrough, which Frances called a blessing, was that Ellen had started joining them for dinner. She even managed to work on a small plate of food each time. Frances gave Ruby a big wink the day Ellen took her first bite. Frances later said it was an occasion "beyond joyful."

OK, Frances. But it drives me nuts to watch Ellen pick at her food. I want to scream, "Just scoop up a good forkful and eat it, for heaven's sake." But I don't. I'm afraid anything I might say could push Ellen right back into eating those candy bars all the time. Frances would be crushed, not to mention furious with me, if I caused that to happen.

Perhaps the nicest of all Ruby's personal blessings was the one that came through the front door this morning: Father Hannaford had come to call. She was positive it was a sign from God. Father said he had been praying for her in morning matins and had missed her at early Mass, so he hoped she didn't mind his coming by without calling first.

"Of course not, Father," she had told him. "You feel free to mosey in here to see me whenever you have time. As you can see, I am unable to get to church anytime soon." Father Hannaford was still a handsome man at sixty-two, although Mother had always recoiled when Ruby mentioned his attractiveness.

"You're not supposed to look at priests in that way, Ruby. It's disrespectful and can only lead to trouble," she'd say. Mother had pursed her lips, looking as if she had just taken big gulp of moldy sour cream as she chastised Ruby about it. "Always view priests as holy statues, each wonderfully created and sculpted, but not to be approached too closely. Most importantly, they're never to be touched."

Standing at the foot of her bed, good-looking Father Hannaford opened a slim black-velvet-lined carryall that looked a lot like her old flute case. What a responsibility it must be carrying the body and blood of Jesus around under his arm.

"Would you like to take communion, Ruby?" he asked.

She said certainly, she'd love to receive the sacrament. As he opened the case, her heart beat faster. This would be a banner day. She'd never before had the chance to get an up-close look at the delicate crystal cruets for the water and red wine, the traveling silver chalice, the freshly starched linen chalice cloth used to wipe off any saliva she might deposit, and the small round silver box of tasty hosts.

With the late morning sun creating a halo effect around his head, Father Hannaford moved alongside Ruby, his eyes closed, leaning in just a little to hear her short confession. Stranded in this bed, she didn't have much to tell. The usual unkind thoughts and not loving God with her whole heart, soul, mind, and strength came predictably out of her brief self-examination. He absolved her sins and gave her three Our Fathers and six Hail Marys to say in penance.

"Unkind thoughts lead to unkind actions, Ruby," he said quietly. "Ask God to help you find the good in others. Pray for His help every day. God will guide you. He will show you the way, if you ask in the name of His son, Jesus Christ." He stood up, his mini sermon about to end, his hands ready to wave the sign of the Cross over her. Looking wearily into Ruby' eyes, he spoke the lesson he had delivered thousands of times. "Most of all, remember that God loves you. Be obedient to His will for you. In that obedience you will find peace in Him. In the name of the Father, and the Son, and the Holy Spirit. Amen."

She loved that Father Hannaford. He was such a nice man, his very presence an encouragement. She had often wondered what kind of penance he would give to a confessed murderer, or a serial killer. Sadly, it never seemed like the right time to ask, and today was no exception. She was sad to see him go, his special portable case gripped tightly in his hands, more shut-ins to absolve of venial sins, more stories of bad health to endure. She had enjoyed his visit.

Untying the too-frilly satin ribbon of her bed jacket, wanting to take it off now that Father was gone, she was interested to see Beulah McDonald hurrying down West Fifth, fighting the wind, her coat collar pulled up tight around her ears, her hands pushed down into her pockets, nice long brown boots covering her legs up to her knees.

Beulah is a sensible woman, honest and unaffected, just like me. That's not prideful to say. I'm just following Father Hannaford's advice, finding the good in others. I think Beulah and I share the same qualities of levelheadedness and humility. I'll have to remember to call her when I get home and invite her in for a short visit around the Thanksgiving holiday. She doesn't have much family left in Oswego. She'll enjoy a little White Zinfandel and my onion dip.

Settling back down, Ruby was warmed by her love for the Catholic church. She couldn't imagine life without it. She took pleasure in the idea of Jesus dying, then sitting up there at the right hand of the Father, with Mary solidly alongside, hand on His shoulder, seeing everything and deftly nudging her son, giving Him good advice about women and their lives, urging Him to be thoughtful, to see things from their perspective, to help them out.

Hail, Mary, full of grace. The Lord is with thee. Blessed art thou among women, and blessed is the fruit of thy womb, Jesus. Holy Mary, Mother of God, pray for us sinners, now, and at the hour of our death. Amen.

The Holy Spirit was harder to understand. Ruby thought of it as a kind of powerful masculine wind that blew through people's hearts, forcing them to be stronger in their faith. She was glad people talked about the spirit these days instead of the Holy Ghost. Ghosts come out of thin air at night or, worse than that, as a deathly cold spot right in the middle of your staircase. Who wants to invite something like that into your heart? She didn't really pray to the Holy Spirit. She mentioned it from time to time, just in case it was critical to God, but she never felt comfortable bringing that eerie testosterone presence into things.

Probably the most difficult concept for her was when the priest turned the communion wine into the literal blood of Jesus, and the wafers into the literal body of Jesus. "It's a miracle," the nuns had said. "You cannot question it." But she did. It seemed too voodooish, not to mention gross. The very thought of the wine as blood made it hard to swallow at the communion rail. She didn't do well with eating the real flesh of Jesus, either. She smiled now, thinking about the catechism classes she took in preparation for her first communion when she was eight years old. Sister Camilla had instructed them in the nuances of how to receive the host.

"Get your saliva going good before the priest gives you the host," Sister said. She demonstrated best practice by moving her cheeks in and out, rolling up a juicy wad of spit. She waited for them to follow suit. When she was satisfied that their mouths were full, she said, "Open, receive the sacrament, and chew! Now swallow! See how easy it is? That's how you do it so the host will melt quickly and not stay in your dirty mouth too long."

Sister Camilla's host-eating program never worked for Ruby. Most of the time the thin wafer got stuck to the dry roof of her mouth and she had to tongue it down. It always wound up in a pasty ball; hard chewing was the only way to get it moving fast. She didn't think Jesus would like her munching away at His body, but what could she do? In the end she let it go, the whole doctrine of transubstantiation making no sense to her. She could never believe that Jesus wanted to be treated that way.

"Try to hold on to the things you can know and accept the things you will never understand," Sister Ignatius had said when Ruby shared her concerns. "These great ideas are way beyond your ability to figure them out, Ruby. Let your faith dispel all of your doubts. Hold on to God's hand, in faith."

Over the years she happily held on to the church rituals and tried to keep the days of her life holy without any further theological inquiries. She decided to trust the Pope and let the rest go. It had worked just fine, except for the troubling times of Vatican II. She had been jolted in the 1960s when the Holy Father and his College of Cardinals decided to update the church. After an entire childhood of eating fish on Fridays, going to confession before Holy Communion on Saturdays, and twenty-four-hour fasting before taking that communion on Sunday, the new encyclicals erased those strict disciplines. She was deeply unnerved to think that what she had been carefully taught was suddenly untrue.

Explaining her confusion to Lizzie when they both were home from college, Ruby referenced a painful experience she'd had when she was ten, an episode that had permanently marked her. Even now she could feel the hollow despair of that Easter morning decades ago. It had started when Mother came walking into the kitchen just before Mass. She looked beautiful in her charcoal-gray suit, a cream-colored silk blouse under the long jacket, and her new daisy hat that nested on her head like a well-fitting wig. Mother stopped and stared at Ruby, asking her, "What are you chewing?" Ruby was just swallowing a walnut from the coffee cake they'd have after Mass.

"You've broken your fast," Mother had said. "That means your body is now impure. You may not receive the sacrament today. Your thoughtlessness has ruined your Easter Sunday." Ruby instantly vacillated between feeling guilty about sinning and knowing she had not made a conscious decision to sin. "I didn't even think about it, Mother," she cried. "I just saw that little walnut and took a bite! It's not a meal or anything and I didn't think of it as eating. Doesn't it make a difference if you don't mean to sin?"

Mother said it made no difference. "A sin is a sin whether you intend it or not," she said.

The most humiliating part was having to stay in the church pew while her family crawled over her to get out into the aisle. They didn't look at her as they joined the line of devout parishioners on their holy march to the communion rail. Miserable in her gay Easter outfit, her white gloves and light wool coat with the mother-of-pearl buttons covering her, but not protecting her, Ruby had wondered what people thought when they saw her sitting alone in the pew like the last colored egg in the basket, not allowed to join the Eucharistic family on this day of all days. She knew they'd ask themselves, "What has Ruby done?" Then they'd reason, "Surely a child of ten couldn't commit a mortal sin! Why, she could go right to confession and clear things up, even if she had. Had she missed confession? Stayed too long outside playing so that she missed Father Stangel's confessional times? How could she have been so careless? On Easter week, of all times!"

Years later Ruby was still upset by her mistake. With the reforms of Vatican II, she told Lizzie, now they could gorge themselves on a full buffet before communion and still be pure enough to take the body and blood. How could it have been so wrong once, and now be perfectly all right? Lizzie said the church had become more modern, that's all.

"Life will be easier for us now," she said. "Just think about the new rules like you were buying a new car: You still have an engine, four tires and a steering wheel. But the outside is sleeker, newer, more in keeping with the times. Not to mention nicer upholstery—have you seen the white leather in Nancy Walker's new Buick? It's gorgeous! Just enjoy the changes and stop fretting about what happened ten years ago, little sister."

Ruby took Lizzie's advice—eventually—and once again embraced her church. She still looked forward to the musty fragrance of incense on high holy days even though it filled up her sinuses faster than an alter boy pulling off his cassock after Mass. She knew it was sheer luck, an accident of birth that she was part of the one true religion, and she was grateful. When she questioned why everyone didn't have the same chance for heaven, the nuns said, *everyone does*.

"God has given all people the gift of free will, Ruby. That means everyone can choose to study and learn about God. When the priest says they're ready, that they understand the rules of being in the one true church, then they can join us," Sister Elizabeth Mary said. "Won't that be wonderful when we get to heaven together? Then we can spend all of eternity praising God just as the Bible says, sitting at His throne, singing His praises all through the day and night!"

Ruby sat up in bed again, wishing she had a nice full glass of sherry in her hand. She didn't even want to think about just sitting around all day and praising God. Honestly, she felt the nuns got that part wrong. God wouldn't want all of that hoopla, and besides, He would know it was boring as manna for people to sing His praises all day and night long. Not to mention the fact that most of the faithful couldn't sing well, or even on key. No, she didn't believe any of that eternity-of-praise business for a second.

She turned toward the door, certain she heard Frances moving around in the library. She listened carefully in case she fell and needed help or something. Ruby was very relieved Frances had become a Catholic. She didn't want to be in heaven without her. Who knows where she would have wound up if she had stayed a Baptist? Ruby wasn't sure about Ellen and her religious side. She never went to a church and didn't talk about God or Jesus, or saying her prayers, or praying for others like Frances and Ruby did. How could she get through life without religion? Who did she lean on when things got tough? How did she manage to be OK thinking that this life was it—that there was no heaven? How did she cope without a Father in heaven to talk to? How could chocolate bars be enough? She certainly couldn't imagine that kind of life. *Count me out.*

Ruby flicked the breakfast crumbs from her comforter just as a gusty wind swirled down West Fifth, nudging cars along, their drivers gripping the wheels tightly. She saw the Kaslowskis' dog earnestly cantering along home, his short legs keeping him close to the sidewalk, a grounding stroke of luck in the pushy wind.

Well, what she knew for sure—as Oprah would say—is that she would obey the rules of the Catholic church to the best of her ability so that when she died, she'd fly straight up to heaven to be with Mother and Father again. She'd wave to Ellen on her way up, and pray that one day she'd be able to join them.

She could hear Henry making his way down the front hallway, his black nails clicking along the hardwood floors. Wherever Ellen was, Henry was never far behind; she guessed Ellen was on her way to Frances. Henry was a great dog. Nothing to be scared of, that's for sure. He was just a good-natured baby, really. She pretended to be aghast when he'd jump up on the side of her bed to say hello. She'd let him stay a minute if Ellen was busy with Frances. She loved to feel the silky fur on the top of his head and smell his warm Alpo breath. Before nudging him back down, she always looked right into his dark eyes, sure that he was loving her back.

Ellen wasn't such a bad egg either, she supposed. She'd like to know what went on with her before she came back to Oswego. She bet that was a pretty good story right there. Ellen was as quiet as Apple Annie about her past life. Ruby didn't know if she'd ever get the full story.

Apple Annie. *What a great movie. I need to watch that movie again when I get home. I love watching Bette Davis being transformed into the wealthy dowager. The original makeover. With Glenn Ford at his sweet and funny best, her Svengali. He seemed more like Santa Claus than a gangster in that movie. I need to make a note or I'll forget. Where's my pen?*

Pulling open the nightstand drawer, she spotted her Swiss Army knife along the back. Grabbing it quickly, she rolled it around in the palm of her hand, kissed the red enamel inlay, then put it back.

Ruby did think Ellen seemed marginally happier these days. She was always glad to see Ellen's attempts at self-control, her urge to cry over every little thing held at bay; she was getting better at keeping herself in check. In fact, the last couple of weeks she seemed much brighter, more interested in living than sleeping. Maybe she was getting over that divorce after all. Ruby had enjoyed seeing her lighthearted side yesterday, when Ellen went out to get the morning paper from the front porch and saw Derek Simonson riding down West Fifth with the top down on his '56 Mustang.

"Look, Ruby! His hair is standing straight up, nearly frozen in place from this wind. What is he thinking? It's thirty-one degrees this morning!"

Ruby grinned back at Ellen. She told her Derek was famous for riding in his Mustang in all kinds of weather. "It's his claim to fame. For the last twenty-eight years Derek has made it his business to put the top down on that old car at least once a week and drive it around town. He's his own Guinness World Record attempt. Far as I know he's never missed a week."

Ruby talked loudly so Frances could hear. She wanted her to notice, too, that Ellen was perking up. "The *Pall Times* does a story about him in February or March when the snow's piled high and there's nothing to see but Derek's foolish head sticking up in that bright blue car as he rides up and down Bridge Street in a blizzard. We all have to read about his antics once a year, right along with news about those crazy polar bear swimmers, don't we, Frances?"

"Yes we do, Ruby. You'll probably think me silly, but I look forward to Derek's story. I think he's a mighty interestin' man."

Ellen said she admired his determination. Ruby began to hand-press her hair, trying to straighten the curls around her forehead with the natural oil in her palms.

"Fools are always determined, Ellen," she said. "Being an idiot doesn't come naturally to most people."

"Oh, Ruby, dear, surely you don't mean that!" Frances called out. "Daddy always said idiots aren't fools. 'They're just us in our birthday suits,' he'd say. Daddy was so naughty sometimes."

"I stand corrected," Ruby replied. "He was right. I wish I'd known your daddy!"

"He was very good-hearted," Frances said. "always tryin' to understand people. You both would have liked him."

Ellen walked away, smiling as she passed Frances's door. "I know I would have," she said.

Ruby hoped Frances and Ellen were in Daddy's good-hearted, understandin' mood when they discovered she had snuck out of this Recoup Hotel. She hoped they realized Ruby was neither an idiot nor a fool for getting away. She could hardly wait for nightfall. Her escape plan was ready. So was she.

Twenty-One

Frances wondered if she'd ever be able to stand up comfortably for more than ten minutes at a time, or use her right arm fully. Fortunately her speech was nearly restored and her facial expressions were normal again. Dr. Ireland said she had an ischemic stroke as opposed to a hemorrhaging one. He showed her a chart of eleven indicators used to predict the outcomes or severity of the stroke she experienced. Her condition and progress to date gave her a rating of nine.

"All things being equal, that means you have an excellent chance for a nearly full recovery within twelve months," he told her. "You improved very quickly the first few days, Mrs. O'Reilly. That was a good indicator of what you could expect in terms of your continued progress. These past weeks we've seen steady improvement. I believe we are on track for a complete recovery."

"Thank you, Dr. Ireland. Now if I could just trust my right hand to hold a cup of tea I'd feel much better."

She gently laid aside the duvet cover and pulled one leg at a time over the edge of her bed. She wanted to open the drapes so she could see the rain falling. She could hear it, of course, but seeing it would be even better. Rainy days were welcomed, even if they were deeply dreary in November in Oswego. Between the damp cold and the icy raindrops, a long rainy day could be quite depressing. She wouldn't give into it. Instead, she embraced the idea of the trees and bushes taking a good long drink in preparation for the arduous winter days ahead.

Pulling on her robe and slippers, she edged slowly to the window, pushing herself hard to get the tall, soft, green silk drapes open. With just that little effort she felt limp as an unstarched collar, ready to flop down again. She moved to the chair by the window, the one Ellen liked to sit in when reading Garrison Keillor's book to her. It was one of the sweet highlights of her day. Ellen had such a lovely way with the words, her tone with just enough inflection to make it interesting, but not theatrical. One could get theatrical reading Keillor and that wouldn't be good. Frances was loving *Pontoon*.

The expensive chair was designed to swivel, which is why Frances bought it all those years ago, placing it by the windows so that she could turn and look out on her side gardens.

I think I like this cheerful upholstery as well as any of the three fabrics that have been on it. Pushing one of the pins back into the arm cover, she noticed the fabric needed dry cleaning. *I probably need to get all the arm covers done around the house. Before the holidays. Certainly nothing to worry about today. Today I will just enjoy this wonderful feelin' of sitting in a tropical paradise in the pourin' rain. Such a comfort.*

She drew in her breath sharply. The punishing wind and rain had tossed her black chokeberry bushes into the fence, twisting them into tortuous positions, bullying them into cruel configurations.

Isn't that a most disturbin' sight! Hang on, darlings, bending won't kill you. Your roots will keep you from breaking! Oh, and look at you, my brilliant orange cones of sneezeweed! In the midst of this terror you stand so bravely next to those beautiful full mounds of purple asters.

The wind swirled through the willow tree in the back of the garden. She had planted that willow the year they moved into their home. She had told Alan she wanted something that she could look at every day, something that would remind her of her roots. He had chided her that he'd agree to the willow so long as she didn't weep along with it.

The rain was beating hard against the high windows. She could barely see.

What am I to think, my sweet chrysanthemums? Are you dead? No! There you are! How clever to keep your blossoms closed tight to all of this. You will outwit this nasty storm. You all are brave beyond words. I wish I could come out and hug you, my darling children.

"Are you all right, Frances?"

"Why, yes, of course, Ruby. Thank you. I was just encouragin' the asters to be brave in this storm. I must sound very foolish! Please, forgive me. I hope I didn't wake you from your nap."

"You didn't wake me, Frances. I've been wide awake for at least an hour with that rain pounding away. I was just resting, thinking about the roast pork and bread pudding we'll have this afternoon. I have to say, Ellen is an excellent cook, don't you think?"

"Absolutely," Frances said. She stood up and walked easily into the front parlor.

"On another subject, I thought you had very good news from Dr. Davis yesterday, don't you?" Frances said. "He seems very pleased with your remarkable progress."

Ruby said yes, it was all good news. The better news would have been if she were healed enough to get up and walk around safely right now.

"You will heed his advice not to walk on that sprained ankle for a few more days, won't you, dear? He seems to think that is very important."

Ruby rubbed her ankle and looked up at Frances.

"It's almost 100 percent healed now," she said clearly. "Sometimes I think Dr. Davis just likes to have control. You'd think he was a surgeon or something, and not just a good old family doctor. But I'll do what's best. You can trust me. You know that."

Frances looked over the top of her reading glasses at Ruby.

"I don't like the sound of that answer," she said quietly. "I do trust you, Ruby, but I also know you don't always follow Dr. Davis's orders to the letter. I do believe you should in this case. To the letter."

Shamelessly changing the subject, Ruby replied, "I've been enjoying this yellow color in the tray ceiling, Frances. It's very pretty with the rose. All of my ceilings are white. Having spent hours staring at the ceiling these past weeks, I may paint mine a color when I get home."

Frances laughed and pulled open the drapes along the end of the parlor. "I think your white ceilings do a fine job as a setting for your vivid Oriental rugs and the elegant Victorian furniture in your rooms," she said. "I wouldn't change a thing."

Ellen walked in, glad to see Frances up and walking around and Ruby still in bed resting her ankles. It was about the time that Ruby needed help with the commode, but she didn't want to embarrass her by asking out loud.

"I was just thinking about you, Ellen," Ruby said. She pulled the covers to one side. "I think I need your help, if you know what I mean."

"I do, Ruby." Ellen helped Ruby out of bed, easing her into the motorized power chair they were able to rent for her.

Frances also knew what Ruby meant.

"I think I'll just get myself a small glass of milk," she said. "The walk to the kitchen will do me good. May I bring you back a little juice, Ruby?" Ruby said no, she still had some left from breakfast.

Frances turned into the hallway, taking her time, pacing each step carefully, not wanting to trip. She and Ruby embraced the mantra of the Recoup Hotel: no falls, no broken hips. In fact, Ruby had created a comical short song about it to the tune of the old Perry Como hit, "Round and Round," rhyming with *no down, down, down.* She was such a clever woman.

"I'm told we're having something quite delicious for dinner today, Ellen," Frances called back. "Roast pork on a Monday?"

"Ruby requested it and I'm happy to oblige." Ellen walked alongside Ruby's chair as they crossed the hallway to Alan's study. She had moved the commode in there for added privacy when Ruby's power chair arrived. Henry immediately sat down next to the commode, waiting for Ruby.

"Roasted vegetables, too, I understand. How lovely," Frances said. She held on to the hall banister, turning to wink at Ellen. "You are spoilin' us rotten. I'm afraid we'll never be the same! I hope you will be joinin' us for our delectable feast?"

"I shall. It actually sounds good to me."

Ellen settled Ruby into place. They barely spoke during this awkward time. Ruby was getting heavier, a natural consequence from eating good food and not exercising. Ellen had suggested they do green salads for lunch every day, but Ruby had balked. "All that lettuce gives me gas," she argued.

Walking briskly out of the room, leaving Henry standing guard behind the commode, Ellen went across the hallway to tidy up Frances's bed. She was nearly finished when Ruby rang the bell.

"Do you have that Ace bandage I had on my knee when I left the hospital, Ellen?" she shouted.

"I do, Ruby. Do you need it now?"

"Well, I'd like to have it on hand. Dr. Davis said I'll be ready to walk on that left ankle pretty soon. I wouldn't try it without that bandage for support. Could you bring it to me?"

Ellen picked up Frances's laundry bag and went into Ruby's room to get hers. She could get a load started before dinner, and finish it up tonight. They both needed fresh underwear.

"Certainly, Ruby. You did hear Dr. Davis warn you not to walk on that ankle for a few days, right?"

"Of course I did. I just like to be prepared. That bandage is mine anyway, and I'd like to keep track of it. Please bring it to me the next chance you get, will you?"

Settled in bed again, Ruby asked if Ellen had been able to get a nice pork loin at the Price Chopper.

"I didn't even try. I called Garafolo's this morning and they cut and rolled us a nice roast. I like their meats and cheeses better, so I just did our shopping there today. I didn't need too much. Just potatoes, onions, bread, and some raisins. "

"I have to say, Garafolo's costs a lot more than the Price Chopper, Ellen. We need to be careful with our money. Extravagant spending isn't a good idea for Frances and me." It wasn't the first time Ruby had called Ellen on her spending. She and Frances contributed to the cost of living each week, splitting the food and housekeeping bills equally. In the previous two weeks Ruby had given Ellen $150, although that did include two trips to the pharmacy. Ruby knew she could eat for $25 a week with just the slightest effort.

"Oh, well. You're such a good cook, I guess I shouldn't complain," Ruby said. She didn't want Ellen to change her mind about roasting that pork loin. "I'll have broiled hamburger patties and Betty Crocker scalloped potatoes back in my life soon enough."

"And money in the bank," Ellen said.

Frances returned with an Oreo cookie in her hand. She turned it on its side and carefully separated the layers, the white icing staying on one side of the cookie, the other wafer nearly bare.

"Will you share this with me, Ruby?" She handed her the iced side. "I know you love them this way, and so do I. Fortunately, you love the icing and I love just the chocolate cookie."

Ruby slid the icing along her bottom teeth, pulling it off in small chunks, enjoying the wads of sweetness. The dense chocolate cookie was almost a relief from the sugary filling. She put the wafer on her tongue and sucked it slowly. She loved chocolate, all kinds and every type.

Ellen went into to Frances's room, leaving the pocket doors open slightly so that she could hear if Ruby needed her. She should be fine now for an hour or more. Ellen picked up *Pontoon* and raised her eyebrows at Frances, who had settled herself on the window seat next to Ellen's chair.

"Ready to see how Barbara is coming along with the arrangements for her mother's funeral?" she asked.

"Certainly! You know, I got to thinkin' about Barbara after the last time, and Ellen, I just don't know what I would have done if my mama had left instructions to be cremated and poured into a bowling ball! Of course, Mama never bowled. She would never wear multicolored shoes. She could be such a snob at times!" They both laughed, eyes closed, shaking their heads at the thought of Frances's elegant mama wearing bowling shoes.

Ellen read for forty-five minutes, right up to the point when Mr. Hansen handed Barbara a county permit, which allowed her to place Evelyn's ashes in the bowling ball, seal it in a watertight container, and drop it straight to the bottom of Lake Wobegon. Noting the strange request, Mr. Hansen said he wasn't surprised, really. He had come to know Evelyn over the years. She was an original, he said.

"She sure was!" came a loud voice from the parlor. "Oh my good Lord, what a funeral she's going to have!" Ellen and Frances looked at each other in silence. Neither one had ever heard Ruby laugh like that.

"She certainly was unusual, Ruby," Frances said. Joining in her laughter she got up and walked through the pocket doors. "I am so glad you will join us to see just how Evelyn's wild funeral will actually come together."

Sitting up instantly, Ruby covered her pink cheeks with her hands. "Oh, don't count on me, Frances," she said. "I don't know if I'll have the time." Frances said she wouldn't take no for an answer.

"We will make our *Pontoon* reading time fit your schedule," she said. Cupping Ruby's face in her hands, Frances looked at her without blinking. "Ellen and I can easily move into the front parlor and sit by your bed if that suits you. Or you can get on that clever motorized chair and ride it right into my room and sit by the window with me. Either way, you are most definitely going to be part of Evelyn's funeral party."

Ruby felt guilty for the first time in years. Frances had no idea Ruby was about to betray her and Ellen both. They were good women, really nice women.

They honestly care about you, Ruby, and you know it. They trust you, and you will violate that trust tonight by stealing away and abandoning them. They will feel lied to. When they find your empty bed in the morning they will think they have failed you, that you dislike them somehow. Why did she go? they'll ask each other. What did we do to make her feel so horrible about staying with us? Where did we go wrong? What did we do to hurt her? They will feel betrayed.

They would never understand and she would never tell them. She only knew that she was Ruby Bainbridge and she lived on her own, on West Fifth Street, in the house that was home to three generations of Bainbridges. She would never tell Frances and Ellen that she had given up the idea of living in other people's houses when she was eleven years old, on a warm summer afternoon when Phillip had discovered her in his room pretending to be an Altdorfer, pretending to live in their big brown house, talking out loud, telling Papa Altdorfer about her upcoming piano recital where she'd play Tchaikovsky's "Dance of the Sugar Plum Fairy." Mama Altdorfer was asking him to close the store early next Friday so they could all go together at five o'clock, and afterward go on to

Vince's Steak House to celebrate. Papa Altdorfer was thinking about how he could keep the store open Friday night and still get away to the important recital to hear his talented daughter play. Ruby was holding her breath, not even touching her hot crossed bun as she waited to see if Papa Altdorfer could come. It would mean the world to her.

Phillip had come in so quietly that she never heard him sneak up behind her. He put his hand up the back of her light cotton blouse, making her jump. His other hand went over her mouth, not too hard, as he told her to be very quiet. "Don't make a sound."

"Say good-bye to the Altdorfers, Ruby," he whispered. "You and I are going to play house now, and it will be much more fun than sitting around with fat old Mama and Papa Altdorfer."

She wanted to scream, but Phillip wouldn't let go. She tried to wiggle out of his grasp but he was too strong for her, holding her wrists behind her, unbuttoning her blouse. She couldn't get her hands free to stop him. She didn't scream because no one would hear her. Mother was at bridge club and Father was at the office. The bedroom window was open to the summer breeze, as were her neighbors' windows. She would rather die than scream to them for help, putting family business out into the street, as Father would say disparagingly of quarrelsome neighbors.

"I'll tear the blouse off, if I have to, Ruby, so why don't you just cooperate?" Phillip said. He didn't sound like Phillip just then. His voice was soft and seductive, like Tommy Edwards singing 'It's All in the Game.' "I won't hurt you, I promise. You're my sister, cutie-pie. This will be just some fun between the two of us. You'll like it, I promise."

He got her blouse halfway unbuttoned and pulled it up over her head, the buttons hurting her ears, the blouse ripping under the arms, she could hear it. Oh, Mother was going to be upset. It was her best blouse, used for special occasions and church. She had put it on to visit the Altdorfers, never thinking it might get ruined. She couldn't look at Phillip as he turned her around roughly, facing him now in her white training bra. She wanted to slap him until his face was purple, pull his hair out at the roots until he begged her to stop, until he screamed bloody murder.

"Just a peek, Ruby, just a small peek. Like Mr. Altdorfer does with Mrs. Altdorfer when she gets ready for bed. Take off your bra, Ruby, come on. Just a peek. Oh, that's nice." He drew back, pretending his hands were a camera, putting his fingers together to form a viewing lens, moving his hands left and right to look from different angles. "You are growing up nicely, little Ruby. Now, let me take just a touch. Just a small touch. That's right. Stay calm. I won't hurt you. Just a little kiss with my tongue now. It won't hurt at all, Ruby. I'll just lick you a little on the tits. Do you even know they're called tits? Just a little suck on them now, Ruby. Doesn't that feel sweet? C'mon, tell me it feels good. It does to me. Just a little harder now, feel my fingers. Too hard? OK, little sister, I'll be gentler. How's this?"

She froze in his grasp, stiffer still when he laid her down on the floor and pulled down her shorts. She closed her eyes, her hands in hard fists. She was beyond terrified, her back hard against the thin carpet, her legs lifted in the air, her ankles on his shoulders.

"I'll just lick you a little right there and massage it a little, Ruby. Don't worry. I won't go in."

He barely kept that promise, wiggling his finger against her skin. He asked her if she was feeling the pleasure, and should he go inside now? Ruby slammed her legs down hard on his back and ankle-kicked him.

"No, you may not go in," she said, kicking him harder now. "Get out of there! Get away from me! It hurts, Phillip!" He lay down on the floor, rolling away from her a little.

She heard him moving fast, doing something to himself. She wouldn't look. Minutes later he let out a big *ahhhh* sound and moved farther away, giving her room to sit up. She grabbed her blouse and yanked up her shorts, hanging on to the windowsill as she stood up. Phillip was zipping up his pants when he warned Ruby what would happen if she ever told anyone about their time together.

"I'll tell Mother and Father you came to me, my weird out-there sister. I'll tell them you undressed right in front of me, asking me to feel your body. We all know how strange you are with your secret lives through the windows, little dream girl. I'll tell them you said you had read a book about having sex and you wanted me to show you how it's done. That sounds like something you would do, don't you think?"

He was grinning now, enjoying himself. He looked at her like she was an imbecile as she tried to cover up her breasts with her torn blouse. "Keep your big mouth shut because that's what I'll tell them. Don't doubt for a moment that I won't be totally convincing. I'll make sure they believe me. They will, too. They always do."

Her head was pounding as she struggled into the hallway. Ruby knew he was right. She took three deep breaths and tried to calm down, to think. Holding onto the walls, she made her way slowly to her bedroom, shivering now, shaking as she closed the door behind her. In one swift movement she turned the key, locking her bedroom door for the first time in her life. She looked into the delicate oval mirror, laced in thick pink velvet ribbon, over her dresser. Her face was pasty white, like the white-faced pantomimes that performed at her school last year. She didn't look like herself anymore. She started to cry, furious as she examined herself, hating herself for letting this happen.

You are such a jerk, such a baby. Pretending to be an Altdorfer, thinking life could be made up like that. Look where it got you. Look at you! How stupid you are. I never should have gone into his room. I never should have trusted him to be decent. Oh, how I hate you, Phillip. I hate you so much. I want Mother and Father to know what you did. I will scream at them to punish you, to cut off your finger and tear out your disgusting tongue. I will make you pay for this. I will. Oh, you stupid idiot, Ruby. You know you can't! You can't do anything like that. You know it! How could you even look at them and say it? How could you stand the look on Mother's face when you describe it? How could you say such things in front of Father? Even if you could get it out, they'll believe Phillip. They'll think you just went over the edge with your weirdness, with your made-up lives and too many books. They will never think their perfect son could attack his little sister. Not their darling. Not their wonderful, brilliant Phillip. Not in this family. Oh, God, there's no one to tell, you stupid little Ruby girl. Phillip has won, as usual. He always wins. He's the strong one, the winner, and you are just the weakest of the weak, the scrawniest of the scrawny. Damn it all to hell. Hell. Oh, may he burn in hell forever. I will pray for that every day for the rest of my life. Hear me, God! Burn that disgusting animal in hell. I hate him so much.

She pushed her arms through the sleeves of her thick bathrobe and closed the robe tight in front, tying a hard knot so it couldn't possibly fall open. She pulled wildly at her thick socks, yanking them up past her knees.

Face it, little Ruby. You can't do anything to make him pay.

She stomped her feet on the floor, feeling the pain searing into her ankles, her soles taking a beating. She sat down and put her knees together, arms around the top, holding herself tight.

The only thing you can do now is to make sure it never happens again. Think, Ruby. Not ever. Not ever again.

The next day she let Phillip know she had the Swiss Army knife from her Girl Scout camping gear with her. She told him she would carry it with her constantly, even to bed. She had practiced all night long opening and closing the knife quickly, showing Phillip how good she was at it, expertly demonstrating how she could instantly change from the large blade to the scissors, from the scissors to the corkscrew, and from the corkscrew to the fish scaler in three quicksilver moves. She told him she would use it to cut off his tongue and his fingers if he ever touched her again. Phillip saw the look in her eyes.

"I was only kidding, little sister, really. Anyway, you're not that good, to tell you the truth. You're too small and way too flat to get a man get excited. I wouldn't touch you again even if you begged me. Don't come crawling into my bedroom looking for it."

She spit right in his face, hurling the saliva at him in a big ball that landed on the top of his nose. He stood there, shocked, his hand rushing up to his face, the spit sliding down in a slippery dance to his top lip. She turned and walked away holding the Swiss Army knife in her hand, spinning around briefly to flash it at him. Phillip never touched her again.

She had never told anyone that story, and she wasn't about to start now. She had learned to live with that awful memory, and she was all right. The best thing to think about now was her plan for tonight. It was thrilling to know that tonight she would be back in her own house where she could lock the vestibule door, bolt the inside door, and crawl into her own bed.

Tonight she would get back to her little kitchen radio and big band music, to her elegant dancing partner and simple little nourishing meals on a tray table in that cozy alcove with her TV. Tonight she would return to her noisy backyard family of hungry birds and unpredictable, screaming squirrels. Most of all, tonight she would get back to a place where no one could sneak up on her.

She turned away from Frances, saying she needed a little nap now. Closing her eyes, she could hear the voice of Phillip, the tenor voice that taunted her for months after the attack. He'd walk into a room singing it, or come to the dinner table humming it, telling everyone it was his favorite Bing Crosby song, asking Mother to play it on the piano every chance he got.

Oh, you must have been a beau-ti-ful ba-by . . . you must have been won-der-ful child . . . when you were only star-ting to go to kinder-gar-ten, I bet you drove the lit-tle boys wild . . . And when it came to winning blue rib-bons . . . You must have shown the other kids how! I can see the judges' eyes, as they han-ded you the prize . . . you must have made the cutest bow! Oh, you must have been a beau-ti-ful ba-by . . . 'cause ba-by, look at you nowwww!

Mother would giggle with pleasure at her son's playful nature. Father would say, "That's enough, Phillip," but he had a smile on his face when he said it. Ruby would put her fingers around the knife in her pocket.

"Shall I show you all my Swiss Army knife tricks?" she'd ask.

"Now, Ruby. You don't have to one-up your brother, little sister," Mother would say, gently. "It's all right. You have other talents we enjoy. Let your brother sing! He's not hurting anyone."

Twenty-Two

Larry Robinson blew into his hands as he waited for someone to answer the doorbell. With Thanksgiving just a week away, the Oswego winter had begun in earnest and Larry had been awake most of the night listening to the howling winds, wondering if his twenty-two-year-old roof could stand another rough season. He had meant to have a new roof put on last summer, but he'd left it too late, once again. Tomorrow morning he'd see if Jack Rabyson could come out and take a good look at it. Jack had the most successful construction firm in town, and he owed Larry a few favors. If anybody could find some roofers who didn't mind working in the cold, it was Jack.

Shivering in his light topcoat, he reminded himself to dig out his heavy coat this weekend. Next year he'd buy a small condo in Florida and get the hell out of this crazy cold. Shaking now, the wind coming along West Fifth with the meanness of a case of shingles, he peered into one of the side windows around the front door and saw a woman coming from the kitchen wiping her hands, using the front of her apron as a napkin. Maybe this was the caretaker Frances O'Reilly had hired? He stood back and straightened his shoulders, finger-combing his hair into place.

Ellen hadn't seen Larry Robinson since high school. Of course he'd aged, but his tall good looks were still in place, his big brown eyes and dark blond hair, now graying at the temples, topping the athletic body all the girls had wanted to touch. He was still in great shape, a tribute to his wholesome vanity, she suspected. *He looks tired though,* she thought, *and cold,* as she opened the door and motioned him inside.

"Hello, Larry," she said. Smiling, she extended her hand in welcome. "It's so good to see you again after all these years."

"Gosh," he replied. He stepped into the front hall and looked quizzically at Ellen. "I feel as if I know you. But honestly? I couldn't say how. I feel awful about that. Can you help me out, please?"

"Of course, Larry. We knew each other in high school. I'm Ellen Varner. Does that ring a bell?"

"Ellen? Is that you, Ellen? Well, of course it is! How wonderful you look. Gosh, it's great to see you! Heck, it's been thirty-five years and you still look terrific. You know, now that I think of it, someone told me that you were back in town a while ago! I guess it just didn't register. Are you back in Oswego for good, or just visiting? What are you doing here today? Are you working for Frances now?"

Ellen explained she had moved back to Oswego after her long marriage had collapsed.

"I bought the little house next door. The old Elliot place."

Larry's mind finally kicked into gear. Next door. Across the street from Ruby's home. This was the owner of the dog who attacked Ruby. This was the "Ellen with the dog" Ruby talks about. What the heck was she doing in this house?

"Frances and I became friendly as next-door neighbors. I had committed to caring for Frances after her stroke, and when Ruby became incapacitated, Frances and I wanted to help. It made sense to have them both here in one place. I've been with them now for more than a month. It seems to be working out just fine. Does that bring you up to date?"

Larry said, "Yes, thanks, it does." Then he paused, pushed back his shoulders and looked at her squarely.

"You know I represent Ruby in the negligence case."

"Yes, Larry, I am fully aware of that. I have received your letters. Would you like to talk with Ruby now? I can shut the parlor doors. That will give you plenty of privacy. I'll be busy in the back of the house, in the kitchen."

"That would be fine, if you're sure it's not a problem for you," he said.

Ellen looked at him carefully, just as he had been doing to her. Not a shred of trust interfered with their concentration.

"It's not a problem. I was just getting a loin of pork and a bread pudding ready for the oven," she said. "Ruby has regained her appetite, and Frances and I aren't far behind. Just ask Ruby to ring the bell when you're ready to leave and I'll see you out."

Larry took a breath. A pork roast and bread pudding. It had been years since he'd had a really good home-cooked meal. He had gone home every year for his mom's Thanksgiving turkey and Christmas roast beef, but she had died eleven years ago. Since then the closest he had come to Mom's cooking was when Sally O'Mara invited him to dinner on St. Patrick's Day. She had filled his plate with slices of pretty good corned beef, but then ruined it with overcooked cabbage and watery boiled potatoes. Women didn't seem to feel they needed to cook these days, much less cook well, he had decided. Take out or eat out was the new rule. He envied Frances and Ruby if Ellen could get a pork roast right, not to mention the bread pudding.

Opening the door to the parlor, Ellen stepped aside to let Larry pass. "You've got company," she told Ruby.

"Well, hel-lo, Ruby," Larry said his voice booming, his long legs striding confidently into the parlor. Ellen thought he must think Ruby's injuries affected her hearing.

"How are you, my brave friend?" he bellowed.

Ruby stiffened at the sight of him. *How interesting*, Ellen thought.

"I am getting along just fine," Ruby said. She poised herself on the hospital bed as if it were a chaise, arching her eyebrows like Joan Crawford in *The Bride Wore Red*, her eyes hard and cold. "What brings you here today, Larry? Before you begin, I must ask you to be brief because I have an appointment I cannot miss at 12:30. I don't have much time."

Ellen nearly gasped as she closed the door and stepped back into the hallway. "Appointment I can't miss," Ellen repeated to herself. "You wily coyote. Your only appointment at 12:30 is with Jack Abbott and Victor Newman and their wild and nefarious soap opera families on *The Young and the Restless*. Ruby, Ruby. You are priceless."

Hanging up Larry's light coat in the hall closet, she wondered if it was heavy enough for him in this thirty-degree weather. *Men have such trouble with the change of seasons when they have no woman to switch out their closets for them.*

Frances had told her Larry's wife left him years ago.

"Not everyone can adjust to Oswego," Frances explained about Larry's wife, Julia. "She was a beautiful girl from a prominent family in Dobbs Ferry, down in Westchester County, and Larry was absolutely mad about her. He met her in New York City when he was in law school at Fordham." Frances stood up, crossing the room to look at the oil painting over the fireplace. It was the formal portrait Alan had commissioned to commemorate her fortieth birthday—"While you've still got your looks," he joked.

"Larry and Julia had a heavenly wedding downstate," Frances continued. "After a trip to all the major art galleries in Europe, they moved to Oswego and Julia turned that handsome house on the corner of West Fifth and Bridge, the old Flanagan place, into a showcase." A look of sheer delight softened Frances's face as she remembered Julia's sophistication.

"She gave beautiful parties. People came from out of town for weekends, but Julia used to say she didn't know what to do with them. 'Where can I take them around here, Frances? The Stands?' As it happened, everyone seemed to think lakeside dining with those spectacular Texas Hots from The Stands was the highlight of their visit! But in the end Oswego just wasn't enough for her. She left Larry to live in Manhattan after eight years of marriage.

"She is such a talented artist," Frances said. "We used to have coffee together every week. She was a darlin'." The last she had heard, Julia had a studio in Soho and a strong following for her work. "I think she's workin' with fabrics now. She did send me an invitation to her weddin' about ten years ago. I saw the write up in the Sunday *Times*. She was back in her element with a life she knew how to live. That's the way things generally work out, don't you think?"

Ellen didn't feel qualified to comment on anyone's element, actually, considering the mess she had made of her life. But she certainly could sympathize with Julia.

When she saw Ellen hesitate, Frances decided to try another tactic to get Ellen to open up.

"Do you think you'll be able to find what you need in Oswego at this point, dear?" she said. "I don't mean to pry, but I do wonder sometimes if you are findin' your way, getting what you need, now that you're back."

"I'm not sure I know what I need, Frances," Ellen said. "If you ask me today if I can be happy in Oswego, I might say yes. But if you ask me tomorrow, I might say no, *never*, not ever."

"I am so sorry, dear. Truly, I am. I know just what you mean."

Chopping fresh rosemary and sliding it to the side of the cutting board, Ellen picked up the pork loin and rolled it in olive oil. To add flavor she pierced the fat on top in a dozen places and wedged slivers of fresh garlic into the shallow cuts. She seasoned it with salt and pepper then patted the fragrant rosemary all over the outside, drizzling it lightly again with oil as she set it on the rack in the roasting pan. The ladies liked to have their dinner meal around two o'clock these days, with a small supper of leftovers or a light soup around six. That worked fine for Ellen since it allowed her to run errands in the morning or late afternoon and settle down early in the evening, which she suspected was a concession the ladies had discussed and agreed to make for Ellen's sake.

She slid the roast into the oven and reached for the bowl of stale bread and rolls she had torn into bite-sized pieces yesterday, leaving them to dry out overnight, intending to make breadcrumbs out of them. They worked perfectly for the bread pudding instead. She mixed eggs, sugar, melted butter, cream, raisins, cinnamon, salt, vanilla, and pecans together and poured the mixture over the bread. She buttered the baking dish and poured in the pudding, covered it, and put it in the fridge. Later it would bake for forty-five minutes, with brown sugar on top, when the roast was nearly done. She had a nice bottle of maple crème for the light drizzle when it was served warm for dessert, with a dribble of half-and-half. Unfortunately for Frances, the pudding would be too rich. She'd have fat-free vanilla frozen yogurt with a handful of red raspberries for her dessert, and as always, Frances would say it was exactly what she wanted.

Henry scratched at the kitchen door just in time for his meal, which he ate around noon each day. She flipped the top on a can of Alpo beef chunks and spooned it into his bowl, mixing a teaspoon of Sunflower oil in to help with his dry coat. She grabbed a bag of frozen peas and put a cup of them into the microwave to defrost. Some days she gave him finely chopped carrots or green beans, but today he would get his favorite peas mixed in. She scooped out one level cup of organic dry food and sprinkled it around the meat, then broke a Milk Bone in half, putting the pieces along the sides of the bowl. He liked to crunch on that after the meal. Ellen liked to think he was brushing his teeth after eating. She let him inside and asked him to stay as she set his bowl down. Henry waited until she said *mange* before attacking his meal.

Looking at her watch, she wondered if Ruby realized the time. In just fifteen minutes the drama would pick up where it had left off yesterday. Ellen completely understood Ruby's addiction to the soap. She had been similarly addicted for many years when her boys were growing up. They'd have their lunch around eleven thirty and go down for their naps when they were infants and toddlers, and Ellen would curl up in her favorite chair and watch Katherine Chancellor, Nikki Newman, John Abbott, and their assorted husbands and wives create havoc in each other's lives. It was addictive and comforting to have that crew of characters in her life every day. Thanks to her VCR, it was the family that stayed with her wherever she went. She suspected it was like that for Ruby, too.

She took off her apron just as she heard the summoning bell ring sharply, with an urgency she had come to recognize. She walked quickly down the hallway, knocked, and went into the parlor. Henry trailed behind her, trotting over to Ruby and jumping up on the side of the bed so Ruby could look into his eyes and pet his head. The other day Ellen had been shocked to walk in the room and find Henry all the way up on Ruby's bed, soaking up the extra attention as his head lay in her lap, his tail wagging in three-quarter time. Seeing Ellen, Ruby had gasped, the look on her face like that of a child caught taking her mother's best perfume. She had unceremoniously pushed him off the bed, much to Henry's surprise, telling him he was a very bad dog indeed.

"Are you ready to wrap things up?" Ellen asked.

Raising a hand to his forehead, his fingers curling over one eyebrow shielding his right eye like a visor, Larry looked pained. "Ruby?" he said. "Is that your dog?"

Ruby sat up tall, obviously frustrated herself.

"Why, no, Larry, for heaven's sake. I don't own a dog. This is Ellen's dog. Henry."

"The one that knocked you down the porch?"

"Well, yes, of course. But as I've told you so many times, I think it was only reasonable that he jumped on me. I had that big smelly lamb bone in my hand at the time. As you can see here, he's not a bad dog, just frisky." She nudged his paws down off the bed.

"Has this dog been living with you these last few weeks?"

"Certainly, Larry. Wherever Ellen goes this dog goes. Everybody in our neighborhood knows that."

"Could you give us just another minute, please, Ellen?" he asked.

"Absolutely, Larry. C'mon, Henry, let's go see Frances!"

She closed the pocket doors tightly behind them as Frances broke into a wide smile. Ellen put her finger to her lips, then threw up her hands to let Frances know she had no idea how things would go.

"Now, Ruby. Am I to understand that you actually get along with this dog now?"

"As I said, Larry, he is not a bad dog, as it turns out. Grabbing that lamb bone was what any dog would do under the circumstances. Don't you agree? I'm afraid a judge and jury will think so."

Larry stared at her for a moment. He had lost her, if he ever had her, and he knew it.

"Shall I withdraw your lawsuit, Ruby?"

Ruby looked left to right, fussing with the comforter, wanting this to be over so she could see if Nikki had fallen off the wagon again. It seemed like every time the plot got stuck, the writers made Nikki change from a fully-in-recovery alcoholic to a sad, desperate dry-drunk who walked right into bars to stare like crazy at liquor bottles. It was nuts, but she still wanted to know if Nikki was going to take that first drink today or not.

"Oh, Larry, I am so sorry. Really I am. It's just that I never felt right about suing Ellen because of what her dog did, and I've told you that a dozen times. She never asked me to come visit, much less with a lamb bone in my hand. At this point, well, how could I sue her, in all good conscience? Ellen has been so good to me and honestly, I don't think it had anything to do with the lawsuit."

"What about your out-of-pocket expenses and the damage to your home as a result of the fire, Ruby? Don't you think you should at least recover those monies? You must need $50,000 or more for all of that."

"Actually, Larry, I am able to absorb any costs involved," Ruby said. "Mother and Father left me in good shape. I can take care of myself easily for the rest of my life without worrying. In answer to your question: *yes*. Please get busy and drop the lawsuit. Furthermore, don't hesitate to send me a bill. I fully expect you to charge me for the time you have invested in my case to date. Will you do that today?"

Larry said he would. "However, legally, you don't have to pay me anything, Ruby. I took this case on a contingency basis. I didn't expect to be paid unless you won in court."

"Oh, horse-puckey to that, Larry. Go on and bill me for the time you've put in. It's only fair. I am called a lot of things, as we all are, but hopefully no one will ever be able to say I was not fair with people. Go on now and make up your bill. Just be sure it's reasonable. I can still add and subtract like my father."

She rang the bell firmly. "Ellen, would you please show Larry out? He's got a lawsuit to withdraw, and a bill to prepare."

Ellen walked over and handed Ruby the remote control. "She hasn't taken a drink yet. But she's about to, I think." Ruby pushed the power hard enough to turn her thumb white.

Twenty-Three

Ellen heard the dishwasher kick into gear. *The kitchen is now officially closed,* it said, and she was grateful. It was only five thirty and the whole evening stretched before her. She was tired and happy to have the rest of the night to herself. She needed time to sit with her thoughts, which seemed to be shifting gears these days. Change was coming, she could feel it.

She grabbed the broom from the mudroom and swept the leaves off the back porch, carefully moving down the steps, clearing out each step so neither she nor Frances would slip and fall. The backyard was one broad carpet of leaves, the vibrant red and gold hues tossed together in thick piles around the edges of Frances's garden. She'd have to see if Mario Simonson would come back this week and rake as well as cut the grass. She just hoped she hadn't left it too late. Mario seemed to be the only teenager willing to rake leaves anymore; he was probably booked solid by now. That meant she'd have to get a landscape service to do it. *I'll have to check with Frances to see how much she usually pays for this kind of work.*

She stopped sweeping to take pleasure in the late afternoon chill, a lake county girl through and through, a lover of the cold weather. She edged up to the fence, stepping over the last of the marigolds and oregano, to take a look at her own back garden. She'd have to get those leaves raked, too. Sadly, it wouldn't be such a hard job this year. The old maple tree, which had been the main leaf thrower for decades, was now a pathetic-looking stump. Its gnarly roots were still clearly visible under the hard-packed dirt, running along the fence and out into the yard. The black chokeberry bushes were taking greater control of the fence line already, moving into the sunshine, branching out into the once-shady space of the overhanging tree branches, seizing the opportunity to grow.

She breathed deeply, enjoying the musky smell of autumn. It was her favorite time of year. As a teenager she had looked forward to the fall with its promise of a fresh start, the back to school feeling of anything being possible with new things to try, new responsibilities to take on, more and more privileges to enjoy each year. Those years had been heady times of testing ideas and pushing limits, despite the warnings from adults. Now she embraced the season for its guarantee that things would settle down. In the winter days ahead, Oswego would become a culture of TV and movie watchers, book readers, quilt makers, and ice skaters.

We'll tuck in and enjoy good music by the fire, and eat cream of wheat for breakfast and hearty vegetable soups for lunch with oyster crackers floating on top, and have steaming hot cups of chocolate for a treat in the afternoon. We'll bundle up against the frigid early morning to go out and warm up cars in the driveway for five or six minutes, even though the car dealer said it isn't necessary anymore.

She thought about how they'd all prepare for the holidays, decorating and cooking roasts and pies, side dishes of thick mashed Buttercup squash with real butter and cream, moist turkey dressing, celery stalks, and good black and green olives on the table. They'd even put out gravy boats at Thanksgiving and Christmas and let the cholesterol counts soar for a day or two. *Hardy lake dwellers don't know of any real substitute for rich homemade gravy on mashed potatoes and dressing. We'll roll the dice and see if it clogs our arteries or not.*

She rubbed her shoulders, chilled by her inactivity, the broom leaning against her chest. She enjoyed thinking about it all. More than that, she was happily surprised that she had included herself in the "we."

Moving down along the garden beds, she scooped up the assorted piles of weeds she had created and called to Henry. He came charging at top speed from the side garden where he liked to pose for Frances, who responded by knocking on the window at him. She never failed to give him a big wave, calling out his name with praise. He seemed to adore the big fuss she made. What a ham. Ellen sat down on the back porch steps to watch the twilight coming on, the grayness slowly darkening, the air damp and cold.

"I have to tell you something, Henry," she said when he sat down next to her, his chin on her leg. "After all these months of dragging around, I think I am ready for some change. What change, you ask? Well, no more staying up all night reading books about other people's lives, then sleeping all morning, for one. No more hiding out in our house and avoiding people. I'll have to eat real food again. That's important. I have a whole list of things I need to do. The main thing is, I think it's time I got my act together, don't you?" He just looked at her.

"What was it the Anne Tyler character said in *Ladder of Years*? I like a fresh start, or something close to that. Know what, Henry? I've come to realize that I feel the same way. I know we're supposed to stay committed to everything and everyone forever, but I like change. So there it is. Your best pal likes a clean slate. It feels good to be able to say it and be OK with it."

On one level she knew Ruby's decision to drop the lawsuit was part of her fresh start. When Ruby told Larry to prepare his final bill, she had wanted to shout *yes* at the top of her lungs. She realized now that the lawsuit threat had terrified her all these weeks, adding to her emotional limbo. She'd have to let her insurance agent know what was happening. He would be delighted to hear the news. A couple of weeks ago he had told her she was covered for the rebuilding of her garage. The flip side was, she wasn't covered for the tree work, which came to $3,400. Since the garage was a $16,000 repair, she'd happily pay the tree bill and be done with it. Her agent wasn't happy, however.

"No offense, Miss Varner, but I have to say again that you're probably going to lose that dogsuit, big time. I hate to think of what they might award Miss Bainbridge with all that she's been through. I'm not looking forward to this." She'd call him later tonight.

Another real surprise was in finding her appetite again, after nearly a year without one. It was a slow change, with only a half-dozen bites of food possible in a meal, but she was encouraged. She had stopped dropping weight, and her hair showed signs of coming to life again. *Who knows? I may just be in full-press divorce recovery after all.*

"Let's go, buddy," she said. Leading Henry to the garage, she reached for the garbage can to wheel it out to the curb for pick up in the morning. With the large heavy-duty plastic container trailing behind her, she stopped at the end of the driveway. Across the street was the old Scanlon house, the original white façade now painted a lovely taupe-gray by the new owners, with fresh black shutters, creamy-white trim, and a black front door. She had admired the house as a child, but found the friendliness of Mr. and Mrs. Scanlon a little terrifying. They loved to invite her inside the big, dark house for cookies and pop. The only time she accepted, they told her they would give anything to have a little girl just like her, a little girl to live in their house and play the piano and dance in the playroom off the upstairs bedrooms.

"Wouldn't you like to live here?" they said. "What if we never let you go? Aw, go on, don't cry! We were just kidding!"

While she knew they weren't about to kidnap her, she got out of there as fast as she could. They were just plain spooky. From then on she tried to find an excuse every time Mrs. Scanlon called to her. "Come and sit with me on the porch a minute, Ellen, honey. I just made cookies." Ellen adored those buttery, powdered-sugar wedding cookies, so she went as far as the porch steps a couple of times before she avoided Mrs. Scanlon completely, walking on the other side of West Fifth on her way home from school, pretending not to hear Mrs. Scanlon calling her, even though her stomach was rumbling. The cookies were not worth the weirdness.

Such funny memories. Oswego childhood, you called me back. I answered. What's next?

She squared off the garbage can with the road and hurried back up the driveway. The sun was sinking, giving way to the dangerous time of twilight and darkness. Henry sat very still waiting anxiously as she grabbed his leash, put two pooper-scooper bags into her jeans pocket along with a Heath Bar, just in case, and turned to hook him up. He whined, pulling her toward the door. He was as ready for a walk as she was.

The sun gone now, the bitter cold pinched Ellen's bare ears as they stepped out onto the back porch. The temperature gauge screwed on the wall by the kitchen window read twenty-eight degrees. Standing up the collar on her pea coat and tying a wool scarf around her neck, she thought warmly about the mild, sunny fall season in Nashville. It was her favorite time of year there, the sweet vibrant days lingering from September right up until Christmas when rain was likely to greet Santa on his sleigh, not snow. Clean slate notwithstanding, she felt a hard sadness for what she had left behind.

No looking back. Fresh start.

As they crossed the street to walk under the streetlights, Henry pulled and tugged, sniffing into the hedges in front of Ruby's house. It was too late for moles or baby rabbits to be hiding there. Probably just another dog had left his calling card, which grabbed Henry's interest. She liked to think that all his determined sniffing was tantamount to his reading a daily newspaper, discovering what had gone on while he was away, finding out who had visited his neighborhood, and what they'd been up to in his absence. She smiled to see him get his nose right into the dirt, digging like a pig for truffles.

Ruby's house was in darkness. The front porch light had burned out several days ago. She'd have to get over there in the next day or two to replace it because Ruby gave every sign of being ready to get back home just as soon as the doctor gave the green light. Ellen didn't want her trying to climb a ladder to change the bulb, that's for sure. She noticed that the light on the back porch was still working, illuminating parts of the side and backyard at least.

Ellen hadn't seen many home security signs in the front lawns along West Fifth, and that surprised her a little. She had grown used to seeing them sprout up like lawn art in Nashville, even though Nashville's crime rate was relatively low. She suspected the age of dual-working couples leaving homes empty all day was the reason for a thriving home security business in Nashville, particularly in the high-end suburbs. Fortunately, Oswego also had a relatively low crime rate. Homicides were rare, although burglaries by young people desperate for drug money were becoming more common. Reading a story in the paper last week, Frances had been appalled at a home invasion two blocks over, down on Third Street.

"I know we can't leave our screen doors and front doors unlocked at night anymore," she said, "but to think that someone would burst into a house at two o'clock in the afternoon, right in broad daylight! The paper says that two young men in stocking masks walked into the living room and put a knife to Millie Hasbrouck's throat, telling her she'd better give them all her cash, or they'd slit her throat. *Imagine!* A knife at her throat, of all things! Right in broad daylight."

Ellen agreed that crimes were bolder, even harsher today. In her heart, she didn't think she could ever feel unsafe in Oswego. There was something about her history here, her childhood of knowing everyone, the strong linkage among families and neighborhoods that gave her the courage to believe it was a safe haven, a place where windows still could be left wide open at night without harm coming to sound sleepers. Despite this confidence, twilight time always made her edgy. She knew enough to keep her wits about her when she walked with Henry after dark. She was nearly to the end of the long block when he stopped short, his ears pushed forward to listen, his eyes intent on something in the Walpoles' front yard just ahead. A low, gravelly growl churned in his throat.

"What is it, buddy?" she whispered, a shiver shooting up her neck.

Peering over the tall privet hedge, she heard their voices before she saw the two boys on the front porch. They looked like teenagers, one a couple of years older than the other. They were shouting now, pushing against each other, back and forth, until the older boy threw a punch at the younger one, hard in the face, blood spewing out instantly as the younger boy stumbled against the porch railing, grabbing it for support, staying on his feet, touching his nose, wiping blood away with his bare hand.

"You son of a bitch. I'm bleeding, you motherfucker," he said. The older boy charged at him again, fist raised, punching him quickly, knocking him down. Ellen recognized the aggressor. It was the grass cutter, the lawn boy, Mario Simonson. The sound of the young boy's screams reached the street.

Ellen yanked Henry around. Bending down behind the hedge, she started to inch back down the street. She could hear the boys fighting still, hating each other with four letter words, throwing punches as they both tumbled down the front steps. She crept along, pulling Henry behind, frightened to be this close to the violence. Fistfights terrified her. She had stumbled on one like this when she was ten years old. The terror was imprinted deeply.

It had happened on a normal snowy afternoon, the school day over, with the light just beginning to fade in the late afternoon. Ellen was feeling good, having just finished her homework and an hour of piano practice, when Aunt Eleanor called her into the kitchen. She gave Ellen a dollar and asked her to walk down to Schneider's Market and buy a pound and a half of ground round. Ellen was happy to do it. The ground round meant it would be savory meatloaf tonight, one of her favorite dishes. Besides, she had run this particular errand many times before. It would be fun to get outside.

"I've already called in the order. Mr. Schneider is expecting you," Aunt Eleanor said. "When you get there, be sure to tell him it's a pound and a half I want, no more and no less. You may keep the change for a stick or two of licorice. But no chocolate. That goes without saying, doesn't it? Now don't you eat the licorice until after dinner. I don't want you to spoil your appetite. Go straight to Schneider's and come right back home. It's going to be dark soon."

When Ellen left the house it was still light enough that she felt safe to take a shortcut rather than stay on West Fifth to Bridge Street, then down to Eighth Street where Schneider's store sat on the corner. She was humming to herself, the notes of "Fur Elise" still in her fingers as she cut through the Mackins' backyard, then through the Jensens', bringing her right over to Seventh Street. Head down, her mind full of arpeggios and the interpretative nuances Miss Eddy had told her to practice, she wasn't paying attention as she headed to Bridge Street. She heard the angry voices first. Wary, not knowing exactly where the voices were coming from, she slowed down.

It startled her to see bright red blood sitting in puddles in the snow, like the pools of rare roast beef drippings her Uncle Samuel liked to sop up with white bread. Blood-gravy bread, he called it. Specks of red spattered the gray snow, as if someone had sneezed blood, bits and spurts of it uneven, splashing down to the sidewalk. She felt queasy, sensing that she was walking into something dangerous. The loud voices came closer, but her legs wouldn't move. Nothing could give her cover; the trees and bushes were bare.

Just then, Joey Serentino and Sammy Cordova came wrestling each other around the corner, pushing and shoving, shouting about knocking each other's teeth out, falling down in the street just near the bus stop bench. They were only six feet away from her now. Joey Serentino struggled to his knees holding his mouth, blood oozing out, as the street light came on. Ellen was stunned as she watched him trying to catch the blood with his bare hands. Sammy looked right at Ellen just before he turned and kicked Joey hard in the head. Joey fell over in the snow bank, moaning, his ear bleeding now, blood all over the place.

Sammy slid onto the bus bench, exhausted, and looked straight at Ellen one more time. He never said a word, but for weeks afterward, Ellen lived in terror as she waited for Sammy to come and get her. She was the witness, the little girl who could get him in trouble. But he never came. In time Ellen understood that Sammy didn't have a clue about who she was, or where she lived. He was a teenager and she was ten. They were worlds apart. She had had bad dreams about that fight for years. The loud sounds of an argument and the sight of blood terrified her to this day.

The shouts from the Walpole front porch seemed to have peaked. Easing around the tree to take a look, Ellen knew it was time to make a move. Henry couldn't stay put much longer. He started to bark. *Oh, no. What if they saw her? What if Mario recognized her?* Shushing Henry, she wondered why none of the neighbors, or someone inside the Walpole house hadn't come out to stop this? Surely they could hear as well as she could? *Oh, damn it all to next Tuesday.* It was up to her. She pulled out her cell phone and started to dial.

Just as she was hitting 911, she heard the police siren wailing down West Fifth, the car's blue and red lights flashing. She straightened up to see a police officer pull into the Walpoles' driveway.

He grunted as he propelled himself out of the car, jogging across the front lawn, yelling at the older boy, "Get your hands off of him; get the hell off of him right now. I mean it, Mario, stop it now or I'll have to taser you." The officer struggled to untangle them, but the boys were too engaged, too wrapped up with each other, legs twisted together, hands and arms flailing in the air, the younger boy screaming with each punch, the older boy snorting and wheezing as he pummeled him over and over.

"I am gonna tell you one more time, Mario. Get off your brother right now! All right, it's your choice! Here it comes."

Ellen watched intently as the officer aimed the taser gun at the older boy just as he looked up. She'd never seen one used before, except on TV. The officer shouted once more for him to get off his brother, but the boy didn't move. The laser beam must have hit him in the right place because the boy yelped and fell over instantly, like a half-cooked soufflé. The officer sprinted over and pushed him on his stomach, handcuffing him easily.

Ellen couldn't tell if the younger boy was moving. How in the world does this kind of thing happen on West Fifth? Right here in little Oswego, New York, for Pete's sake. Hot bile bubbled up into her throat and she spit it out, coughing. Henry pulled at the leash, wanting to go back to the scene, the smell of blood and tissue begging him to go and have a good look around. She wasn't having any of that.

"Move it, Henry, *right now.*" Startled by her aggressiveness, he put his ears down, his tail between his legs, and moved steadily alongside her. She picked up speed, wanting nothing more than to get home and disappear into that upstairs bedroom where she could hole up in peace. As they passed familiar houses, lights coming on all along the block, she realized she had been holding her breath. She let it out in one big *whoosh*. Her chest felt as if someone had put a match to it. A wad of poker-hot bile rocketed into her mouth and she leaned over and hurled it out, bathing the exposed roots of Ina Schmidt's horse chestnut tree in vomit.

What a mess. What a horrible, big, fat, sour-milk mess.

Moving like a rusty old wagon behind Henry, Ellen knew it would be days before the images of that scene would fade and weeks before she could close her eyes at night and not see that young boy and his brother tearing each other apart, young bones snapping to pieces, terrible things being said, old memories melding into new terrors. Two boys settling things with their fists, just like before.

At least I know these boys didn't see me. They have no idea who I am. I can put that fear away. I will not let this get to me. I am a grown woman who knows those boys can't hurt me. What was that? The wind was picking up. It was nothing. Get a grip.

She took the porch steps two at a time, eager to get into the house, out of the dark.

Twenty-Four

Ruby heard Ellen come in the front door. That was strange. Ellen always took Henry through the kitchen door so that she could hang up his leash and her coat in the mudroom.

"You all right?" she called out.

"Yes, Ruby, I'm all right," Ellen said. "Just give me a minute and I'll come in and see you, OK?"

Frances got up to see what was happening. Like Ruby, she recognized something was amiss for Ellen to come through the front door. She walked gingerly back to the kitchen to investigate. She found Ellen hunched over the kitchen sink, either hiccupping or retching, she couldn't tell which exactly.

"Is something wrong, dear? Why, you're shaking! What's happened to you?"

Ellen wiped her mouth with the back of her hand and straightened up. She turned to look at Frances, the lovely, kind, sweet Frances who now lived five doors down from a violence so raw it made her heart want to split open.

"Oh, Frances, it was horrible. Ugly and horrible. I was walking Henry when I heard voices, angry voices, and then two boys, teenagers I'm guessing, got into the most brutal fight on the Walpoles' front porch. They were shoving and punching each other until they both fell down the porch steps. Terrific screams came out of the younger boy. There was blood everywhere. Then I realized it was Mario who was the aggressor. *Our* Mario, the boy who does our yard work. He was brutal. Then the policeman came and used a taser on Mario to make him stop. I couldn't stop watching. I was terrified. Then we snuck away. I was so afraid. I threw up all over Ina Schmidt's tree."

Frances hugged her, lightly squeezing Ellen's limp arms.

"What a ghastly experience for you to endure, my darlin' Ellen. I surely do wish you'd never even had a glimpse of such an awful scene. But you're home now, and safe. It can't follow you here."

Ellen lifted her head, her swollen eyes barely open. She squinted at Frances, trying to focus.

"Follow me here? But of course it's followed me here. Don't you see? It's inside me now, Frances. It always will be."

Frances didn't reply. Instead, she put her arm around Ellen and guided her to the back stairs, telling her she'd be up in a few minutes to help her with a good hot bath. Ellen looked like a frightened child as she let go of Frances's hand.

"You will come up, for sure?" she asked.

"Yes, dear, of course. I just want to speak one little minute with Ruby, to let her know what's happened. She'll be wantin' to know you're all right. Go on upstairs now. I'll be along shortly. You just draw the water for a nice hot bubble bath, and I'll come along in just a bit."

While Ellen and Henry headed upstairs, Ruby listened to Frances intently. She was shocked by the news.

"Well, for one thing, it's not the Walpole house anymore," she said. "But I know the one Ellen means. The Walpoles retired to Florida three years ago and sold the house to Tony Russo. He turned it over to his daughter, Angelina. She lives there with her two sons, Angelo and Mario. They seem like nice kids. Something must have gotten into them to fight like that. I wonder if Angelina was home. She must not have been, or she would have put a stop to it."

Ruby told Frances that Mario, the elder brother, was just out of high school. He had delivered groceries for Garafolo's last winter.

"He is always polite, always well spoken. In fact, I had him come in for a cup of coffee several times on his run. I offered him hot cocoa but Mario said he didn't drink 'that baby stuff.' Black coffee was what he wanted." Ruby said Mario's brother was probably a couple of years younger.

"I remember when Jack Simonson married their mother. Angelina was an Italian beauty with her black hair and shapely figure. A big smile on her dimpled cheeks all the time. A very nice girl, too, everyone said. Jack was the catch of the season with his blond hair, blue eyes, and six feet of charm. He had the most beautiful strong white teeth." Stretching to take a look toward the Walpole house, Ruby said the marriage had failed.

"It's hard to mix a strong Italian Catholic family like the Russos with a Lutheran Scandinavian like Jack. We all wondered how long it would last," she said, adding, "We hoped for the best, of course."

Within a year of their wedding Angelina gave birth to Mario. A couple of years later, Angelo was born.

"We were quite surprised when Jack upped and moved to Boston three years ago. Angelina's an Oswego girl from start to finish, but Jack wanted to see more of the world, I guess. At least that's the story Angelina told people when their divorce came through."

Frances said she hoped the boys were all right after their awful melee. She started toward the front hallway.

"I am so deeply sorry for Ellen," she said. "What a terrible thing to experience. I need to get up to her now, to help settle her down. You'll be all right, won't you, my dear?"

"I don't like the idea of your going upstairs, Frances. You haven't attempted those stairs in weeks. You don't know what you can and cannot do on that staircase. I think you should let Ellen get herself bathed, then come down here so we can see that she's all right. We don't need you falling."

Frances's shoulders drooped at the mention of falling. "Of all the sweet things to say Ruby. I am so appreciative of your thinkin' of me and my tender state. You are exactly right. I probably have no business climbing those stairs this evenin'. I'll call up to Ellen and let her know. Oh, what a distressing business. I am simply flabbergasted by it all."

Ruby hated the upset the fistfight had caused for Ellen and now Frances. She'd have to find out what prompted Mario to knock his brother around like that. He must have had a good reason. She liked Mario. He was a hard-working kid who got a bad break when his father left. Just when Mario needed him most, she suspected. On the sunny side, she could use this unhappy scene to her advantage. When Ellen was finished bathing, both women would be ready for a nice strong scotch and soda, followed by a good night's sleep. Ruby would happily prepare their nightcap. She'd make the drinks good and strong, adding to her chance for an uninterrupted escape tonight. Tonight was the night.

Rod Stewart, sing me home.

She could hear Frances at the bottom of the staircase calling loudly up to Ellen, explaining it was as far as she could go. Ellen seemed to be all right, lightly shouting back that she was in the bath, and that she'd come down to the parlor when she was finished.

Ruby shifted herself off the bed, a sense of control sliding down her spine. Settling into her scooter chair, she motored over to the bar in the butler's pantry and set up the scotch and soda tray. She drove out to the kitchen and filled the ice bucket, then made three trips from the pantry to the parlor, setting up the drinks table by the fireplace. She felt like Bette Davis on a mission, all strong and in charge. "Fasten your seatbelts, ladies. It's going to be a bum-py night."

This was working out perfectly. *Thank you, Mario.*

Twenty-Five

Ruby lay wide awake listening for the sounds of snoring. It was just before two in the morning, the ideal time to make her escape. The house was coffin-still, the rich mantle of sleep settled over her friends. At least she hoped so. Frances usually fell asleep within thirty minutes, and tonight had been no exception. Ellen was another matter. Since she was upstairs with Henry in the front bedroom, it was difficult to detect snoring, much less heavy breathing. Still, she knew that once Ellen settled down, she would sleep through the night. Ruby decided to go with the history and assume Ellen was deep into a dream state by now.

When the digital clock hit 2:00 a.m. she slid carefully off the bed and, in one turnaround, landed squarely in her scooter chair. Her biggest issue would be getting the chair up and down two sets of porch steps. She had gone over and over the logistics in her mind, devising what she hoped was a doable plan. It had to work. Step by step, she'd make it work.

First of all, she didn't intend to take much with her tonight. Once the ladies realized she was back home, they would bring everything to her. At the foot of her bed she tugged hard, her muscles not as tight as they could be, until she managed to pull off the Hudson

Bay blanket. It was bitterly cold out, and while her good winter coat and hat were in the hall closet, every door opening and closing brought the chance for discovery. This blanket would serve her well; she would keep things simple. Standing up, she bundled herself in it, then plopped down to wrap her left ankle tightly with the Ace bandage. The swelling was nearly gone today, and the extra support felt good as she rolled her wool sock back over it. She stepped her feet into thick lambskin slippers. With their nonskid soles, those slippers were ideal for the trip across the street.

She put two bottles of medicine in the side pocket of her scooter along with her house keys and the latest issue of *Star* magazine. The magazine had been coming to her in the mail every Monday for eighteen years. Normally she couldn't wait to take it to bed just after supper and read it cover to cover. She had been too distracted to read it tonight; it would be a nice reward tomorrow. She reached into the nightstand drawer and took out a white envelope and laid it on the bed pillow. Reaching in again, all the way to the back, she put her fingers around the Swiss Army knife, easing it into the scooter's small inside front key-pocket. She had everything she needed. Now all she wanted was a little luck.

The scooter hummed quietly down the front hallway. She steered it carefully, determined not to bump into the walls. Her escape route would be through the back door, not the front, because she wanted to maximize the distance between her and the ladies. Easing through the kitchen, she faced the first of several hurdles: the three steps down into the mudroom. Stopping the scooter close to the door, she stood up and gripped the doorframe before sitting down quickly on the top step. Her ankle didn't seem to mind the weight she was putting on it. Good things were happening.

She twisted around and brought the scooter behind her and went down the first two steps on her fanny, sliding as lightly as she could. Reaching back, she grabbed the scooter and pulled it toward her with both hands. It bounced down slowly at first, then picked up speed, landing nosily on the mudroom floor. She was sweating in the blanket, the stress and physical exertion already taking its toll, the scooter heavier than she thought, its loud landing capable of giving her away. She sat still to listen for sounds of movement in the house. She heard none.

She took a deep breath and pulled herself up, shuffling over to the back door. Unlocking it carefully, she pulled it toward her all the way, then pushed it halfway to the wall. She opened the storm door and dragged the scooter behind her as she went out onto the back porch, still on her fanny. Six long steps to go down. She pulled the two porch doors closed behind her. She didn't like leaving them unlocked, but it was only a few more hours until daylight. Besides, this was Oswego, for heaven's sake. It was still the safest place on earth, despite the events of the past week.

She went down a step at a time, standing after each one to lift and pull the scooter along behind her, holding it tight. She managed not to fall despite her precarious balance on the narrow steps; she stopped several times to catch her breath. The weatherman had been right for once. The frost was heavy tonight. Within seconds she was shivering. A sharp wind slapped her in the face; another blast lifted her hair, shooting cold air into her ears. She'd have a good old earache tomorrow. She sat herself down in the scooter chair, the blanket around her shoulders. She tented the blanket over her head, tucking it in at her waist, and took a deep breath, relief spreading over her. Step one had been successful.

Keep going, Ruby.

Although she hadn't spent much time in Frances's backyard, the back porch light gave enough illumination for her to find her way around the side of the house and down the driveway. Moving steadily, she noticed the front porch light wasn't on at her house. Oh well, she hadn't intended to go in the front anyway; too much exposure and too many steps. Coming to a dead stop at the end of Frances's driveway, she checked for cars. At this hour West Fifth Street was quiet, not a car in sight. She hoped none of her neighbors was having a sleepless night. She could only imagine what they'd think if they saw her scooting into the road, the blanket over her head, her bulky slippers sitting in the foot carrier, the scooter moving in high gear at a nutty five miles an hour. Thankfully, the little engine managed to jump up over the worn curb of her driveway and push her on her way. She patted the scooter like a much-loved pet.

Chugging up the driveway her heart quickened. *Yes!* The back porch light was on. It was a small light, just an inexpensive forty-watt bulb; it was good enough for the porch. She had no interest in lighting the whole backyard as some of her neighbors did now.

Landscape lighting, my foot. What a waste of perfectly good money.

Ina Schmidt had thrown a special party last summer just to show off her new lights. She said she wanted to create a special backyard ambience. Ina needed a good trip to France; when she saw how those French people treated Americans, she'd be done with her *ambience*. Besides, who wanted to sit outside with lights on all over the place, attracting every mosquito for miles around, every stagnant pond from Minetto to Fruit Valley loaded with larvae in the summer drought? Ina had an answer for that, too. She installed electric mosquito killers so they could all sit and listen while hundreds of bugs sizzled to death. It certainly wasn't Ruby's idea of a fun summer evening.

Moving forward again, Ruby eyed the five steps leading up to the back porch door. She slowed down, hesitating, then stopped. *What was that?* She turned her head, tilting it like a dog listening to a coyote howl, head forward, intent, not moving a hair. Something wasn't right back there. Behind the garage? Turning around, she went to investigate.

The large three-car garage took up half of the backyard space. Father had built it in the 1950s to house his car and Mother's. Additionally, he built a third bay for Phillip to play basketball inside, out of the rain and snow, the backboard and net erected in the center bay, on the rear wall. With Father's car gone each day, there was plenty of space for all three children to play. Mother encouraged it. The garage provided natural light from two sets of six-foot windows Father had ordered for each of the side and back walls. Mother was a great one for fresh air and well ventilated rooms. Those windows provided both for the garage.

After Father and Mother died Ruby had walled off the interior into two large rooms. In one side she stored the summer porch furniture, the lawnmower, brooms and shovels, and assorted boxes and old household items she was saving until she could figure out what to do with them. On the other side she parked her twelve-year-old Oldsmobile, which still looked new. With only 22,549 miles on it, she never intended to buy another car. That Olds could take care of her needs right up until the day she died. She also had thick wooden blinds installed to stop any snooping around by neighbors or kids. The blinds stayed closed all the time, except for spring and fall airings.

She headed the scooter down alongside the garage, moving carefully on the old concrete walkway. A narrow line of soft light from the room at the back of the garage spilled into the yard. *Why was the light on?* Pulling up alongside the second window, she saw it was broken, the bottom half smashed to pieces. The cold wind pushed the wooden blind back and forth, banging it like a drum against the window frame. She stopped and sat very still in the dark, listening for sounds of an intruder. She peeked carefully into the window as the blind lifted and dropped. And then she saw him.

He was sound asleep on the old couch along the back wall of the storage bay, curled up in a fetal position, big basketball sneakers hanging over the edge. He looked young, but she couldn't tell for sure because he was turned away from her, on his side. He must be freezing. She had the urge to yell at him to go and get a blanket from one of the boxes in the other room, the dope. "You broke my big window, for heaven's sake. You may as well break into my linens!"

But she held her tongue, remembering the two violent episodes in the neighborhood this week. She needed to be careful. She gripped the handle of the Swiss Army knife.

How do I handle this? Do I try to take care of him myself, or do I try to get into the house and call the police? I don't think I can get up the back porch steps without making a lot of noise. Chances are he'll wake up and come after me, and I'll be compromised on the steps or in the back porch. I'll be in a position of defending myself, and that's not a good idea. Wait a minute. Why am I on the defensive? What gives him the idea that he can just barge into my garage and take up space? Well, he can't. This is my home, my garage, and I have a right to be safe in them without interference from anyone. I need to get the police over here.

For a moment she regretted not having a cell phone. She had never wanted one, preferring her standard black rotary-dial telephone on the little rosewood shelf next to the Altdorfer grandfather clock in the front hallway, and another one by her bedside. But tonight she wondered, briefly, if she would pay a price for her dislike of all things electronic. Oh, probably not. She was on her own, and she was fine with that.

Taking a deep breath, she shouted at the top of her lungs through the window. "I am calling the police as we speak." He wouldn't know she didn't have a cell phone. "Come out of there right now, or you'll have more trouble than you can think about!"

The boy rolled over slowly and sat up, then jumped up and peered out of the window trying to wake up, trying to see who was out there.

"Who are you?" he said. He was hopping up and down now, flapping his arms to warm up, the wind blowing right through that broken window into his T-shirt. "I didn't do nothing. Please don't call the police. I don't want no trouble. *Please.* I'll get out of here right now. Just don't call the police."

Ruby told him to come out the way he went in, through the window. "Don't give me any trouble or make any quick moves, mister. I am armed and I know how to use it!"

He waved his hands out the window. "I'm coming, I'm coming. Don't shoot!"

He climbed out and Ruby told him to stand still right where he was so that she could get a good look at him. She held up the knife like a gun under the blanket, the cutting blade protracted. He looked at her in disbelief. "What the hell?" he said.

"Oh, my sweet Mother of God, the Father, Son, and Holy Ghost," Ruby said. "Is that you, Mario Simonson? Am I looking at my young friend, Mario, who sat at my kitchen table and drank my coffee and ate my best Archway chocolate cookies all winter long? The young man I gave a personal reference to for community college? Have you broken into my garage as a way of saying *thank you*?"

Mario squinted at her. "Is that you, Miss Bainbridge?" Officer Kavanagh was nowhere in sight. "You look weird in that blanket getup and the motor chair, Miss Bainbridge. But I guess that's you under there." He stood up crossing his arms over his chest and planted his feet solidly. "And no, this is not my way of saying thank you for helping me out. I got into some trouble at home tonight and I can't stay there right now. I knew you were over at Mrs. O'Reilly's for a while. I thought you wouldn't mind if I parked myself in your garage for a night or two, until I could figure out what to do, ya know?"

"No, I don't know. I don't know why you'd think I have any responsibility whatsoever for boarding you at my home, Mario Simonson." She lowered the blanket and closed the knife, keeping it in her hand. "What's more, what makes you think I would want to board a young man who beats up his own brother so violently that the police have to intervene? Yes, I've heard about it already. What in the world was that all about? Your own brother? On West Fifth of all places, Mario."

Mario said it was family business. "My ma don't like us discussing family business."

"Well then I suggest you call your ma and let her know her elder son is homeless tonight, unless she gives you permission to explain yourself." Ruby waited, feeling the cold. Mario paced around, got out his cell phone and punched a button, then put it back in his pants pocket.

"All right, Miss Bainbridge. But you have to promise me you won't tell nobody, if I tell you. I mean it. My ma will kill me if she knows I told ya."

Ruby shifted in her chair, pushing the blanket off her head.

"Let me tell you something, young man," she said. "I have heard stories about people in this town all of my life. If you had any idea how many dark secrets are contained in this gray head of mine, you'd be shocked. That being said, you don't know me well enough to trust me to keep your secret, and I don't know you well enough to be sure you will tell me truth. So there we are. Where do we go from here? Make up your mind, Mario. It's too cold to stay out here testing each other."

Mario turned away. He clenched his fists and furiously shook his head as if he needed to get water out of his ears. Pacing back and forth in small steps, he mumbled to himself, pulling at his hair. Finally he turned to Ruby, raising his hands up then slapping them down hard on his thighs.

"All right, Miss Bainbridge. I guess I have no choice. I'll tell you what happened tonight, but you gotta promise me you won't tell nobody nothing. Promise?"

"I promise you I will not divulge your secrets to anyone, unless they are secrets that will harm you or others, Mario. In other words, I will not break your confidence unless I feel it's the right thing to do. That's as good as you get."

Mario sputtered something, then sat on the ground. Ruby wanted to tell him it was too cold to sit there, but she said nothing. She waited for him to begin.

"Ever since my dad left town I've been the man of the family," he said. "My ma expects me to watch over my brother and keep him on the right road."

"Nothing wrong with that," Ruby nodded. "Go on."

"I've been watching Angelo get close to some pretty bad dudes at school the past few months. I've been asking around to some guys I know, trying to find out if he's doing what I think he was doing. Well, I found out tonight that my instincts were right. A couple of my buddies told me that Angelo and three of his new friends were selling drugs over in East Park this afternoon. Right in the park where the cops check all the time. Right in broad daylight. That's a felony, Miss Bainbridge. It's a trip to the big house. Angelo is sixteen now. The cops don't play with sixteen-year-olds when it comes to selling drugs. How stupid can he be?"

Ruby closed her eyes for a second. This was bad. She had no idea what to tell him. Drugs were everywhere, she knew, but not in her life. She simply had no experience with this kind of thing.

"So you confronted him and beat him up?"

"I didn't mean to beat him up. I meant to shake him up, sure. But he started mouthin' off at me, sayin' stuff about my not being his dad, and how he was his own man now and he could sell drugs all day long if he wanted. Crazy, stupid stuff like that." Mario was mechanically pulling at the grass with his long fingers, jerking it out of the ground so hard that Ruby wanted to tell him, "That won't help. Killing the grass won't help."

"I don't know," he cried. "My mind just snapped, I guess. I started pushing him, like I could push the stupidness right out of him, and it got out of control. He ran out of the house saying he wasn't coming back, and there was nothin' I could do about it. I showed him I could. I know it was wrong to give him such a beating, but like I said, I just seemed to snap."

They sat and looked at each other. Ruby knew she had to be careful how she responded. She thought about Jack Simonson's beautiful teeth and blond hair, his tall good looks, his way with the girls. Mario took after his mother with his dark hair and dimpled smile. He had a sweetness about him that must have come from Angelina. Jack Simonson has a lot to answer for leaving his sons at this crucial time in their lives. She'd have a hard time minding her own business if she ever saw him again.

"Well, Mario, I don't know what to say exactly. I do know that I am very glad you told me, and I understand why you got so upset with your brother. Dealing drugs is a horrible way to live. Prison is worse. I understand why you were so hard on him. I just hope you managed to knock some sense into him. Do you know if he is going to be all right? Physically, I mean."

"Yeah. He's got a hard head. They put him in the hospital for overnight observation, Ma said. He'll have some big shiners, a few stitches, and a headache for awhile, but he'll be OK. I think his wrist is broken, so at least he won't be able to toss around bags of shit for a while. Sorry, Miss Bainbridge, I didn't mean to talk like that in front of ya." Mario said his ma wanted things to cool down before he could come home.

"A time-out, she called it. My brother was talking big about filing charges against me, but Ma said that will never happen. The police said they'll do whatever Ma wants, since this is the first real bad thing I ever done. I've been trying to keep on the straight and narrow. I'm all set to start Onondaga Community College in January, ya know? I hope I didn't blow it."

What lives children face today, Ruby thought. She was profoundly grateful she had grown up in a time when divorce was scandalous news and drugs were for Beatniks.

"I hope so, too, Mario. It sounds as if things will turn out all right. Your ma's support must be a great comfort to you. I am glad you have that. She's certainly right to separate you two for a few days, until tempers can settle down. It makes good sense."

With that, Ruby was finished. "Now I have to tell you that I am bone tired, Mario, and it's nearly three o'clock in the morning. I'm ready to make a deal with you. If you help me get into the house, you can stay in the garage for a couple of days while you figure things out. However, I insist that you call your ma to get her permission. If she approves, then we have a deal."

Mario didn't like the part about calling his ma, but he was in a tough spot. He agreed. Ruby stood up and rolled out of the Hudson Bay blanket and gave it to him.

"Here. Take this to keep warm. There are more blankets and pillows in the boxes marked *linens* on the shelf in the front of the garage. Help yourself. There's no sense in freezing to death."

An hour later Mario was back in the garage and Ruby was in her favorite chair in the kitchen alcove. She had insisted Mario clean up after they each had a bowl of Hormel chili with beans. It was lucky she still had a couple of cans left in the pantry. Mario offered to pick up an order for her tomorrow at Garafolo's, if she wanted, since the kitchen cupboards were bare.

"Don't you keep no food in this house, Miss Bainbridge?" he asked, wiping down the sink. "I mean canned food and nonperishables, ya know? Things my ma calls staples? You ought to, just in case, living alone like you do. I mean, stuff happens."

"When stuff happens, Mario, I manage quite well," she said. "Besides, it isn't good to spend money on just in case. I prefer just in time."

"Whatever, Miss Bainbridge," he said. Grabbing his jacket on his way out the back door, he turned to her. "Maybe you got the right idea, ya know? I mean, my ma says you're rich as Croesus."

Ruby smiled all the way to sleep.

Twenty-Six

Henry was the first to discover Ruby was gone. A creature of habit, he went down to see Ruby first thing in the morning, even before Ellen or Frances woke up. It was the only time of day Ruby would let him jump up on her bed and stay there awhile. Once up, he'd roll over on his side and Ruby would give him a tummy rub for a good ten to fifteen minutes. Then she'd give him the signal and he'd jump down and run back up the stairs to be ready for Ellen. No one knew their secret.

Trotting into the parlor this morning, Henry headed for Ruby's bed and jumped up on the side with both feet, asking permission to come aboard. He sniffed the empty bed, one end to the other, then dropped back down to the floor and went around to the other side. He sniffed some more, particularly where she kept her scooter chair. He went around the parlor and followed her scent halfway down the front hallway before he gave up and went back upstairs.

Ellen turned over as he came into her room. He sat by the bed and whined. She dropped her hand, assuming a morning head pet was what he wanted. But he kept whining until she asked, "What *is it*, Henry?" He went over to the bedroom door and looked back at her, moaning now.

"For the love of eight o'clock mornings, do you have to go out?" she said. It was unusual for him not to be able to hold his water until eight, but occasionally he did drink too much in the night and needed an early out. She got up and put her sweater on, stretching her legs to get them moving. "All right, buddy. I'm up. Let's go."

Henry ran straight into the parlor and sat at the side of Ruby's bed. Ellen was already headed down the front hallway when she realized he was neither ahead of her, nor behind. "Henry? Where are you?"

He barked once. *The parlor?* "Oh, shush, Henry! You'll wake up Ruby, you silly dog. Come on, get out of there now." When he didn't come, she went back to get him. Ellen stared at the made up bed and the white envelope on the pillow. "*Ruby?*" she whispered. "What's happened to you, Ruby? Where are you, you crazy woman?" The motorized chair was gone, too, along with the Hudson Bay blanket.

Ellen picked up the envelope and slid it into her sweater pocket. She had a pretty good idea what it said; she'd wait until later when she and Frances could read it together.

The pocket doors opened and Frances came through. She looked at the empty bed, then at Ellen. "So she's run away from home?" Frances said. "I had an inkling last night that she had a little mischief in mind. She was entirely too insistent with you about that Ace bandage, and about us havin' that second scotch and soda." Frances smiled. "Not that it wasn't pleasant. Now I am thinkin' I should have said something, just to let her know I realized she was fixin' to do something foolish. Well. Here we are." She smoothed the sheet with her hand. "Ah, my darlin' Ruby, what have you done?"

"I imagine we'll find her sleeping in the kitchen across the street," Ellen said. "I just don't know how she could have made it home. How did she manage to get up and down all those steps? My first thought was that she had an accomplice, but that doesn't make any sense. No one ever visited her here in the past six weeks except that priest, and he wouldn't be part of anything like this. What am I not seeing, Frances?"

Frances said Ellen's vision was perfectly fine.

"We are seein' just what Ruby wants us to see, sweetheart. She is letting us know that we have been livin' with a woman who will find her own way home no matter what anybody tells her, no matter how difficult it is."

Frances went to the head of the bed and tenderly picked up Ruby's pillow.

"This is all the Recoup Hotel can expect to keep from a woman whose home is so much a part of her that everywhere else is simply purgatory." She put the pillow down and moved decisively over to the front windows looking for a light in the big house across the street. She didn't see one.

"Come on over here and sit next to me by the bay window, Ellen. We'll keep an eye out for signs of life at Ruby's. If we don't see any in the next hour, you'll have to go on over there to make sure she's all right. Do you agree?"

Ellen said that would be fine, but wondered if she shouldn't go right away. "Don't you think I should at least check to be sure she's not outside in the back or something?"

Frances said she thought Ellen's first instincts were right. "I imagine she is fast asleep in that TV chair in the kitchen. Ina Schmidt gets up at seven every mornin' to feed the birds and squirrels. She checks Ruby's house front and back after she's done with that feeding. If Ruby were facedown anywhere, we would have heard somethin' by now, don't you think?"

Ellen couldn't argue with that. She had seen Ina do her inspection sweep many times. The woman certainly was thorough. "You're right. Let's give Ruby a chance to sleep in a bit after her daring night." She settled into one of the wingback chairs next to Frances. They faced the windows together.

"I still don't understand why Ruby would be so desperate to get home," Ellen began. "She was only a couple of days away from doing it right. If she had been that determined to go sooner, I would have helped her. Why would she risk doing it in the night—and without telling us after all our time together?"

Frances knew why, after nearly fifty years living across the street from Ruby. How could she explain it to Ellen in less than an hour?

"Let me see if I can capture Ruby's essence so you might understand," Frances said. "Surely you've seen *Gone with the Wind*, Ellen?"

"Certainly," Ellen answered.

"Well, it is one of our Ruby's all-time favorite pictures. She has talked to me about it more than a hundred times. Do you wonder which character she loved the most? Well, I know you can guess. Miss Scarlett, of course." Frances looked down West Fifth. She was glad to see the dimmed headlights of the milkman's truck coming along, parking now next to her driveway. She heard his steps around the side of the house, the *clink* of the glass bottle as he set it down on her back step, just outside the kitchen door. She loved it that Byrne Dairy continued the option of home delivery to longtime customers like her, Ruby, and Ina. Frances was down to just a Tuesday delivery now that Alan wasn't sharing the milk, cottage cheese, and sour cream that milkman Johnny brought to her doorstep.

"Anything wrong, Frances?" Ellen asked.

"No, dear, not at all! I was just listenin' to the milkman making his stop. Where was I?" Frances looked at Ellen. "I remember! Miss Scarlett. Well now, to say that Ruby admired Miss Scarlett is somethin' of an understatement. She was overjoyed by the way Miss Scarlett took no guff from Rhett Butler or anyone else. She often talked about the way Scarlett stood her ground in a man's world, doing it her way. She particularly admired the way Scarlett just *adored* her family home and wouldn't let anyone take Tara away from her.

"Now, I know that most northerners think Miss Scarlett was the epitome of the southern belle," Frances continued. "But I tell you this truly, she was *anything* but a true southern belle."

Ellen was interested in hearing how the stereotype was false. "I'm not sure why, Frances. Will you explain it to me? I enjoy unraveling northern–southern misunderstandings!" Frances nodded and looked directly at Ellen.

"First of all, northerners do not comprehend that in the traditional South, a belle is a young woman who is carefully trained to live in the background. She is brought up to be gentle and kind, doing good works for others when she can. A real southern belle would never display a temper like Miss Scarlett did, or try to compete with men and their business."

Ellen had to admit, she had never thought about it this way. She turned to the table next to her and lifted the top of the silver box. She picked out a pale green thin mint. "Go on," she said. "I'm fascinated."

"All right, dear. But you stop me if I'm wearin' you out. Alan used to ask me, 'Will I be *alive* at the end of this story?' I can go on a bit, I'm afraid." Frances put her hands together, interlacing her slim fingers.

"The traditional southern belle is unobtrusive, a woman who loves and supports her husband and takes care of her family life, doing everything she can to create a beautiful, happy home. In *Gone with the Wind* the true southern belle was Miss Melanie Hamilton, the sweet-natured young woman who married Ashley Wilkes. She was all that a real southern lady should be—lovely, peaceful, without guile, and a good Christian soul."

Ellen was quiet for a minute, the mint tasting fresh and sugary as it melted into her tongue. "What you are saying is a revelation to me, Frances. I am just this minute realizing that you are absolutely right. I knew a few of those true southern belles in Nashville. To be honest, I thought they were terrible phonies at first. It seemed to me they were totally passive-aggressive, and I can't stand being around that type of woman. However, over time, I came to understand that those belles were just nicer than I was. Sweeter somehow. No, *genuinely nicer.* I finally came to the conclusion that while I could never be one, I was glad they were around."

Frances leaned over and touched Ellen's arm, giving it a gentle squeeze.

"I am eternally grateful to hear you say that, my dear," she said. "It is comfortin' to know I have at least one human being in this town who understands the southern psyche, and moreover, one who can appreciate it. I have spent the last forty-eight years subduing mine, and sometimes I wonder what my life would have been like if I had stayed in the South, among my own people."

Ellen concluded that the moral of the story was that Ruby was a renegade, like Scarlett, not a well-bred dutiful lady, like Melanie. Ruby would defy convention and do exactly as she pleased, fighting for what was hers until the end. It made sense.

Satisfied, Ellen turned her attention to the street again. She saw that Ruby's house was still dark. She told Frances she'd give it another twenty minutes then go over there, light or no light. In the meantime, she suggested they brew some coffee. "I could use a piece of toast, too," Ellen said. "We have some excellent rough-cut marmalade. You interested?"

Frances put her arm around Ellen as they walked toward the kitchen.

"It feels a little like we've been slapped in the face, doesn't it, Ellen? Her leavin', I mean. I don't want it to, but it does." Ellen agreed, as Frances continued, "We'll just have to get over that feeling, won't we? It wouldn't be fair to Ruby not to. She was only doin' what she had to do."

They were in the middle of cleaning up the kitchen when the front doorbell rang. Ellen went to answer it, wondering who would be calling at this early hour. She opened the inner door and stepped into the vestibule, looking through the glass.

Oh my god, it's crazy Mario Simonson! Violence had found its way to their front door. Her hand flew to her mouth as she stared at him.

Frances called from the kitchen, "Is everything all right, dear?"

"No!" Ellen yelled back. "Come quickly. I need your help."

Frances walked as fast as she could, surprised at how fast that was, really. It was encouraging to know she could rise to the occasion when necessary. "Here I am, Ellen. What's got you in such a terror?"

"It's Mario from the fight. Look at the bruises on his cheeks! What do we do, Frances? We can't let him in!"

Frances told Ellen to step aside; she'd take care of it. Opening the door, she smiled at Mario, recognizing him as her grass-cutter and the delivery boy. "Why, I do believe you're the young man from Garafolo's," she said. "But I don't know that we've ordered anything today, Mario. In fact, I feel sure we haven't. Are we in the middle of a misunderstandin'?"

Mario shifted in place, hands deep in his jeans pockets, one foot keeping time with his nervousness.

"Uh, Miss Bainbridge sent me over, Mrs. O'Reilly. She wanted to let you know she got herself home last night. She said you'd be worried and she wanted you two to know that she was fine and safe inside her house."

Coming alongside Frances, Ellen felt bolder.

"How do you know what Miss Bainbridge did last night?" she said. "Why are you her messenger?"

"I was sleeping in her garage when she buzzed home on that crazy scooter. I explained to her why I was there, and then we talked things over. She agreed to let me stay there awhile. My ma said it was OK, too. I'll be helping Miss Bainbridge out for the next couple of days. She needs things like groceries and help getting up and down the stairs."

"Aren't you the boy who got into that horrible fight on the Walpoles' front porch last night?" Ellen asked. "We heard there was a terrible fracas there." Mario said he was, and it was the Simonson house now, his family's house.

"How is that boy you beat up?"

Mario narrowed his eyes at Ellen. He put his hands on his hips and looked at her like she was someone not worth his time. He wanted to tell her she was a nosey little twit, but he held back.

"He's gonna be fine, ma'am," he said. "He'll be out of the hospital this morning. He's my brother. It was family business we were fighting about. It's all over now. Anyway, Miss Bainbridge said she's tired out this morning after her trip last night. She said to tell you not to come and see her until she's had a chance to get some sleep. She said she'd call you when she's ready to receive visitors."

"Visitors?" Ellen looked at Frances, who didn't seem to be surprised at being called *visitors*.

"Thank you, Mario, for delivering the message," Frances said. "Please tell Miss Bainbridge we are awfully glad to know she is safe and happily ensconced in her home once again. Kindly let her know we will be telephonin' her later today, will you?"

Mario gave a small salute as he turned to go, taking the porch steps two at a time, crossing the street as if his pants were on fire. "Do you think Ruby's safe with him?" Ellen asked.

Frances said she felt fine about Mario. "I don't believe he would do a thing to hurt our Ruby. As he said, he had a family disturbance and it had nothin' to do with her. Ruby has known his family for years from church and doing business with Angelina's father. Actually, I feel lucky that she has Mario to look after her for the next few days. I think they'll be just perfect for each other."

Frances and Ellen moved into the parlor. They stood still looking at Ruby's bed, not saying a word. Frances broke the silence.

"Well, it's all changin' again. I can't blame Ruby for going home. Not one little bit. But I was gettin' used to her being here. You too, Ellen. I supposed you'll be on your way now that the real patient is gone."

Ellen nodded, trying to think of a pithy aphorism, which might help Frances, and herself.

There is nothing so constant as change. All good things must come to an end. All is flux; nothing stays still. To exist is to change. Things do not change; we change.

All of them were true. None of them helped much this morning.

"It is what it is, Frances. Change happens every second we live, I guess." She pulled the pillows off Ruby's bed. "Right now I am looking at all the work we have to do in breaking down this Recoup Hotel. I think I'll get started, if you don't mind."

She stripped the bed, dropping the sheets on the floor, and pushed the hospital bed against the window. She'd arrange to have it picked up later today. She took the portable TV off the wide plant stand so she could bring it back to the rental place. She had seen an old duffle bag in the hall closet that could hold the rest of Ruby's things. Maybe Ruby could send Mario over to pick them up later.

Frances went into the living room to get busy, too. She pulled up the duvet cover on her bed and put the pillows in place.

"I don't know how you'll feel about this, Ellen, but I've decided I'll continue sleepin' downstairs for a little while longer," she said. "I am perfectly fine about being alone again, but I still feel uncertain when I think about going up and down that staircase. Have I become my mother, do you think?"

Ellen laughed. "No, of course not, Frances. In fact I think the downstairs plan is perfect. It makes me much happier knowing you are not tackling those stairs. It's so cozy in the living room, and your garden will spring to life again before your very eyes, and that will be thrilling to watch. I think it's a wonderful plan."

"Oh, I don't intend to stay here until spring. My word, no. Bless your heart, Ellen, I am not takin' to my bed. I simply want another week or ten days before I fully return to managin' the whole house."

"I'm glad to hear that, Frances. I wouldn't let you give up on the world just yet, even if you wanted to."

Ellen picked up the sheets and pillowcases and started toward the laundry room just off the kitchen. She had a lot of errands to run today. Plus, she needed to open up her own house and take stock of things. Her refrigerator would need cleaning after this six-week hiatus. Her bed would need clean sheets, and her bathroom, fresh towels. The whole house would need an airing out. Nothing was worse than walking into dead air. She'd be busy for a couple of days.

Coming into the kitchen to get a cup of tea, Frances looked at Ellen.

"So what do you think you'll do?" Frances asked. "I mean, have you thought any more about your plans, dear?"

"Actually I have, Frances. I've been thinking about my life and what to do with it for weeks. The timing of Ruby's exit is interesting, because it was just last night that I decided I need to get a job. I had thought maybe in another month, but it looks as if I can start the search right away. It's exciting in many ways, but it's also pretty scary."

Frances poured water into the electric teapot and turned it on. She reached into the tall cupboard and took down a cup and saucer from her favorite Limoges china. The cup was patterned with delicate pale blue *fleur de lis* with silver encircling the rims of both pieces. She always felt good just bringing it to her lips.

"Scary, Ellen? What would scare you about it? I think of you as one of the most capable women I know. I am thinkin' you can do anything you want to do."

"Thanks, Frances. You're very kind. But it's scary because I don't know what Oswego can offer me, and vice versa. Living here is so different from living in the Sunbelt where everything is booming with growth and corporate headquarters, and convention centers and football franchises, and bigger houses and downtown condos, and lots of jobs—particularly if you've lived there twenty-three years, as I did, and you've developed a good network."

Ellen stopped. The washing machine was working too hard. It was chugging so loudly that Ellen knew Frances would have trouble hearing her. Ellen hoped she hadn't overloaded it; she couldn't leave Frances with a damaged machine. She lifted the lid to check if all the sheets were immersed in water. She pushed the linens down into the water all around the tub. When she closed the lid the appropriate sloshing noises began in earnest. Everything seemed to be in order now.

Turning back to Frances, she picked up where she left off.

"The truth is, Frances, the South is turning cartwheels while our little Oswego is barely holding on by its economic toenail. Plus, I don't know anyone in my hometown anymore. Thirty-two years is a long time to be away."

"Do you plan to stay in Oswego, dear?" Frances poured honey into her tea. A fresh lemon was next in line.

"Yes, at least through the winter. Then I'll see where I am. It may work out for me here, and it may not. All I know for sure is that I feel as good as I'll ever feel about my divorce. I'm ready to engage in life again."

Frances put her cup down and turned to Ellen. "If there's anything I hate to do, it's give advice. But you are so important to me that I cannot keep my ideas to myself this time. Forgive me if I'm oversteppin', but here's what I've been thinking."

She walked over to Ellen, putting her hands carefully on her shoulders, face-to-face now.

"You should use your marvelous cooking skills to open your own small restaurant, or start your own caterin' business right here in Oswego," Frances said. "We certainly could use a place with unusually good food, and we absolutely could use a fine caterer for the parties we all have. Holiday parties, Easter egg hunts, family reunions, weddings, anniversaries, and special birthdays. We all entertain on those occasions and we don't have many options when it comes to food, Ellen. Not to mention the university and its many needs for caterin' services as well, particularly in the president's house."

Ellen wiggled out of Frances's light grip and went over to the kitchen counter. Henry trotted in, his morning way off track, his walk an hour overdue, his post-walk treat still in the cabinet. Ellen crouched down to hug him. *Poor boy. Change is tough on us all, isn't it?*

"I've thought about that, too, Frances. I'm not sure I have the stamina, or the will, and god knows the critical element, the passion, to create a business around food." she said. "The restaurant business becomes your life."

"Perhaps that is just the point," Frances said softly. "It could be your life, *for now.* The timin' certainly seems right. You know I'd be more than delighted to enlist all of my friends in helping you to build your business. Just think about it, will you?"

Henry's patience was exhausted. He jumped on Ellen, letting her know he was all done waiting.

Ellen gave Frances a warm smile. "I will think about it, of course. Thank you, Frances, for even caring about it, and for caring about me. I feel so much better just knowing you're in my life. You have no idea how good it is to feel your strength and wisdom behind me."

She let Henry out the back door telling him she'd be with him shortly.

She turned slowly then and, like a magician, pulled the white envelope out of her sweater pocket with a small flourish. "Now! Are we ready to read the note Ruby left us? I wanted us to do it together, so I secreted it away this morning until we were ready."

"Oh my, yes. Let's get us a glass of wine and sit in the front parlor, shall we? In Ruby's room, as I'll always think of it now." She opened the cupboard and took out two fine old etched crystal wine glasses.

Opening the cocktail cupboard, Ellen asked, "Will Cockburn's port do?"

"Perfect! A lovely cordial before lunch!" Frances said, marching toward the parlor. Henry barked at the door, seeing Ellen leaving the kitchen. She let him in and grabbed his bag of chicken treats to bring with her. He happily followed Ellen to the blue chair by the bay windows and settled down at her feet, delighted with the chicken strips. Frances pulled a small mahogany table between them and they poured the wine. Looking across the street, they lifted their glasses.

"To Ruby," Frances said. "May you remember the Recoup Hotel with fondness, for that is how we think of you, our darlin' friend!" They each took a sip, feeling the warmth of the fortified wine all the way down to the soles of their feet. Ellen slid the envelope onto the small table. Frances demurred.

"My glasses are in the livin' room and I am too nicely settled here now to get up and get them," she said. "Please, you read it aloud."

Slipping her finger through the sealed envelope, Ellen eased out the letter. She had never seen Ruby's handwriting. It was elegant. She must have been a Palmer Method student, her hours of going round, round, round, swing a-round, round, round, evident in her cursive skills. Ellen cleared her throat and read the note slowly.

Dear Frances and Ellen:

By the time you read this I will be back in my own bed. I hope I haven't caused you any worry, but the simple fact is, I need my own house again. I can't explain it any better than that. You both have been more than good to me, and my departure has nothing to do with you. It has everything to do with me. I am fine to take care of myself now anyway.

I thank you both for your generosity. I will certainly miss Ellen's cooking. I'll have to stock up on Lipton's Dry Onion Soup and Hamburger Helper when I get home. I would like to learn how to make that bread pudding, Ellen. Maybe you can show me sometime. Anyway, we'll talk soon. Don't be mad at me. Thank you again.

With my best personal regards,

Ruby Bainbridge

P.S. If you decide to finish that Garrison Keillor book, I wouldn't mind joining you. We could meet over here for a change of scenery. OK, I admit it. I am curious to see what happens at Evelyn's funeral. She sure is a character.

Frances let the Port sit on her tongue, savoring the rich flavor before its warmth filled her throat. Ellen got up and went into the living room. She picked up *Pontoon* and brought it back with her, sitting down again next to Frances.

"Shall we save this for Ruby?" she asked.

"Oh my. I think so, don't you? It wouldn't be the same without her now."

"I agree, Frances. It wouldn't be the same at all."

They decided to surprise Ruby with cinnamon raisin scones and good sweet tea the day of the reading.

About the Author

Rick Campen

Martha Nelson has carried around stories in her head for sixty years, but *Black Chokeberry* is her first novel. Born and raised in Oswego, New York, she loved growing up on the shores of Lake Ontario. She is a graduate of Syracuse University and Lipscomb University and is a retired nonprofit executive, educator, award-winning journalist, and chef. She plays the piano and harp and used to play the flute. She has two grown sons, Terry and Billy Schiff, two daughters-in-law, Emily and Alicia, and two grandchildren, Riker and Seldon. Martha lives in the greater Nashville area with her husband, Mark, two dogs, Bart and Lulu, and Hank the cat.